What Others Are Saying about
The Amish Wanderer...

The Amish Wanderer grabbed me on the first page. I had to keep reading and couldn't put it down. Laura V. Hilton's unique characters and unusual plot twists kept me guessing until the last page. *The Amish Wanderer* reminds us that even when we think God has abandoned us, we're forever on His mind.

—Kate Lloyd
Author, The Legacy of Lancaster Trilogy

story! Laura Hilton tackles appalling situations with grace and love, leaving her readers with the certainty that even the darkest night has a dawn.

—Naomi Miller

Laura Hilton's characters are so relatable. You'll find that to be true in *The Amish Wanderer*. The lessons Bethany and Silas learn are life-changing. You'll find this book well-written and enjoyable!

—Linda McFarland

Laura V. Hilton has once again addressed social issues that exemplify emotional and heartbreaking circumstances. Woven throughout are difficult social mores revealed in a sensitive and poignant manner. Her characters are credible and well-developed, stirring the heart and soul of the reader. Ms. Hilton has exceeded my expectations through this heartrending book. I have already read this book twice!

—*Nancee Marchinowski*

Ms. Hilton proves that faith can free us from our shattered pasts.

—*Charlotte Hubbard*

Laura Hilton can be counted on for rich, multilayered characters and plots that inspire. *The Amish Wanderer* is no exception. Hilton's stories will warm your heart and transport you to a gentler way of life. You'll find yourself remembering her characters long after you finish the book.

—*Mary Ellis*
Author, *Magnolia Moonlight*

Laura V. Hilton took me on an emotional rollercoaster ride with this powerfully gripping story.

—*Cheryl Baranski*
https://cherylbbookblog.wordpress.com

THE AMISH WANDERER

THE AMISH WANDERER

LAURA V. HILTON

W

WHITAKER
HOUSE

Unless otherwise indicated, all Scripture quotations are taken from the *New King James Version*, © 1979, 1980, 1982, 1984 by Thomas Nelson, Inc. Used by permission. All rights reserved. Some Scripture quotations are taken from the *Holy Bible, New Living Translation*, © 1996, 2004, 2007. Used by permission of Tyndale House Publishers, Inc., Carol Stream, Illinois 60188. All rights reserved. Some Scripture quotations are taken from the *Holy Bible, New International Version*®, NIV®, © 1973, 1978, 1984, 2011 by Biblica, Inc.® Used by permission. All rights reserved worldwide.

THE AMISH WANDERER

Laura V. Hilton
http://lighthouse-academy.blogspot.com

ISBN: 978-1-62911-798-0
eBook ISBN: 978-1-62911-799-7
Printed in the United States of America
© 2017 by Laura V. Hilton

Whitaker House
1030 Hunt Valley Circle
New Kensington, PA 15068
www.whitakerhouse.com

Library of Congress Cataloging-in-Publication Data (Pending)

1 2 3 4 5 6 7 8 9 10 11 ᵂ 24 23 22 21 20 19 18 17

Dedication

To my maternal grandparents, Joseph and Mertie,
who made the decision to marry and leave the Amish,
thus beginning the rest of the story.
To God be the glory.

Acknowledgments

They say that no one can write a book alone, and that is absolutely true. I would like to thank...

Whitaker House, for taking a chance on me.

Courtney Hartzel, for being a great editor.

Cathy Hickling, for all the hard work she puts into promoting my books.

My street team, for helping get the word out.

Nancee Marchinowski, for making herself available as a beta reader.

My daughter Jenna, and her husband, Steve, for editing the book before anyone else.

My critique partners, especially Candee Fick, for not going easy with the red pen. (Candee, you make me a much better writer!)

The rest of the critters who take time out of their busy schedules to read and mark up my manuscripts.

Thank you all.

Glossary of Amish Terms and Phrases

ach:	oh
aent/aenti:	aunt/auntie
"ain't so?":	a phrase commonly used at the end of a sentence to invite agreement
Ausbund:	Amish hymnal used in the worship services, containing lyrics only
boppli:	baby/babies
bu:	boy
buwe:	boys
daed:	dad
"Danki":	"Thank you"
der Herr:	the Lord
Gott:	God
großeltern:	grandparents
dochter:	daughter
ehemann:	husband
Englisch:	non-Amish
Englischer:	a non-Amish person
frau:	wife
grossdaedi:	grandfather
grossmammi:	grandmother
gut:	good
haus:	house
hübsch	pretty
"Ich liebe dich":	"I love you"
jah:	yes
kapp:	prayer covering or cap
kinner:	children

koffee:	coffee
kum:	come
maidal:	young woman
mamm:	mom
maud:	maid/spinster
morgen:	morning
nacht:	night
nein:	no
"off in den kopf":	off in the head; crazy
onkel:	uncle
Ordnung:	the rules by with an Amish community lives
rumschpringe:	"running around time"; a period of freedom and experimentation during the late adolescence of Amish youth
ser gut:	very good
schatz:	sweetheart
sohn:	son
verboden:	forbidden
"Was ist letz?":	"What's the matter?"
welkum:	welcome

For I am persuaded that neither death nor life, nor angels nor principalities nor powers, nor things present nor things to come, nor height nor depth, nor any other created thing, shall be able to separate us from the love of God which is in Christ Jesus our Lord.

—Romans 8:38–39

Chapter 1

November

The sky is falling, and I'm searching for somewhere to hide. We need someone to help, but all I see are clouds in everyone's eyes. If only my fears could be forgotten....

If only I could get out of this town.

An unidentified sound, loud in the relative silence, jarred Bethany. Her blue pen made a squiggly line across the page in the fat little notebook where she wrote down her thoughts. Maybe she should've found a more secluded place to write than the pile of hay at the base of the loft ladder, but she was usually undisturbed here.

She raised her head and listened. Heard nothing more, except for the squeak of the wood doors in the back of the barn as her younger brother, Timothy, put the cows out to pasture. The soft lowing of cows. The clucking of free-range chickens.

Hopefully, he was too busy to notice she'd left—and wouldn't look for her.

But there came that sound again, from somewhere overhead. A sound that didn't belong amid the soft lowing of cows and the clucking of free-range chickens. A creak and a thump.

Hopefully, it wasn't Hen. She would've heard if he'd gotten out of jail, ain't so? A thread of fear ripped through her, unraveling the fragile sense of peace she'd been able to find.

Bethany capped her pen, shot to her feet, and hid her notebook under a loose floorboard. Then she scampered up the ladder to the lower loft.

Nothing.

She climbed higher, to the upper one, some thirty feet above the main floor. Peeking over the edge, she scanned the areas in view.

13

There—someone was wrapped in the ratty old blanket Daed kept for "strays," as he called them. Mamm called them "wanderers," and she wouldn't be happy to learn that one had bedded down in their loft while Daed was gone—incarcerated, in a sense, in a mental hospital after he'd set out to kill all the black cats in the district.

The cats all lived. Their species had nine lives, ain't so? But Daed was institutionalized, and Hen Stutzman, the man who had actually carried out his deranged wishes, was in jail, awaiting trial for arson.

And here, Bethany had thought Hen's frequent visits were for the purpose of seeing her. Even when she'd kum to dread his presence.

Her head, and heart, were permanently bowed in shame. Now nobody would ever kum calling.

Especially if they ever found out….

Nein. They couldn't. She would never tell.

Life would never be the same.

Okay, maybe she was being a bit overdramatic. But still….

Bethany's eyes burned. She blinked to clear the watery haze.

What were they going to do with Daed gone?

A black Amish hat covered the face of whoever dozed on the hay-strewn floor of the loft. His body was wrapped tightly in the blanket, putting her in mind of a newborn boppli in swaddling clothes. Except this was a man. Not a boppli.

And definitely not Hen. This man was taller and much thinner. Relief flooded her.

She started down the ladder. It wouldn't do for a vagabond to discover her there in the loft with him. Not even if the image reminded her of the live nativity scenes she'd seen downtown at one of the Englischers' churches. The carol ran, uninvited, through her thoughts: *The little Lord Jesus asleep on the hay—*

A ladder rung snapped in two under Bethany's weight, and she dangled there, her feet flailing, hanging tight to the top of the ladder. Too far to fall without breaking a bone. Or killing herself.

When her fingers started slipping on the worn wood, she let out a strangled cry. The slumbering man bolted upright, his hat falling away to reveal shocks of sun-streaked light brown hair. He struggled free from the blanket and scrambled to the edge of the loft. "Hang on, I'll pull you up."

Up? In the loft, alone with him?

Nein.

His hands closed around hers. They were strong. Warm. Work-roughened. She glanced at his fingers, curled around hers, as unexpected sparks shot through her. The sensation had nothing to do with the fact that her life hung in the balance. Or maybe it did. She looked down again at the floor, thirty feet below. And whimpered.

Clinging to him seemed a gut idea though. And if it'd save her from falling....

Her shin made contact with the broken rung a moment before her tennis shoe found another ladder rail. She let out a breath she hadn't realized she held. "I'm fine." Now. She pulled her hands free one at a time and lowered herself. A step. Two. Three....

He stepped onto the ladder and started his descent.

Where was Timothy? There was safety in numbers. She was going to call for her brother but became sidetracked watching the quick climbing of the handsome stranger. In her haste to escape, her feet slipped off the rung.

A faraway-sounding scream reached her ears. She recognized the voice as her own as she plunged through the air. Her body hit something. Two arms enfolded her, and then...darkness.

Until....

"You shoved her!" Timothy's voice sounded from somewhere above her.

She was safe. Gut. She dared relax.

Hands ran over her arms and legs. Not Timothy's hands. These were bigger and stronger, yet gentle. Hands that left tingles where they touched. Strange, this reaction to a stranger. To anyone.

"I didn't shove her. She slipped and fell. I was trying to help." The stranger's voice seemed familiar, in some way.

"She could've died, and then her blood would've been on your hands," Timothy almost shouted.

Bethany's head throbbed, especially in the front. Probably more from tension than from the fall.

"Who are you, anyway?" Timothy demanded. "And what are you doing in our barn?" His voice cracked and changed pitch, a clear sign of his adolescence.

"I don't think she broke anything." The stranger rolled her over and brushed his hand down her spine. As if he'd be able to feel a broken back. He moved her again, his hands investigating her ribs, brushing against her curves. This checkup was going too far. Too intimate. Who'd given him such liberties, anyway?

Bethany forced her eyes open and locked gazes with the stranger. He looked as lost and confused as she felt. She sat up, ignoring the wave of dizziness that overtook her as she stared into his hazel eyes. Eyes that were also familiar.

Could it really be…? "Silas Beiler?"

⟿

Silas stared at the woman sitting on the barn floor, just beside the hay bale that had spared her from hitting the hard ground when she plummeted from the ladder. Her kapp had fallen off, and her reddish-gold hair was still in a bun, albeit a messy one, with bobby pins sticking out from it in every direction. How did she know him? He hadn't expected anyone here to remember him. His family had moved away six years ago. If only he could recognize her, could recall her name….

"Bethany Weiss." She gave a hopeful smile. "You took me home from a singing once. Brought me lemonade at the frolic beforehand."

He sat back on his haunches and studied her. Her dress was still pooled immodestly around her hips, revealing her long, shapely legs. He gave them an admiring glance. *Ach*, he was beginning to remember. That happened back when he'd dared to dream that things could be different. That he would court a maidal and think about settling down.

Nein point in thinking of that now. He wasn't staying in Jamesport but only passing through on his way to his onkel's haus in Pennsylvania.

He turned his attention back to Bethany. "Are you hurt?"

She glanced down at her body, as if expecting some part of it to wave and say, "Me, me!" Then she tugged at her dress so that the fabric covered her legs. "My shoulders are a little sore. My upper back, too. But I should be fine."

Silas stood up and held out his arms toward her.

She hesitated a moment, then put her hands in his. "Danki."

Something jolted through him at the contact.

Her brother scowled. "I'm going back to work." He disappeared out the barn doors.

Silas released Bethany's hand and stepped toward the ladder. "I'll just grab my bag and be on my way, then."

"Nein! I mean, you should let us serve you breakfast first. Daed always says we might be entertaining angels unawares."

Silas almost snorted. He wasn't an angel. But his stomach sat up and took notice at the thought of food. Maybe she would even pack him a lunch for the road.

"Well, he used to say that, before...." Bethany choked back a weird-sounding sob, and shook her head.

Silas swallowed. "I'm sorry about your daed." The loss must have been recent. It would explain the slightly run-down appearance of the farm.

She nodded. "The diagnosis was a shock. At least we have hope that Gott will heal him."

So, her daed was still alive but sick or injured. "You don't have to feed me." Silas's stomach rumbled in protest. "I should really be getting on my way. I need to search for a temporary job so I can earn some money for the rest of my trip." Money for food. For new shoes, since he'd worn gaping holes into his soles. And for thick socks, to provide extra padding for his poor, blistered feet. It was a long walk from the western side of Kansas to northern Missouri, and not many drivers stopped to offer a ride. Plenty of drivers did pelt him with fast-food wrappers and empty cups, however. Oftentimes, the cups still had soda and ice in them, leaving him a cold, wet, sticky mess.

"A job? That's nein problem. We'll hire you. Timothy has to go to school, and we need tons of help around here. The community has been pitching in, but they all have their own farms, so our place is just getting a lick and a promise…which is better than nothing, ain't so?"

At least Bethany's tongue hadn't been injured in the fall.

"Wouldn't your daed want to weigh in on hiring me?"

She pulled in a deep breath. "He's in the hospital right now, and we don't yet know if he'll be put in jail—"

"Shut up, Bethany." Her brother marched back into the barn pushing a wheelbarrow. A shovel bounced along inside it. "You don't need to air all our dirty laundry."

Silas hitched an eyebrow.

Bethany gathered her cloak around her shoulders. "I'll go fix breakfast."

Silas followed the bu, intent on helping out. Maybe he could earn his breakfast, even if a job here were nothing more than a pipe dream.

⌒

Upon entering the warm kitchen, Bethany was greeted with the mouth-watering aromas of oatmeal with maple syrup and brown sugar, fresh-baked biscuits, fried ham, and koffee.

Mamm paused in her bustling. "There you are. I wondered where you'd gotten to." She stirred the pot of bubbling oats.

"We have a guest. He bedded down in the loft last nacht." Bethany removed her cloak, brushed the hay off of it, and hung it from a peg, then bent to remove her shoes, resisting the urge to groan with the pain.

Mamm sighed. "If only your daed were home. I guess he can eat on the porch. Maybe that'll incline him to move along sooner."

"Actually…I offered him a job. You were talking about hiring someone, and he's looking for work. Temporarily."

Mamm stopped in her tracks and shut her eyes. She began shaking her head slowly from side to side. "Bethany Suzanne. I wish you wouldn't have done that. We can't trust wanderers. We don't know what he's like. Or what kind of influence he may have on your sisters and brother."

"It's Silas Beiler."

Mamm stilled her shaking head but kept her eyes closed. Her lips tightened. Nein doubt she remembered the sheets of note paper Bethany had scribbled on all summer long. "Silas and Bethany" inside of hearts of various sizes.

More recently, her scribbles had been "Hen and Bethany," but that seemed just as much of a dream. More like a nightmare.

And Hen had never gone out of his way to be as nice to her as Silas had.

"Silas Beiler." Mamm's eyes opened, and she gave the oats another stir with the spatula. "Is his family back in the area?" A slight wariness had crept into her tone.

"Um, it's just him, I think." Otherwise, he probably wouldn't have needed to sleep in their barn. "And he's just passing through."

"Where's he going?" Mamm flipped the ham in the skillet. "Pour some juice, please, and set another place for Silas."

Bethany grinned. He would be joining them inside. "He didn't say." She flexed her sore shoulders and arched her back to get the kinks out.

"Breakfast is just about ready. Where are your sisters and brother?" Mamm peered out the window.

Bethany began filling the glasses with juice. "Timothy's in the barn. The girls are supposed to be collecting eggs and taking care of the chickens."

"And what were you doing?" Mamm spooned the oatmeal into a serving bowl.

"Milking the cows." And writing in her journal. "Guess I forgot the milk in the barn. I'll go get it, and tell everybody that breakfast's ready." She put her shoes back on and grabbed her cloak, then headed back to the barn, her excitement mounting. Hopefully, Mamm would hire Silas, and Bethany would have a chance to get to know her first love all over again.

Maybe things would be different this time.

And maybe Silas Beiler would be her ticket out of town.

Chapter 2

Silas's stomach rumbled again as he followed Bethany's brother into the cow barn. How long had it been since his last meal? His supply of granola bars had run out three days ago. The thought of a home-cooked breakfast seemed to have enlivened every cell in his body.

The cow barn smelled of hay and dust. A three-legged wooden stool waited at the bottom of the steps beside two pails of milk covered with aluminum lids. The bu had picked up a shovel and headed toward a pile of manure in one of the stalls. The cows were gone—and a door stood open at the far end of the room. A wheelbarrow waited just outside the barn door.

"I'm Silas." He walked down the stone steps leading into the room.

"I heard my sister call you that. I'm Timothy." The young man stopped working, rested his fists on his hips and stared at Silas. "Look, I don't understand how she knows a *stray*...." A sneer accompanied the word.

A stray? But it perhaps was appropriate, based on his sticky, stinky, rumpled clothes. Besides, he had snuck into the barn after the light went off inside the haus. It hurt to be judged so soundly and quickly, though. *A stray. Really?* What did he know?

"But you know, right now, with things the way they are, it isn't a gut time."

Silas cocked an eyebrow. Nein, he didn't know exactly how things were. Except their daed was in the hospital and might soon be incarcerated. He didn't know how to word a question in a casual, nonintrusive way to find out, either. A direct question would earn an equally blunt, "None of your business."

And it wasn't. Not really. But it might be helpful to know. When he decided how to ask it, he wouldn't go to Timothy. He'd catch Bethany alone and ask her. Maybe.

Then again, did he really need to know? He'd be moving on, and it wasn't as if he were still on speaking terms with his parents.

"I'll carry the milk to the haus." Silas picked up the pails. Daed would've never tolerated milk being left in the barn, not even covered, while the barn was being cleaned.

Timothy shot him a dark look.

Silas pressed his lips together to keep himself from saying things he shouldn't. He wasn't responsible for Timothy's opinions or thoughts. And the bu didn't know Silas's story.

He carried the milk pails to the main level of the barn and through the double doors in front. A gust of frigid wind howled around the corner of the building, bringing tears to his eyes, and he blinked to clear his vision. Another gale whipped his black hat off his head. It tumbled along ahead of him, until Bethany ran past him and snatched it out of the air. Then she waited for him to catch up to her, a grin on her face. "Breakfast is ready. You'll join us, ain't so?"

"Jah, danki."

Smiling, she matched pace with him as he walked toward the haus. "So, why are you here instead of there? Wherever 'there' is."

Silas hesitated.

Maybe too long. She glanced at him.

"Kansas. That's where my family is. I'm backpacking across the country." It was the truth. Just not the whole truth.

She sighed, her warm breath fogging in the cold air. "I can't say I blame you. Being free has a certain appeal." Wistfulness filled her voice.

He kicked a stone out of his path. "So does having a home." He immediately wished he could retract his words. He might've said too much. He swallowed. "You know what they say…don't grumble when you don't get what you want. Be thankful you don't get what you deserve." That was a quote from Daed—the last thing he'd said before Silas grabbed his backpack and walked out.

Bethany pressed her lips together and gave him a narrow-eyed glance.

He'd definitely said too much. He carried the milk pails up the porch steps and waited for Bethany to let him in the haus.

Heat rushed out the open door. It would be hard to leave this haven and get back on the road.

Beside the door, the dinner bell clanged with a piercing noise that made his ears ring.

Two girls looked up from their task of setting dishes on the table and gawked at him.

Silas paused on the rag rug and held up the two pails of milk. "Where do you want these?"

"Just set them down for now," Bethany said. "We'll take care of them after breakfast." She brushed against him as she passed. His arm burned where it'd touched her. She stopped mere inches away from him and hung his hat on a wall peg, then took off her cloak and hooked it on the next peg before kicking off her shoes. "Here, I'll take your coat."

"Uh, okay." He lowered the pails to the floor, then shrugged off his coat. He handed it to her as Timothy thundered in through the door, two little girls on his tail. One of the girls carried a wicker basket. When she spotted Silas, she stopped and stared. The basket swung wildly, and Silas recognized the sound of eggs banging together and cracking. The other little girl stuck her thumb in her mouth.

⌒

Bethany grabbed the basket of cracked eggs from Rosemary and yanked Caroline's hand away from her mouth. "Quit doing that. Your thumb is dirty."

Caroline's eyes welled with tears, but she pressed her lips together and didn't cry.

Bethany hadn't meant to sound so harsh. They'd thought Carrie had broken her habit years ago, but it'd resurfaced over the past months, following Daed's "arrest"—or whatever it was called. Bethany wasn't sure. All she knew was, he'd been taken away in the sheriff's vehicle and had ended up in a mental hospital. Because he was the bishop, everyone in the community was aware of what had happened, and Bethany hadn't needed to field any invasive questions. Instead, she'd been treated with pity. Judgment. And poorly veiled whispers that she might be as crazy as Daed seemed to be.

She longed for things to return to the way they had been.

Failing that, a chance to start over, somewhere else.

Did the Amish ever use mail-order brides? The thought came out of nowhere, but the idea appealed to her. Marrying a stranger, far away, where she could write her own history....

She sighed. It wouldn't work. The Amish grapevine stretched across the nation. There would always be someone who knew someone, and within twenty-four hours, tops, her whereabouts would be easy enough to find for anyone who cared. And if the grapevine wasn't enough, there was always the Amish hotline—a phone chain for gossip, essentially, though nobody would call it that. Of course, there was also *The Budget*, as well as other Amish-based news publications.

Too many ways for people to track her and discover her tainted past.

But plenty of options for uncovering information about Silas, and what he'd been up to in the years since he'd left.

Another sigh. If she would resent the violation of her own privacy, Silas was bound to feel the same.

"Bethany?" Mamm's voice broke into her consciousness.

Yanked from her dangerous thoughts by Mamm's sharp voice, Bethany glanced at the table. Her brother and four sisters were already seated. Silas stood behind her chair, having pulled it out for her.

What a man.

Her eyes skimmed his blue jeans. His royal blue T-shirt. Why hadn't she noticed his Englisch clothes earlier? Mamm's eyes must've popped to see an Amish man dressed like that.

But wow, he looked nice. Beyond "nice"—amazing. Amazingly handsome.

A smile played on his lips, and his blue eyes showed amusement as he watched her. His grin revealed a dimple.

Her heart tripped as heat flooded her cheeks. She shook herself out of her daze and hurried across the room to the sink. She set the basket of cracked eggs on the counter, then washed up before approaching the table. "Danki." She slid into the chair Silas stood behind, then watched him as he strode around the table...and sat at Daed's place.

Her heart stuttered. Broke.

Timothy glared at Silas.

But Mamm had set the table. She was the one who had reserved the space for Silas.

Bethany glanced at her. Mamm's mouth was set in a firm, tight line. One that meant, "Don't you dare question my decision."

And that decision, in this case, was to hire Silas. Mamm's positioning him as she had meant he would be welkum to stay and would hold a position of authority…likely over the running of the farm. Maybe over the family devotions and prayers, as well.

"Bethany Suzanne." Once again, Mamm's voice jolted Bethany out of her musings. How many times had she tried getting her attention before adding her middle name? "Apologize to your sister."

Bethany's face heated at being scolded in front of Silas. What was she supposed to apologize for? And to which sister? She tried to think… but couldn't remember. She summoned a smile. "I'm sorry…." She glanced at each of her sisters in turn: Sarah, Emma, Rosemary, and Caroline. Ach, Carrie! "Really sorry, Carrie. I shouldn't have snapped." She quickly bowed her head for the silent prayer, without waiting for direction from either Mamm or Silas.

"Let us pray," Mamm said, a second later.

Bethany stared at her food a moment, then squeezed her eyes shut. *Lord, danki for this food. Please let Silas agree to take me with him, but let him stay until the weather warms up.*

"Amen." Mamm broke the silence.

Bethany opened her eyes. Was her prayer selfish? Probably. She closed her eyes again. *Not my will but Thine be done.*

Timothy grabbed the serving dish of oatmeal and spooned some into his bowl. Mamm helped herself to a biscuit, then passed the basket to the right.

"So, Silas. What brings you back to Jamesport? Will your family join you soon?" Mamm spoke in her too-sweet voice—the one she used with unpleasant church members.

⌇

Silas took the platter of biscuits handed to him, and held it a long minute. "Uh, nein. They're moving to Nebraska. The whole family is. Except for me. I'm going to Pennsylvania."

Bethany's mamm raised her eyebrows. "Why aren't you going with your family?"

"Too many reasons to mention." He kept his tone polite, even though it wasn't any of her business. He took a biscuit, even though his appetite threatened to desert him. Who knew when he'd see his next meal? He passed the platter to Timothy and accepted the bowl of oatmeal.

Silence fell, but he could imagine that eyebrow inching higher the way Mamm's did when she was about to—

"Bethany said you're looking for temporary work."

He jumped at the unexpected words. "Jah. I'm...backpacking cross-country." Because bus tickets weren't in the budget. "Supplies need replenishing." He spooned oatmeal into his bowl and caught a whiff of maple syrup. His stomach growled.

"What kind of supplies?" The woman's stare was direct.

"Oh, you know. Food. New shoes. Stuff like that."

"I suppose we could use your help here for a while. I'm sure you've noticed we're behind on chores and repairs. Timothy has been working very hard"—she nodded at Bethany's brother—"but it's a lot for one young man to handle. My ehemann is...laid up for the time being."

Bethany ducked her head, but not before Silas noticed her flushed cheeks. Probably because she'd already told Silas about her father being in a mental hospital. Not something the family wanted getting out to strangers. Or to former church members.

So, Silas's family wasn't the only one with issues to hide. "Appreciate it." Silas stared at his food. At least there would be more hot meals in his immediate future.

"We'll talk about arrangements and expectations after breakfast."

He nodded, but he could guess what the expectations would include: A reminder of all his family's worst traits. Would he never escape them?

A lump clogged his throat. He ignored it and shoveled oatmeal into his mouth—a big mistake, he realized, when he almost choked on it. He covered up his sputtering with a fake cough.

"You'll want a shower, of course."

"Jah." He knew he stunk. Nein "probably" about it.

"And more appropriate clothes." The bishop's frau eyed his T-shirt. "Maybe some of Ezra's would fit."

Ezra. Friendly fellow. He'd been in Silas's class the last year of school, when Silas was the new kid in town. Ezra and his best friend, Sam Miller, had been quick to welcome Silas. Invited him to join them in whatever they were doing, even though he was obligated to decline more often than not.

"What's Ezra up to these days?" It felt gut to get the conversation off himself. "Married by now, I guess? Any kinner?"

Silence. Again. This time, heavy. Nobody looked at him.

Ach, nein. His stomach churned as the realization hit. Ezra was dead. Nein wonder his clothes were available.

"I'm so sorry. I…I didn't know." What else had happened while he'd been gone?

Chapter 3

Bethany strained the pails of milk and separated the liquid for making into butter and cheese, also reserving some for cream and some to drink. Then she gathered the dirty dishes and carried them to the kitchen sink. Spying movement out of the corner of her eye, she peeked out the window, hoping for a glimpse at Silas. Mamm was supposed to be showing him around the rest of the farm. She'd already pointed out the "outside" shower. Not that it was technically outside. It was in a makeshift bathroom Daed had built at one end of the laundry room, right by the back door. A must-have for farmers, he'd said—shower and leave your dirty clothes right there in the laundry room. Mamm loved it.

Nobody in sight. Must've been a bird.

Bethany began filling the sink with hot water. Meanwhile, sixteen-year-old Rosemary had begun making school lunches for the kinner using leftover fried ham, a head of lettuce, and a block of homemade cheese. Nineteen-year-old Emma sorted through the recipe box.

Bethany looked out the window again. Mamm and Silas walked past, Mamm pointing toward something as she talked, and Silas nodding, his hat clutched to his side. Bethany's heart rate broke into a gallop. She couldn't see the muscles in his arms, but she'd felt them when he'd held her before she fell from the ladder. His broad shoulders and back tapered down to his narrow waist. His jeans hugged his back end. Not too tight, but tight enough that—

"He is so cute!" Bethany barely contained a squeal. *Oops.* She hadn't meant to say that out loud.

"Jah, he is." Emma opened the pantry and took out the flour canister, getting ready to make their daily bread. "Almost as cute as Roman."

Rosemary scoffed as she sliced the leftover biscuits. "You think your beau is the handsomest man alive. Silas is cute, but you know what Mamm always says: You can't base attraction on looks. They don't mean anything. Don't judge by appearances."

Bethany let out a frustrated breath. "Pure foolishness, because a relationship forms because of attraction, jah? And attraction is based on looks."

"We heard in Bible reading last nacht how man looks on the outward appearance, but Gott looks on the heart. We need to base attraction on what they're like as a person."

Why did Rosemary always have to be right? Bethany added an extra squirt of dish soap to the suds in the sink. "Jah, but we wouldn't be interested in what they're like if we didn't like how they look."

So there.

Emma and Rosemary were silent for a long moment. Rosemary finished making sandwiches and bagged them. Then she added a slightly green banana and a couple of sugar cookies to each paper bag.

"I remember you used to like him when we were in school, but you know what his family is like. And Daed often reminded us, the worm doesn't wander far from the apple."

It was nice of Rosemary to say "us" when everyone knew the comment was directed toward Bethany and her former crush on Silas.

"There is that. Pretty is as pretty does. I guess that'd work for men, too," Emma said hesitantly.

Why did everyone have such gut long-term memories? Silas was sweet. And she'd never seen any displays of temper from any of them, even though his older brother, Henry, caused a bag of flour to explode at the store when he slammed it down on the counter, if rumors were true. Or beat up his ex-girlfriend—

Nein. Silas wasn't that way. He couldn't be. Though he was a man. Maybe it was a male trait.

She'd seen more uncontrolled anger from Hen. Kicking dogs for nein reason. Whipping buggy horses. Slamming his fist into the barn wall. Or punched her when....

Bethany frowned. At least she was free from Hen while he was in jail. Hopefully, by the time he was released, she would be long gone. *Please, Lord, let it be so.* She returned her attention to Mamm and Silas. When they disappeared from sight, she started to wash the dishes.

Her school-aged siblings grabbed their lunches from Rosemary as they ran through the kitchen on their way out the door.

When only the three oldest sisters remained, Rosemary picked up a towel and started drying the dishes. "I just think we should encourage Silas to leave, the sooner, the better. He's dangerous."

"Hurting, I think." Emma pounded her fists into the bread dough with rhythmic beats. "And he is cute. But I agree with Mamm. We need someone older and stronger than Timothy helping us. He should get a chance."

Based on the clouded look in his eyes, Bethany guessed he *was* hurting. Was his family as dysfunctional as everyone seemed to believe? Daed and the preachers had gone over there a lot. Preacher Samuel had expressed concern on many occasions. Maybe Silas had gotten tired of it. Or been kicked out. Why else would a man leave home and backpack across the country?

Her sisters stopped their work and stared at her.

"What?" Bethany dried her hands on a towel.

"You make nein sense," Emma told her. "What does being cute have to do with backpacking across the country?"

Ach. She hadn't meant to say that out loud. Hadn't realized she had.

"I was just thinking." Bethany shrugged. "I...I guess I'll get started on the laundry."

In the tiny bathroom, Bethany hooked up the wringer washer to the sink and turned the water on. As the machine filled, she sorted the laundry. She was getting a late start. Mamm liked having the laundry done and hung to dry before breakfast, but since the girls were needed to help with the farm, the haus-hold chores were often delayed.

The door opened, and Silas came in carrying a small bundle of garments. He stopped in the doorway, his gaze going from Bethany to the hose leading through the bathroom doors and then back again. "I guess now isn't a gut time for a shower."

Bethany peeked inside the machine. "It's full. Just disconnect the hose and toss it outside. I can drain it out there, if you aren't finished." As he moved to do what she'd said, she added, "Seems a little silly to shower before you begin working, ain't so? You're just going to get sweaty and dirty." Maybe she could talk him out of taking one *now*.

Because seeing him in *that* condition, just a closed door away…. Her heart lurched. Her stomach followed suit.

"I don't think sweat is much of a concern today, as cold as it is." Silas gave a wry grin. "Anyway, your mamm suggested it. She said I might feel more like working after a shower. I think it was just her polite way of letting me know I stink."

Bethany giggled. "I didn't notice…much. But I have brothers—a brother. And that is what working men smell like, ain't so?" *Please, not now. Wait till I leave.*

He quirked his nicely shaped lips. "Or maybe, as your brother says, 'homeless wanderers.'"

⁓

Silas's face heated as he turned away. He hurried inside the cleanest bathroom he'd ever seen, hoping she didn't notice. It seemed wrong to take a shower with Bethany not five feet outside the door. He shut the door, and locked it.

She, the woman he'd once dreamed of courting, was in the other room. He could hear her moving around, making preparations to start laundry. As nasty as it was outside, the clothes would probably be strung on the lines inside the enclosed room. Seemed winter was coming early this year.

But then, it was November. Two weeks till Thanksgiving. He'd planned to be settled at Onkel Dan's by then. But now it didn't seem possible. Unless he worked a few days, bought what he needed, and hitchhiked his way across the country. Provided enough people stopped to give him a ride. That hadn't happened much, so far.

Silas turned the water on, adjusted the temperature to the hottest setting, and shed his clothes. He hoped the running water muffled the sounds. This was beyond embarrassing. Why hadn't he chosen a different Amish barn to bed down in last nacht? He hated Bethany seeing him like this. Remembering him like this.

A homeless wanderer. A stray.

He swallowed the lump in his throat and stepped into the shower.

A black bottle of men's body wash was lined up next to a bottle of blue "waterfall"-scented shampoo. Or so it said. He opened the bottle and sniffed. Didn't smell anything like the real thing. At least it wasn't some flowery-scented, girly stuff, like Mamm kept for all the women-folk crowding his home. *Former* home.

The hot water beat down on him, relaxing his tense muscles. He stood there, relishing this opportunity. He squirted some bodywash onto a poufy net thing, and soaped up, working to get all the grime off. It was gut to get a shower. He'd washed off as best he could in various roadside parks, but those had been few and far between.

If only he could wash away all the dirt from the inside of himself just as easily. The heated words he'd exchanged with....

Silas growled. He wouldn't let the past interfere with the present. Okay, he could admit he was wrong. But so were they. And maybe he shouldn't have slammed out of the haus like he had, but....

Nein!

He rubbed shampoo into his hair, working it into lather before he rinsed. Then he turned the water off and stepped out onto the thin towel that'd been hanging over the shower rod, and grabbed one of the well-worn towels from a stack on top of a bookcase. The only other contents were a bag of razors, a couple spare rolls of toilet paper, and an Englisch devotional...?

Silas stared at the book as he toweled off. One of the preachers used to have one he kept in the bathroom, too. He'd been a role model to Silas, welcoming him into his home, into his life, and letting him tag around when Silas had needed to escape his home life. He'd have to find out if Preacher Samuel was still alive. If he was still as gut a man as Silas remembered him being. Maybe Preacher Samuel would even help him get on track to becoming a man some other boy would like to emulate.

He knelt on the thin bathmat. "Lord Gott, let me be that man," came his whispered prayer. "Help me not to become what I escaped. Cleanse me from the inside out."

A big reason why he wanted to get to Onkel Dan's haus. He'd left the Amish. Joined the Mennonites. And now went on regular mission trips. He *had* to be a gut man. Besides, Onkel Dan promised Silas he'd help him get his GED. Pay his way through college.

A major draw.

A thump sounded outside the door. *Ach, Bethany.*

Silas hurriedly dressed himself in Ezra's castoff clothes. What had happened to him, anyway? But he wouldn't risk asking. Not now. He gathered his own soiled clothes and opened the door. "I'm to give you my laundry. Where do you want it?"

Bethany looked up with a beautiful smile that made his heart skip a beat. He stared at her, marveling at the way her eyes lit. *Wow.*

"Put them in there." She pointed at a wicker laundry basket. "And bring me anything else you need to have washed. Since I have to hang everything inside, I'll likely have to do at least a load a day to keep caught up."

"Danki." He dropped the filthy mess into the basket she'd indicated. "I'll get the rest of my things."

"First go into the kitchen and let your hair dry. I'll make you some hot chocolate."

It reminded him of the Bible story where one woman, Rebekah, maybe, went above and beyond when meeting the needs of Isaac's servant.

"Danki, again." He couldn't keep from grinning at her.

Maybe someday, he would be in a position to court a sweet girl like Bethany. But not her. Because he was leaving.

And she wasn't.

⌒

Bethany left the unfinished laundry in the bathroom and went into the kitchen, Silas trailing behind her. Her sisters and Mamm were all busy working. On the counter were several pans of rising bread dough covered with towels. Now Rosemary was mixing cookie batter, from the looks of it.

Bethany checked the water in the teakettle on the woodstove. Still hot. Gut. "Have a seat," she told Silas.

He pulled out a chair. His dark eyes were fixed on her, but they were shadowed. She couldn't read what he was thinking. Did he find her attractive? If he lived here, would he ask to drive her home from singings?

Bethany opened a cabinet and took out a packet of instant hot chocolate with mini marshmallows. Mamm kept a box of Swiss Miss on hand for a quick chocolate fix. The real cocoa was saved for special occasions. Not that there were many of those anymore. Not since Ezra went to a party in Pennsylvania and came home in a casket.

Mamm measured milk into a mixing bowl, then got out the rest of the cheese-making supplies. She'd mentioned mozzarella and cream cheese last nacht when they planned the day and made the daily list of things to do. Mamm was a list-maker. Of course, it made it easy, with a list of needed chores hanging on the refrigerator; they just had to mark off what they did. And the menu was posted next to it, so everyone knew at a glance what was for dinner.

She glanced over her shoulder at Silas as she stirred the contents of the packet into the hot water. He finger-combed his toffee-colored hair—too long, even by Amish standards. He needed a trim. Bethany had cut Timothy's hair when Mamm was busy. Would Mamm object if Bethany trimmed Silas's hair? Would Silas even let her?

Ach, how she wanted to run her fingers through his toffee-colored tresses.

Her stomach clenched with guilt that chased the naughty thoughts away.

Mamm probably wouldn't let her cut his hair, unless she did it when she wasn't home.

Emma's giggle drew Bethany's attention away from Silas. Nobody needed to know that she couldn't keep her eyes off him. That her long-ago crush had returned. Otherwise, they might send him away prematurely.

And that wouldn't do at all.

He had to stay long enough for her to convince him to take her with him.

He simply had to.

Chapter 4

Silas finished his hot chocolate and went outside to start the chores Bethany's mamm—Joe's Barbie, as she'd introduced herself—had asked him to do. He pulled his coat tighter against the cold wind as he walked toward the barn, and wished for a pair of gloves.

A lime-green car turned into the drive, its tires spitting gravel as it skidded to a stop in front of the closed-in porch. Silas lowered his head and turned away slightly as a bubble of panic rose in his chest. But then, the people he feared wouldn't drive a vehicle of that color.

With a whirring sound, the driver's side window lowered. An Englisch man leaned out. "Hey, your cows are loose. And my wife wants to know about the cheese for sale." He crooked his thumb to indicate the woman seated in the passenger seat.

Cheese for sale? Silas hadn't noticed a sign. But then, it had been dark when he'd stumbled in last nacht.

"Just a moment." Relief flooded him as he backtracked to the haus and opened the porch door. Bethany was there doing the laundry. "The cows are loose," he told her. "I'm going to round them up and fix the fence. Do you have a pair of gloves I could borrow?"

"Sure. I'll go get you a pair and help you round up the cows. Let me go grab my coat." Bethany started inside.

"And some people just drove in. They want to know about the cheese for sale…?"

Bethany barely paused. "Tell them to kum in. I'll let Mamm know."

Silas returned to the vehicle and relayed the message to the couple inside, then started toward the road. He heard the car doors slam shut, followed by footsteps crunching across the gravel driveway and pounding up the porch stairs.

Moments later, Bethany ran out to join him, a black bandana covering her head, her coat flapping behind her as she ran. "Here you go." She handed him a pair of black gloves. "Mamm said you can keep them. They're spares."

"Danki. How many cows do you have?" He glanced at her as they hurried toward the road.

"Five."

"Five?" Silas blinked.

"It's for our cheese business. Each cow gives us five gallons of milk a day."

"My parents kept one cow. It was more enough for the family." Both immediate and extended, all crowded into the same haus. At least they would have a little more space without him there. Maybe tempers wouldn't rage so hot with one less person to contend with.

Silas closed his eyes. *Lord Gott, forgive me for my bitterness. Help me—*

"Was ist letz?" Bethany pulled the front of her coat closed. "You look upset."

Silas frowned. "Just…thinking."

"What about?"

Conveniently, they reached the road. A dead tree had fallen on the fence, breaking it and pushing it low enough for the cows to step over. All five of the cows had found their way out of the pasture. A couple of them grazed in a neighboring field. One stood in the middle of the road, a potential traffic hazard. And two headed toward Silas like a bovine welkum committee. He rubbed the nearest one on the nose.

He would have his work cut out for him, between sawing the tree and fixing the fence.

"We have a chainsaw," Bethany murmured.

That would certainly make the job easier. But chainsaws were banned when his family had lived there. "Did your daed change the Ordnung?"

A slight frown appeared on her face. "Nein, but Hen—he's my… um…he might have been my…well, maybe he actually was my boyfriend. I'm not quite sure about that. Anyway, he borrowed it—or, more likely, stole it—from someone and brought it over two winters ago after a big storm. He never picked it up to return it, so we can use it. He's in jail, you know. County jail, awaiting trial."

Silas scowled at her use of the word "boyfriend," even though he wasn't sure why it mattered. He vaguely remembered Hen—or his name, at least. Not too many men were called that. "Awaiting trial for theft?"

Bethany targeted the nearest cow, the one Silas had petted, and attempted to drive it toward the fence. It ran in the opposite direction, stubborn thing. Silas went to head it off.

"Arson…attempted murder…." Her voice caught. "Daed might face the same charges when he gets out of the hospital. Unless they determine he was off in den kopf. He has a brain tumor, you know."

He hadn't known. And the news answered a lot of his unasked questions. It seemed that by making simple inquiries and keeping quiet while Bethany talked would allow him to garner a wealth of information about her family life. But her mamm's description of the bishop's condition—"laid up"—seemed too mild a version of the story. This family needed more than temporary help.

"I'm sorry." That didn't begin to cover his sympathy, but he didn't know what else to say. He helped Bethany drive the uncooperative cow back into the pasture and then went for another one.

Dust rose behind a pickup truck coming up the road. Silas turned his back to it and dipped his head. Anyone could drive a truck. When the vehicle stopped, Silas's heart rate increased. The driver's door opened. Slammed shut. Silas tensed, bracing himself, and clenched his fists.

"Need some help?" The man had the rough voice of a longtime smoker.

"Please." Bethany slapped the rump of a cow, and it ran out of the weeds alongside the ditch. "Silas, this is Mr. Zollos. His wife and their sohn drive for the Amish."

The name sounded familiar. Silas dared to peek at the farmer clad in overalls. He allowed himself to relax. "Nice to meet you." He'd never had need of a driver when he'd lived here.

Mr. Zollos herded the fifth cow through the broken fence, then pulled a cell phone out of his pocket and glanced at it. "I'll wait here while you get your saw. I have a few minutes."

"Thanks. Be right back." Silas hurried toward the barn.

After saying something to Mr. Zollos that Silas couldn't make out, Bethany ran to catch up with Silas. "I'll show you where the chainsaw is."

"Danki. And if he recognizes the chainsaw as his, do I send it home with him?"

She laughed. "Of course. And, just in case, I'll show you where we keep our handsaws. Do you want my help with the tree?"

He glanced at her out of the corner of his eye. "Trying to get out of doing laundry, are you?"

She sighed. "Helping you just sounds like more fun."

He smiled. "Jah." But he didn't want to upset her mamm.

"Besides, we have a several years to catch up on, ain't so? Like how your family is, and what you did in Kansas? Did you move there as soon as you left Jamesport?"

He didn't want to talk about his family. He shook his head. "I'll take care of the fence."

And keep his relatives where they belonged.

In the past.

⟳

Laundry was not Bethany's favorite job, by any means, but it beat baking bread. Her loaves always turned out misshapen and dense—never light and fluffy, like Emma's. Mamm said it was because Bethany didn't have the patience for it.

At least she couldn't mess up laundry.

Much.

One time, she'd accidentally washed a red washcloth with Daed's white undershirts, which had turned pink. Daed hadn't been impressed. His face had turned a scary shade of beet red, and Mamm had made Bethany use her babysitting money to buy material for new shirts.

She'd taken the time to sort the clothes after that.

And Mamm had taken the opportunity to stress that if she quit running her mouth and focused on her chores, instead, the chores would get done correctly, and ever so much quicker.

It was more fun to talk.

Besides, the only way she could learn anything was by talking to people. Listening to them. Open ears and eyes told her lots, especially when people were disinclined to tell her the things she wanted to know. When people were afraid to give her anything more than meaningless answers, because her daed was the bishop, and she might tell on them. But she wouldn't tattle. Not on purpose, at least.

She just needed to have her thumb on the happenings of the community. And most people seemed to appreciate her efforts. Even the ones who grumbled because she asked too many questions. Like the Englischer who'd fired her from his haus-cleaning service because she'd asked questions of a client who'd complained of having her identity stolen.

Bethany sighed. At least she'd gotten paid.

She needed to know the details of any given situation in order to be able to pray effectively about it, ain't so? And if the news spread a little further because she lost track and told too much, then it only meant that more people were able to pray.

At least, that's what she told herself to alleviate the guilt. And she was trying to do better. Really.

On the other side of the barn, blocked from her view, the chainsaw rumbled as Silas worked on sawing up the tree. She wanted to be with him, trying to discern the buggy loads of secrets behind the clouds in his eyes.

The chainsaw fell silent.

She chewed her lip as she spot-treated a pair of Timothy's trousers, then fed them through the wringer.

What was the real reason Silas left home? He seemed to harbor pain and bitterness, if his eyes were any indication. And the way he avoided talking about his family told her a lot. Maybe he would find healing here. She hoped he would. Where was he going? Not that it mattered so much where, so long as she could go along. But it must be someplace great if he was willing to walk the whole way.

The chainsaw roared to life once more.

Bethany fed another pair of Timothy's trousers through the wringer washer, then got bored with them. Washing Silas's clothes would be a change of pace. Slight, but a change nonetheless. She gathered his garments from the basket and brought them over to the wringer.

Why did *she* have to do the never-ending laundry? Why couldn't she perform the more interesting chores, like helping Silas saw up the fallen tree with the verboden chainsaw?

She glanced at the window to the kitchen, where her sisters and Mamm worked away. Oh, to be so content with her lot in life.

Of course, to be honest, it was just as well. It could be worse. She could be mucking stalls with Timothy. Women's work—*laundry*—was better than that.

But not by much.

She ran a pair of Silas's pants through the wringer washer. These were Amish-style: Plain. Old-fashioned. Simple.

The rest of his pants were jeans. Denim. With belt loops and pockets, even in the legs. Whoever heard of such a thing?

She toyed with the flaps of one of the pockets. Would there be clues to his personality stashed inside? Maybe a gum wrapper, or a tin of breath mints, or some hard candy. A receipt or two, showing how he spent his money. Something, to give her a hint as to his likes.

But his pockets were empty. Not even a speck of lint in sight.

Nein answers to her many questions.

Which was unfortunate, because she needed to get his attention. Needed to experience the pleasant tickly feeling in her stomach again, like she had that morgen when Silas knelt beside her on the floor of the barn and ran his hands over her body, checking for injuries.

But she wasn't willing to earn it by falling from a hayloft ladder again.

She would rather win his affections another way. A less traumatic, less dangerous, way.

Like helping him saw up a tree for future firewood.

Or....

She looked down at a filthy pair of jeans. Mud was splattered all over the legs.

Maybe doing his laundry and performing other small acts of kindness would cause him to give her a second glance. Maybe she could work her way into his affections by doing thoughtful things, like she had done for David Lapp when he was the new schoolteacher in town. She'd kept him supplied with homemade trail mix, peppermints, and other goodies, hoping, and wishing...until he'd fallen in love with someone else.

⁓

Despite the frigid, howling wind, Silas shed his coat and tossed it over a portion of the wire fence that hadn't been damaged by the fallen tree. He'd already sawed the trunk and limbs into manageable-sized chunks and moved them off the fence. Tomorrow, he would finish cutting them into pieces small enough to fit inside the woodstove, then haul them to the woodpile to dry.

Right now, the priority was getting the fence fixed so that the cows wouldn't think it was an open invitation to wander off. Even now, the five bovines stood near him, watching him with unabashed interest. Likely looking for another chance to sample the greener grass on the other side of the road.

He'd barely started working on the fallen fence when he heard a horse clip-clopping along the road. He didn't look up. There weren't many people around here he remembered well enough to greet by name.

"Whoa."

The horse stopped.

An Amish man leaned out of the open buggy. "Need a hand there, bu?"

Silas pasted on a fake smile and turned. "I can get it, danki."

The man tugged on his beard. "Seems it might go a bit easier with some help." He hesitated a moment. "Silas Beiler. Is that you?"

Silas stepped forward, finally recognizing the man. His fake smile turned into a real one that spread. "Preacher Samuel. So gut to see you. I'm going to help out the bishop's family for a while. Earn a little money before I move on."

"To?

"Pennsylvania. My onkel's."

Preacher Samuel parked the buggy along the side of the road. "Why not stay around here?"

Silas shook his head. "There's nothing for me here. Anyone who remembers me will remember…."

"Jah, but keep this in mind. Pride isn't too hard to swallow once you've chewed it long enough."

Silas grunted. "My onkel promised to help me get my GED so I could earn a college degree."

"In what?" Preacher Samuel dropped the horse's reins over an unbroken portion of fence.

Silas hesitated. Would the preacher criticize him for wanting to pursue higher education? "I don't know. Something service oriented, I think. Criminal justice, maybe." So he could get people off the street, like—

"Everything you want waits on the other side of your fear."

Jah, that was true.

Preacher Samuel approached the fallen segment of fence. "Let's raise it up, and then we'll get it staked."

Silas nodded. "Danki." The job would take half the time with two doing it.

They worked in silence, until Silas hammered the last fallen stake back in place using a piece of wood. "That should do it. Appreciate the help."

Preacher Samuel brushed off his gloved hands. "You should really consider staying around here. We need you. For reasons I can't go into now."

Silas shook his head. "I can't."

"Just pray about it."

Jah. Because praying had solved a lot of his problems lately.

But then, it actually had. Gott had led him to Bishop Joe's farm, a place that needed his help as much as he needed a job. He'd reconnected with Preacher Samuel. He'd rediscovered his unsettled feelings around Bethany Weiss.

Best to nip those in the bud right now.

"I'll pray."

"Gut." Preacher Samuel nodded. "Sam and I will kum by in the morgen with an ax and a wagon to help you finish up."

"Danki."

Preacher Samuel studied him for what seemed an endless minute. "We'll talk. But…it's not all about you, Silas."

But he was the one who'd ultimately pay.

Silas sighed and nodded.

"Ultimately, Gott needs to be in control."

But….

"Just pray about it," Preacher Samuel said again.

And a tiny bit of hope bloomed. If enough time had passed, maybe Silas could stay.

Chapter 5

After hanging the last freshly laundered pair of pants on the line inside the all-weather room, Bethany dried her hands, then bundled up and ran out to the barn to do some journaling. She wanted to record her emotions and thoughts from that day: finding Silas asleep in the hay. How his unexpected return had awakened her long-dormant hopes and dreams. Hopefully, nobody would bother her before it was time to go back inside and start supper. She reached for her journal, hidden in the hay, sat down, and started scribbling.

Foolishness, Mamm said. Vanity, recording one's thoughts. As if other people might be interested them. Vanity was a sin.

But sharing her thoughts with others wasn't the point. She wanted to keep them private. It simply helped Bethany to process things when she had them down on paper.

She scanned what she'd written, closed her pen, and slid her journal back into its hiding place. Hidden…just like Gott was these days. Had been, for the past year and a half.

Longer than that. Ever since Silas left and Hen entered her life.

Hello, Gott? It's Bethany Weiss.

Silence.

Gott, where are You?

Nothing.

What did it take to get His attention?

I have some things to tell You, but there isn't any point. It's like You abandoned my heart the day Ezra died. You tore it to shreds when Daed got arrested. Why are You silent?

But, just in case You care, I'm trapped in a world that doesn't understand me.

I want my freedom.

Muffled footsteps approached. Bethany jumped to her feet and brushed the hay off her dress. She was supposed to be…what was she supposed to be doing? Milking the cows again? Too early.

Supper. She shouldn't even be in the barn. She would be scolded for daydreaming instead of working. Maybe she could pretend she'd needed to get some more eggs, since the ones Caroline had collected that morgen had cracked. Why hadn't she situated herself in a stall, where she could hide, instead of sitting in plain sight in the main room?

She slumped. Braced herself for a harsh reprimand.

Silas came into view, lugging the chainsaw. He stopped when he saw her.

"I was praying." She tried for a smile but failed. Making an effort to pray was more like it. But Gott hadn't showed up. Again.

He nodded. "The fence is back up. Preacher Samuel came by and helped. He said he would stop by tomorrow with Sam to saw up the tree and haul the pieces to the woodpile." He returned the chainsaw to the shelf Bethany had taken it from earlier.

"Danki. So glad Mamm said you could stay. For a while. Until spring, jah?" Maybe she was pushing it. *Please, don't say nein.*

Because she didn't want to leave until the weather was warmer.

Silas made some kind of noncommittal grunt as he turned toward her. His gaze skimmed over her face and hesitated a moment before catching her eyes with his. She stared into their smoky depths. If only she could see past the clouds…see what he was thinking….

Did he like what he saw when he looked at her?

He approached her, his gaze still holding hers, as he slowly pulled off his gloves, finger by finger.

Bethany didn't dare breathe as he reached for her. Her eyes fluttered shut as his skin brushed hers, his thumb tracing a path across her cheek. She leaned toward him.

A rooster's crow pierced the silence, and the spell was broken.

Silas dropped his hand to his side. "It was…."

Insane. Ridiculous. Crazy.

Seconds of heart-twisting awe.

He cleared his throat. "It was a spider."

～

Silas shoved his hands behind his back, hating that they trembled. Whether from the spider—though it'd been small, and probably not venomous—or from touching Bethany so intimately, he wasn't sure.

Not even twenty-four hours into his return to Jamesport, and he'd touched her intimately more times than the two had had casual contact when he'd lived there.

He had to keep his hands to himself. For more reasons than one.

"I need to go start supper." Bethany's voice wavered, as if she'd been as affected by the exchange as he had.

Impossible.

She inhaled noisily, then exhaled. "Sammy Miller is getting married this Thursday. They were supposed to get married in November, but the date they had picked turned out to be Thanksgiving, so they decided this week would be better. First Thursday in December."

Silas hitched an eyebrow at the random news. He didn't know quite how to respond. Other than to say, *So what?*

But then, Sam Miller had been a friend of his when he lived here. Maybe Bethany remembered that. Or maybe she just thought he should know, since Sam would be coming over the next morgen to help.

Or perhaps she was asking him out in an unassuming Amish-girl way. Saying, in not so many words, *I'll be there if you will, and if you so choose, you can sit with me and take me home after the singing.*

His gaze locked on hers as he tried to decipher her intent, but the mesmerizing blueness of her eyes kept him from gaining any clarity. He grinned, and when she smiled back, his knees weakened.

He wanted to touch her again.

Without either excuse of preventing a fall or chasing a spider.

Instead, he forced himself to look away. "Best get back to work. Your mamm gave me a long list of chores she wanted done today." Not that those were possible now, with the tree and fence he'd worked on a gut portion of the morgen and afternoon.

He hadn't even stopped for lunch, though one of Bethany's younger sisters—he couldn't remember her name—had brought him a sandwich, a banana, and a couple of cookies. She hadn't stayed to talk with him.

Bethany would've. Probably why they hadn't sent her.

Another grin threatened to erupt on his face. He turned away and headed outside. Away from her.

"There'll be a…a…a frolic here on Saturday."

Silas glanced over his shoulder.

Bethany followed him.

"Will there?"

She shrugged. "If Mamm agrees. It's Rosemary's birthday."

He chuckled as he turned to face her. Again. "Maybe you'd better clear it with your mamm before you go inviting people."

Her cheeks pinkened. "I've already invited everyone."

"You have a tendency to put the buggy before the horse, ain't so?"

She looked away. "Well, she can't easily say nein now. But I guess I do need to let her know."

Silas glanced around. "I'll make sure an area's clear for the volley-ball game. But, if I were your mamm, I'd say nein on the principle of the thing."

Bethany sighed. "But it's been ever so long since we had any fun. My birthday frolic was canceled because of Daed's…arrest." Bethany swiped at something just beneath her eye. A tear? "I'd better go fix supper." She turned and strode toward the haus, her skirts swaying.

Silas stopped to watch.

Maybe staying here was an option.

As long as the news didn't get out to the wrong people.

⌒

Bethany hurried up the porch stairs, opened the door, and stepped inside the all-season room. Mamm stood next to the wringer washer, studying the clothes drying on the line. "You did better than I thought you would today. The clothes actually look clean."

Bethany ignored the barb. "I need to tell you something." *Please, Gott, if You can hear me, help this to go well.*

"I know. You aren't over your crush on Silas. Seems you can imagine yourself in love with a bu at will." Mamm pursed her lips.

Bethany swallowed. The only bu she'd ever imagined herself in love with was Silas. "Um, nein, that isn't it. Rosemary's birthday—"

"We won't discuss it."

"I've already invited people."

"Then un-invite them," Mamm snapped.

"But it's been *forever* since we celebrated anything. Not Christmas, not Thanksgiving. Not since before Ezra—"

"We won't discuss him. Or it."

"Just because he's dead doesn't mean we don't have a right to live." Bethany's eyes burned with tears at her own bluntness. She softened her voice. "It's just that, well, Christmas is coming, and it'd be nice to actually make an effort this year—"

"Bethany Suzanne. Stop being so selfish. I lost my sohn and my ehemann, and all you can think of is yourself."

"*I'm* being selfish?" Bethany drew back as tears streamed down her cheeks.

"I'm struggling to make ends meet, and you go and get yourself fired—from the only job you've ever had that paid a decent wage—by talking too much and being too nosy. We *needed* that money." Mamm glared. "At least we have plenty of food on hand. But I'm using your babysitting money to pay that bu."

"But we needed the help."

"I agree. And your babysitting money will be well spent, I'm sure. But the holidays aren't happening. Not this year, not next. Not ever." Mamm's stare hardened. "Now stop crying like a boppli and go fix supper."

Bethany wiped her cheeks with her sleeve.

See, Gott? You don't even care. Why won't You listen?

Silence.

Of course.

Chapter 6

Silas collapsed on the thin, worn blanket covering the pile of hay in the loft, more tired than he'd ever been since leaving home. But this was a gut kind of tired. He earned this fatigue through hard, honest work, instead of by plodding across the Kansas plains and the gently rolling hills of northern Missouri, fighting depression and discouragement every step of the way.

Now he was back where he belonged. Well, in the first community where he'd been accepted, anyway. With his parents yanking up roots every two to three years, it was hard to fit in anywhere. He'd figured the Pennsylvania home base, where his onkel and aenti lived, as well as both sets of großeltern, was the best place for him to go. The place where he would finally fit in. Settle down. Raise a family.

If he could get past his demons long enough to do so.

The likelihood of that feat was debatable. Would anyone raised in his family be able to escape the past?

Nein man can hold another in the gutter unless he stays there himself. Preacher Samuel had answered Silas's question with those words a few years back.

They'd seemed like wise words then.

Still did.

Gut thing he'd started taking the necessary steps toward climbing out of the gutter. Now he just had to make sure he stayed out.

Gott willing, he would not become what he had escaped.

He sat up just enough to push some hay into a higher pile to form a cushion for his head, then gathered another musty blanket over his legs.

Something creaked. The sound seemed to have kum from the ladder.

Silas turned his head. "Who's there?"

"It's me. Bethany."

He sucked in a noisy breath. "Uh...."

"I'm bringing you a sleeping bag, a pillow, and a cot from our last camping trip with the other unmarrieds. Sorry I didn't bring them up here earlier. Honestly, I didn't remember them till now. I had to get Timothy out of bed to help me dig up the cot from the cellar. It was kind of buried."

The dim glow of a lantern lit the loft as she appeared at the top of the ladder. She tossed the rolled-up sleeping bag onto the loft floor, then unstrapped a pillow from her shoulder and set it on top.

Gut thing he'd fixed that broken ladder rung. There were others that had cracked and needed attention. A job for another day.

"You should've kum to get me. I would've helped." He scrambled out from under the blanket and moved toward her.

Her face reddened in the flickering light, and she hesitated as her gaze settled below his neck.

Silas looked down at his ragged long johns, in all their permanently dingy glory. His face heated.

At least he was modest.

Somewhat.

Bethany cleared her throat and met his eyes again. "I still need to bring up the cot."

"I'll get it," Silas said. "Let me just put on some pants." Grinning, he motioned for her to avert her gaze.

Her blush became fiercer as she stepped off the ladder into the loft and turned her body away. "I'll help you set it up," she murmured.

"Maybe you'd better get back to the haus. You don't want your mamm knowing you sneaked out here." Silas hurriedly pulled on a pair of pants.

"She's sound asleep," Bethany said without turning around. "Besides, we're not talking to each other right now."

Silas started down the ladder. "And why is that? You can look now, by the way." At the bottom, he glanced around. Since Timothy had gotten the cot out of the basement, it seemed likely that he would've helped Bethany carry it to the barn. Especially since he'd seemed so protective earlier. But Silas didn't see any sign of the bu, not even lurking in the shadows. Odd.

He lifted the unwieldy box holding the cot, balanced it as best he could, and started back up the ladder.

Bethany watched him, bitterness in her expression. "She said nein frolic for Rosemary's birthday."

Silas chuckled. "Next time, you might want to ask her first."

Bethany shrugged. "Won't make any difference. 'Not now, not ever,' Mamm said."

"Well, you might consider that she's still grieving. I'm not sure how long ago your brother passed, but your daed…he was, um, taken away recently, ain't so?"

She grunted. "My birthday was the end of March. Not so recent. Daed's been gone about eight months, more or less. Long enough."

"Grief has its own timetable. Eight months isn't all that long."

"Where'd you say you were going, again?" Bethany started using a push broom to clear away some straw, probably to make space for the cot.

"Changing the subject, huh?" Silas neared the top of the ladder and slid the box onto the loft floor. "Pennsylvania. But who knows? I might decide to stay around here."

Bethany froze. She muttered something under her breath that he couldn't catch.

"Kum again?" He opened the box and emptied it of the metal bars and canvas topping. From the looks of this narrow, stiff contraption, the hay might be more comfortable. But he wouldn't complain. It was the thought that counted.

"You can't stay here. You simply *can't*. You *have* to take me with you." Her voice was still a mere murmur, but he heard her clearly this time.

He drew in a sharp breath and choked on a mouthful of dust.

She straightened and stared at him as he coughed violently. "Should I get you some water?"

As if he could stop coughing long enough to drink it. He shook his head.

Finally, he recovered his breath enough to rasp, "There is nein chance I'm taking you with me if and when I go. Absolutely none."

Bethany slumped. Tears stung her eyes. "I didn't mean right now. In the spring. After you fall in love with me." Then she snapped her mouth shut before any more words she hadn't intended to say could emerge.

Silas coughed again. Not as hard as before, but his face turned red, either with embarrassment or from the effort of keeping his rebuttal unsaid, she couldn't tell.

Seconds passed. Minutes.

He cleared his throat. "Even if we were to fall in love, I wouldn't take you with me. Walking that far is rough. And hitchhiking is too dangerous for a maidal."

She'd figured they would've gone by bus. But there wasn't any point springing that idea on him. She hadn't planned to spill her intentions in a messy heap in the loft, but maybe it was a gut thing she'd done so. It would give him time to get used to the idea of taking her with him. Because he sure wouldn't marry her. Not if he knew her secrets....

He finished setting up the cot, and she helped him move it to the area she'd cleared of hay. He unrolled the sleeping bag on top of it, and she plopped the fat pillow at the head. "There you go. Sleep tight." She grinned at him.

"Take the lantern with you. I won't need it." The flickering light cast moving shadows across his face.

She hesitated. "But they might notice the light coming from the barn. And then I'd get in trouble for sneaking out to be with you." Her face heated. She shouldn't have kum out here, but she trusted Silas.

"You shouldn't have." He parroted her thoughts. "I can't exactly afford to lose this job."

Bethany looked down. Scuffed her feet in the dusty hay. "I was just trying to be nice."

"Won't they miss the lantern?"

She shook her head. "It's from the shelf on the all-weather porch. Nobody goes out there at this hour of the nacht."

"Except you." Silas hesitated a moment, then sighed. "I'll hold it over the edge while you climb down the ladder. I don't want you falling again."

"Danki."

"Appreciate your thinking of me. The sleeping bag will be a lot warmer than this." He kicked at the thin, holey blanket he'd used the nacht before. A mouse scurried out of it and across his bare foot. Where were all the cats when he needed them?

She nodded. "See you in the morgen."

Down below, the barn doors slid open. A light flashed over the loft. Bethany skittered back into the shadows. Hopefully, out of sight.

"Silas?" Mamm called. "Have you seen Bethany?"

Bethany shook her head, but Silas didn't look at her. He remained quiet for a long moment, staring down at her mother. The lantern swung slightly. It seemed that everything had silenced—even the usual nacht sounds, such as the scratching of mice scratching—while awaiting his reply.

"She's up here," he finally said. "She brought me a cot and a sleeping bag a few minutes ago." He glanced over his shoulder and gestured for Bethany to step forward.

She exhaled sharply.

He got points for honesty.

It hurt when Bethany glared at Silas as she stalked past. She descended the ladder in silence and joined her mamm at the bottom. The two women were quiet until they exited the barn, at which point a heated exchange began. Their words were blown away by the strong wind.

Silas hated getting Bethany into trouble for her act of kindness, but he wasn't going to lie to her mamm—or to anyone. He needed to prove himself trustworthy. To be honest. Wasn't that part of becoming a man of integrity? That, and kindness. Love. Longsuffering. And all the other fruits of the Spirit, whatever they might be. He needed to study up on them sometime instead of relying on a faulty memory. Too bad he'd been forced to leave his Bible back in Kansas.

Danki, Lord, that I have shelter for the nacht. A job, nein matter how temporary. Food. Water. You're meeting all my needs, even now.

Daed had warned him that walking away from the family and the faith was the same as selling his soul to the devil. And he had wrestled the old worn Bible from Silas's hands, claiming Silas wouldn't need it, since he was forever lost.

Not true. He had escaped a living hell and found true freedom.

Another proverb quoted by Preacher Samuel flashed through his mind: "If a man speaks ill of you, live so that nobody will believe it."

Nein doubt Bethany's mamm remembered everything Silas's family had ever been accused of. Despite the façade of perfection his family tried to project in public, the preachers, deacons, and bishop had made enough trips to their home. Issued enough warnings and admonitions. Initiated enough counseling sessions.

Not that any of it did any gut. His parents still argued. The abuse—verbal and sometimes physical—continued. Tempers still raged in the overcrowded haus-hold that was filled to the brim with most of his brothers, their wives, and their kinner. With his married but abandoned sister and her boppli. None of them had moved out. Maybe they were afraid to.

It'd taken Silas a long time to work up the courage to make his escape.

His jaw tightened so much, it hurt. He forced himself to concentrate on breathing. *Relax. Just relax.*

Except the heated exchange of raised voices went on outside the barn. Punctuated by the slam of a door. Loud noises that made him jump.

Silas squeezed his eyes shut. *Be with Bethany right now, Lord.* Then he opened his eyes again. Maybe he should intervene, and prompt his dismissal. He could move on in the morgen, if they let him stay the rest of the nacht. His leaving might calm the tempers some.

He scurried down the ladder, barefoot and without a coat, and opened the barn doors. "Stop! Just stop."

But nobody was there. The only sound was the wind screaming around the edge of the building. The branches of trees banging against the exterior of the barn.

The haus was dark.

And silent.

Chapter 7

Bethany wrestled with her thoughts as she trailed Mamm into the dark kitchen. Should she apologize—a necessary step, either now or later—or sulk a little longer about the unfair treatment?

The flashlight had died when they'd reached the all-season porch, leaving them to feel their way through the blackness, along a maze of still-damp clothes hanging on the line. The same way Bethany groped along through the darkness of her thoughts.

An apology, albeit not a completely sincere one, would be the first step toward reconciliation and restoration. And Gott knew there was enough discord in the family without an extra contribution from her.

Bethany felt her way to the drawer where they kept the batteries. Mamm opened the door of the woodstove to give the room a little light.

"I have the batteries." Bethany grabbed a couple of D cells and set them on the counter. "I'm sorry."

The old batteries clanked at the bottom of the trash can. Mamm stepped behind Bethany and reached for the new ones. "Danki for the batteries. What are you apologizing for?"

"For pushing you. Silas reminded me that grief has its own time-table. And we've been through a lot. You, more than me."

Mamm nodded. "I'm glad you realize that. Since Ezra died, it's been like a nacht that never ends." Her voice softened. "I don't want you to be hurt or to think I don't care, but I do want—need—time to heal."

They all needed that. Probably Mamm more than the rest, since she shouldered the bulk of the responsibility for the family right now.

"We've had a lot of blows," Mamm added.

More than Mamm knew, probably. A wave of nausea rose in Bethany's throat. She pushed her unwelkum thoughts away. "I'll try to find another job. I know you need the babysitting money for more than just paying Silas."

Mamm patted her on the arm. "Ich liebe dich, Bethany." The flashlight flicked on. "It works. Danki, again. I'm going to bed. If you're staying up, please, remain in the haus. You did your gut deed, delivering bedding to Silas. You don't need to tempt the poor bu further. And don't forget to bank the stove." The light disappeared with Mamm.

Bethany reached for a candle and lit it, then grabbed a mug. Hot chocolate sounded gut. She checked the woodstove. Still hot. But she added another log, anyway. She would bank it when she was ready for bed.

Why was Hen the only one who'd kum courting? Not that his treatment of her could really be called "courtship." He'd showed up mainly to talk to Daed. And yet, she'd imagined there was more to her relationship with him. He'd never said he loved her. He'd only told her that Daed wanted them to marry, and she'd accepted his word as gospel truth. And had given herself to him in every way she could.

Or was it that she'd been taken by force? After all, Daed was the bishop. Nobody questioned him, since he was considered being just one step beneath der Herr. At least, that's what Hen had said. Multiple times. Gott talked to Daed. Told him things.

Things he then told Hen to do. Nein questions asked.

Burn barns. Kill black cats.

Hurt my dochter.

Bethany's eyes burned. Her throat swelled shut.

But where was Hen when she was alone in the outhaus, cramping? Crying as a result of their sins left her body, yet feeling strangely relieved?

She didn't intend to make the same mistake twice.

But then, she had. Almost. Practically begging Silas to be her date at Sammy's wedding. Nein wonder he hadn't given her a definite answer—or any answer at all, really, other than a grunt. He was probably horrified by her boldness. And then she'd followed it up with her blundering demand that he take her with him after they fell in love.

She winced.

Okay, so she wouldn't make the same mistake a third time.

Shame filled her.

She flirted entirely too often with too many different men. Viktor. David. Josh. Hen. Sammy. The list went go on and on.

Nein wonder nobody courted her. She chased after any beardless male in suspenders and pants. Desperate for love and acceptance. Mostly looking for an escape.

Ach, the shame.

Bethany bowed her head. But didn't pray. If Gott didn't hear her requests, there wasn't any point in confessing her shortcomings to Him.

She went to the refrigerator and pulled out the pitcher of milk. Hot chocolate tasted so much better made with milk than with water. Richer. Creamier.

The door opened, and the room lit with the glow of a lantern. Silas stood in the doorway. "I…I thought I'd get a glass of water." His gaze traveled upward, above Bethany's head.

She blinked at the pitcher she'd raised in the air like a weapon. Then she lowered the milk. "You were only milliseconds away from devastating pain."

He chuckled. "Death by dairy product."

"You know it." Bethany poured some milk into her mug. "I'm making hot chocolate. Would you like some?"

Silas shrugged.

"Was that a jah or a nein?"

He grinned. "Jah, that sounds gut. Danki." His smile faded. "Will your mamm mind my being inside? The haus was dark, I thought… well, that you all had gone to bed."

"As if that would make it better? Sneaking into an unmarried maidal's haus, after the family went to bed?" And there she went again—flirting, teasing, taunting. Curse her tongue. "Never mind."

"Did you get in trouble?" He came farther into the room, apparently ignoring her run-away words. Her unintentional reminder of the Amish courting practices.

"Nein. Mamm and I…we're gut. At least we're talking again. I apologized, and she accepted. Even offered an explanation. How'd you get so wise, anyway?" She forced a smile, thankful for the change of subject.

Silas slid into a chair. "Preacher Samuel. He's a wealth of wisdom. I'm looking forward to having more talks with him about Gott. I've so much to learn. I need to know how to...." He fell silent.

Bethany filled another mug with milk, then returned the pitcher to the refrigerator. "He's not the Gott of happy stories that came with molasses cookies and grape-flavored juice boxes during school. I don't know who He is." She set the mugs on the stove. "All I know is, He doesn't care. Maybe He isn't even real, and we're just deceiving ourselves."

Silas looked up and blinked. "I don't have it all figured out, but I know He's real. It's real...our faith, I mean. And I'm not done searching. All I know is, He said to trust, and that's what I'm trying to do."

Bethany shook her head. "That's not gut enough for me anymore. I want answers. I want to understand." She ripped the tops off two packets of hot chocolate at once. The violent act did nothing to relieve her frustration. She propped the packets against the cookie jar, hesitated, then removed the lid and lifted out four sugar cookies. She arranged them on a plate, which she then carried to the table. "He doesn't hear my prayers."

"He hears them. And He cares. It's just that, sometimes, He works in the shadows. Behind the scenes. And when He reveals His work, it's perfect. Totally Gott. Believe that."

His voice was barely above a whisper. As if he were telling himself the same thing.

If only she could believe it. Part of her heart seemed to embrace the idea. But the other part pushed it away. *Lies, all lies.* Still, the longing to believe pushed its way to the forefront.

Maybe he wasn't really Silas. Maybe he was an angel Gott had sent to convict her.

As if Gott did that sort of thing.

The milk was hot. Bethany stirred the hot chocolate mixes into the mugs, then carried them to the table and she sat down across from Silas. "Who are you?"

⟋⟍

Silas stared at the miniature marshmallows floating like hard pebbles on the surface of the hot chocolate, apparently undisturbed by the heat that was slowly softening them. Making them more suitable for human consumption.

Was that what he was going through—a softening? Was Gott heating him, putting him through a trial by fire, to make him more pliable for doing His will?

He shivered.

Lord Gott, help me to be receptive to the molding process. Heal me, help me, hold me.

Bethany sighed loudly.

Silas jumped. "Was ist letz?"

And then he remembered. He hadn't answered her question. *Who are you?* But what could he say? She knew him.

He'd wanted to court her. Until....

Okay, so she knew part of him. The public part. She didn't know the real him that suffered at home and longed to break free. To rise from the gutter. To escape the sins that made him turn his face away from anyone driving a motor vehicle until the coast was clear.

"Have you ever watched your dreams slide away?" Her latest query interrupted his thoughts. "Going, going, going...gone."

He was looking at one of his dreams that had slid away. "More times than I can say." His voice cracked. Even staying here seemed an unrealistic fantasy. If the wrong people found out....

"There's a posting in *The Budget* from a widower in southern Missouri, advertising for a frau. Seven kinner. If a woman feels it's the will of der Herr, she's supposed to send a note to the designated post office box. Maybe I should answer it and start over in Seymour, Missouri. Shed the stigma of being the bishop's dochter. The too-talkative one who doesn't know when to shut up. Or maybe I would just be exchanging my problems here for a new set of troubles."

"Uh...." How was he supposed to respond to that? "Why did you say you wanted to kum with me?" Maybe that would be a way to divert her thoughts.

She released a loud sigh. "I'm tired of being the bishop's dochter. I'm tired of the endless questions about Daed and his terrible decisions. I'm tired of people looking at me as if they wonder whether I'm as off in den kopf as he is. I want to escape the shame of some of my actions. If I could pull all the barriers down, I'd leave this town in the dust. But you're the only one I know who's left. The only one who's leaving."

"Ah." Not such a safe topic, after all. "I'm not planning on falling in love and getting married, you know."

She shrugged. "I'm not planning on marrying you."

Well, gut. That was settled.

What wasn't gut was the sharp sting of rejection he felt.

"Do you always go around rejecting girls you hardly know?" Her voice broke. She shoved her hot chocolate away, untouched.

Like his.

But something about the exchange struck his funny bone. He barely held back a chuckle. "Do you always go around proposing to men you hardly know?"

She straightened. Glared. "I didn't propose."

Silas shook his head. "Ach, but you did. You said you were going to go with me after we fell in love. And if I took a girl with me that I loved, it would only be as my frau."

～

So much for that escape route. Another dream was shot. Killed. Murdered in cold blood.

Bethany slumped in her chair and watched Silas down his hot chocolate in one long gulp. Then he stood. "Gut nacht, Bethany."

She reached for the plate of cookies. As if a sweet treat might ease the pain of yet another rejection.

Not that she'd ever been out-and-out rejected before. Just ignored. Passed over. Forgotten in favor of some other girl.

They were all rejections, in essence.

His hand landed on her shoulder. "Don't give up. Bad things will kum and go, but our good Gott will be a constant in your life."

Gott. The One who'd forgotten her. The One whose treatment of her matched that of every other male: ignoring. Passing over. Forgetting. Rejecting.

Except for Hen. He'd forced her. Used her.

The door closed behind Silas.

Leaving her in the room with the single flickering candle.

She put her head down on the table and wept.

Chapter 8

A harsh cough broke the peacefulness of the barn. A snuffle followed.

Silas glanced to the side, removing his head from where it was pressed against the flank of the cow he was milking.

Timothy stood there staring at him as if he'd grown vampire teeth. "Morgen."

The bu grabbed another three-legged stool and the other pail. "Bethany's on her way out. She does half the milking." His voice was hoarse. He coughed again.

"Guess she doesn't need to today. Unless you want her to do your share, since you're sick."

"Doesn't mean you're welkum here." The bu's voice cracked and rose in pitch, foiling the intended effect.

"I know." Silas kept the edge out of his own voice. He hadn't expected to be welkum. Just thought it would be nice.

"But…." Timothy drew in a noisy breath, then coughed again. "Mamm says you're doing a gut job."

Silas raised an eyebrow at the unexpected praise. He was just doing as he'd been told. Caring for the farm as if it were his. It never would be, but he could follow orders and earn his keep.

Timothy positioned his stool next to the cow across the aisle. With his booted foot, he nudged a barn cat out of his way. The cat stalked off, its tail flicking stiffly.

The door behind them slammed against the cement wall as Bethany rushed in. "Sorry I'm late!" Another slam. "Where's the other stool?"

Silas straightened as the cat found its way over to him. He squirted a stream of milk toward the creature, then glanced over his shoulder at Bethany. "Milking is mostly finished."

"Ach, Silas. I didn't mean for you to do my chores, but danki."

Her smile reached deep inside him, warming him. He responded with a grin, then forced himself to look away. Back to the cow and the spoiled cat that demanded another drink with its plaintive "Meow!"

"Mamm's going to visit Daed today." Bethany stopped beside him and leaned one hand against the cow, one hip jutting out.

Timothy stopped working, scooted back, and eyed Silas.

Silas's eyes skimmed her body from the feet upward, noting her seductive pose. The tip of her tongue peeked out, moistening her soft-looking lips. Making him want more than he should. He shook his head, as if that would clear his head of inappropriate thoughts. Why did he need to know her mamm would be gone? It wasn't as if he'd take advantage of her absence. "I'll likely be busy with the tree most of the day."

Her smile dimmed, and a look of distaste crossed her face. "I guess I'm not needed here." She glanced away, her cheeks flaming red. Without another word, she pushed away from the bovine and started for the cement stairs leading to the main area of the barn.

"She has her mind set on becoming a frau," Timothy muttered dryly.

"Well, she's already rejected me." Not exactly the way it had gone down, but her brother didn't need to know the details.

Timothy paused with his milking again and gawked. "You already proposed?"

Silas chuckled and shook his head. "She made it clear she's not intending to marry me." Not that he'd planned on asking. At least, not this time around. Years ago, he might have. Before—

"Well, gut." Timothy's expression relaxed. Softened. "Maybe you'll work out, after all."

So, Timothy had some knowledge of his sister's dissatisfaction.

"Daed decided she's going to marry Hen. And Daed's the bishop, you know. What he says goes."

Despite Timothy's matter-of-fact tone, there seemed to be a measure of doubt behind his words. Maybe he wanted to cling to the familiar for a sense of security as his world unraveled around him.

Who was Bethany's daed to decide whom she'd marry? Silas moved the pail away and cleaned the cow's udder. "She says Hen's in jail."

"Jah, but they won't convict him. He was just following orders." Again, Timothy sounded uncertain.

Silas lifted his shoulders in a shrug. "Gott's will be done," he muttered.

Then he winced. Lately, it seemed he was all about pious-sounding platitudes. He knew all the right answers; somehow, they just didn't mean much. He spoke without true conviction behind his words. Nobody would believe him if they knew how much he struggled. With belief. With faith in Gott. With life. With the unexpected desire to comfort Bethany the only way he knew how.

It was wrong. So wrong.

Silas looked around, searching the barn for something to take his mind off his thoughts. His gaze lit on Timothy, snapping the metal lids on the milk pails. Silas picked up his stool and hung it next to the other one. "I'll take the milk up to the haus, unless you'd rather do it," Timothy said.

"No, you go ahead. I'll stay here and muck the stalls." Because even that undesirable task was better than facing Bethany sooner than he had to.

⌣

Bethany despised herself sometimes. She had the best of intentions. She'd made her decision last nacht. She'd cried herself to sleep at the table, and awakened with a painful crick in her neck. And the very first thing she'd done that morgen was flirt with Silas, letting him know that Mamm would be gone later that day. As if the news would prompt him to drop everything and take her on a long walk. Share a picnic lunch at the pond. Or do any of the other things she used to dream of a beau doing with her.

None of which Hen had ever done.

He'd taken her on short walks, true. To a secluded spot, where she would listen to him go on and on about how wise Daed was, and how blessed they were that he was the bishop. And then she would endure his attentions.

Endured was a fitting word. She'd never experienced the wunder-baar feelings her friends had described when they told her that their special man had taken them by the hand. Stolen a kiss.

Hen's attentions weren't anything special. Tolerable, as long as she didn't resist him.

Ach, the guilt. The shame. The fear.

But a beau—and marriage—those were expected. Gut things. To be desired.

And she was twenty. Almost an old maud.

Though she might rather remain a maud, if marrying would mean being treated by her ehemann the way Hen treated her.

"I will not chase after Silas, or any other man, ever again." She made her statement to any mice that might be listening as she marched through the barn, not even stopping to get out her diary and record her resolution. Not when it resulted from a string of negative self-talk.

She wiped a runaway tear off her cheek and left the barn, bracing herself against the chilly breeze. At least it wasn't quite as cold as the day before.

"They're gonna think you're desperate." Timothy's voice broke into her thoughts as he matched pace with her. "Throwing yourself at all the men like that."

It wasn't quite *all* the men. Just the young ones who'd never been married. The ones that, to her knowledge, had never even been in love. Maybe she'd have more luck if she set her sights on a widower with seven kinner.

She'd write that man in Seymour to-nacht. She could pretend to be the perfect prospective frau, despite her doubts. Despite her history as being the desperate, half-crazy, nosy gossip of a bishop's dochter. Despite her lack of communication with Gott. After all, she had plenty of practice bowing her head in submission. To Daed. To Mamm. To Hen. Even to Timothy, though he was just a thirteen-year-old bu.

"I'm not desperate." Did the objection sound as weak to him as it did to her? "Just tired of being passed over. Forgotten. Overlooked. Or maybe feared because I'm the bishop's dochter."

Timothy made a noise that was somewhere between a snort and a cough. "I get that."

He would. He was the bishop's sohn.

Bethany held the haus door open for her brother. He set the pails down on the kitchen floor, then headed back out with a sniffle.

Mamm glanced over from the stove and raised an eyebrow. "Is he sick?"

"I don't know. But my part of the barn work's all done. I'll wash up and help with breakfast." Bethany eyed the table, where she'd last seen the newspaper. "Where's the latest issue of *The Budget?*"

"In the fire." Rosemary poked at the log she'd just added, then shut the doors of the woodstove as something inside it burst into flames.

So much for writing to the widower. Bethany pressed her lips together, blinked the tears from her eyes, and hurried over to the sink. "What...." Her voice cracked. "What do you need me to do?"

"You can stir the Cream of Wheat. Make sure there aren't any lumps." Mamm expertly flipped an egg. She was cooking them over easy, something Bethany had yet to master. Bethany always broke the yolk.

Bethany picked up the wooden spoon and plunged it into the bubbling liquid. She swirled it around, making sure to get the edges, and smashing the lumps against the sides of the pan.

What would she do now? Silas didn't want her. The widower option had gone up in flames. She cast a baleful glance at her sister. Should she resign herself to marrying Hen, as undesirable as that option was?

It wasn't really an option. Daed had decided, and Hen had agreed. She hadn't been given a choice. Even if all Hen wanted was to use her. To take from her things he shouldn't have. To ruin her.

Nein decent man would have her if he knew the truth.

She'd told him nein. Even tried to fight him off. But he'd reasoned that they were going to be married, anyway. And he'd punctuated his argument with a slap of the hand. Or the fist. Or a kick of the knee.

She wiped another tear from her cheek. Hopefully, Mamm would just think the moisture was steam from the boiling pot.

It'd hurt. Hurt! And she'd felt violated. Afterward, when she'd cried, Hen had called her a big boppli and reminded her that it was her lot in life to become his frau in every way.

She brushed at yet another tear.

Maybe it really would be best if she never married. She wouldn't have to endure that duty, then. But how could she escape if she didn't marry? Hire herself out as a maud or a caregiver? In a different district far, far away?

She'd have to think more about that option. Make a plan. If done right, it might work. Assuming she had the domestic skills to offer.

Well, she could learn. It wasn't too late for that.

The cereal had thickened, so Bethany moved the pot to the back of the stove. "Should I ring the bell for breakfast?"

"Go ahead." Mamm carried two plates of eggs to the table. "Then dish out the cereal."

Bethany headed for the door, but it opened before she reached it. Timothy came inside, followed by Carrie and Sarah. And Silas.

After unbundling, Silas waited in line at the sink. He paused long enough to let Bethany pass in front of him with the bowls of hot cereal. "Smells gut. I love Cream of Wheat." He added a smile.

Bethany's heart warmed and tripped. She grinned back at him.

There was nothing like a man's appreciation.

Too bad he'd rejected her.

⌒

Silas stood by a fallen tree, chainsaw in hand, and watched as the white van carrying Bethany's mamm and her younger sister Emma disappeared into a cloud of dust down the dirt road. Bethany and Rosemary had been left to handle the haus-hold chores. Rosemary had announced that she would strain the milk and start the bread, while Bethany would do a load of the "never-ending laundry." Her words.

Silas grinned as he imagined her filling the machine with hot water and homemade laundry detergent, kept in a big lidded pail like the one he'd seen beside the wringer washer yesterday when he'd gone to take a shower. The orange pail with a label from a hardware store had caught his attention. Briefly. Not even a fluorescent-orange pail was bright enough to distract his focus from Bethany for long.

Preacher Samuel and Sam hadn't showed up yet, but the preacher hadn't specified a time, either.

Silas had cut close to a half rick of wood when Bethany materialized beside him, a Thermos in her hands. She held it out to him as he powered off the chainsaw. He set the tool on the ground and accepted the Thermos. "Danki."

"Careful, it's hot. It's tea. I brewed a kettle and thought you might like some. Or, if you'd rather have koffee, I can make more."

"Tea is gut." He liked it well enough, though Mamm's herbal tea tended to be too weak. He wouldn't be picky now.

"I much prefer it to koffee, myself. Koffee's too bitter for my tastes."

Silas grinned. "Daed always said it puts hair on your chest."

"Then I guess it's a gut thing I don't care for it."

A car approached on the road. Silas shifted so that his back was toward it, then lowered his hat over his eyes.

"Can I help?" Bethany asked.

He nodded toward the waiting wagon. He'd unhitched the horse and led the animal to the pasture to wait until it was time to move the vehicle again. "If you want, you can start loading the wood." He came nearer to Bethany and hefted a log. "Your mamm told me the approximate length she needed these cut."

"That looks about right." Bethany lifted another log and put it in the wagon. "I'm sorry for flirting with you. You don't need to kum with me to Sammy's wedding."

He'd forgotten all about it. "Thursday, you said?"

Bethany nodded. "Tomorrow."

"Preacher Samuel said he and Sam would be by today to help." Silas turned and looked down the road but didn't see as much as a speck of dust rising. He probably shouldn't count on them coming. Not with Sam's wedding scheduled for the next day. But would Preacher Samuel really have forgotten his own son's marriage when he'd promised their services?

"They'll be by, if he said they'd kum." Bethany tossed another log onto the wagon. "Besides, it's the women who take care of all the work—the cooking and the cleaning and such. Though I suppose the men have the benches and tables to set up."

Silas sighed. "I'll be glad to take you to the wedding and bring you home after the singing. If you don't think Hen will mind." Being with her in a public setting would eliminate some of the temptation.

Or so he hoped. Even now, in plain sight of Gott and man, he longed for the kiss he'd always dreamed of sharing with her. Longed to hold her in his arms. To sift the silky strands of her hair through his fingers.

So much for squelching the temptation.

Bethany's face darkened. "I don't particularly care if he minds or not."

Whoa. Silas eyed her as he tossed another log into the wagon. Then another. "I guess you don't, if you're planning on writing that widower looking for a frau." He tried to keep his tone light, though the idea bothered him more than it should have.

She threw a log harder than necessary. "Not anymore. My sister burned the newspaper with the ad in it."

Silas turned aside to hide his smile.

"So, I'm going to find a job to support myself. Maybe as a mother's helper or a caregiver. I don't need to marry. Don't want to. It's not like anyone would have me, anyway. Especially if they knew he—" Another log banged against the head of the wagon.

Silas stopped working and studied her. "If they knew he what?"

He could fill in the gaps between her thinly veiled anger at the mention of Hen, and the rumors and questions about her daed's behavior. Either one would be a deterrent to a potential suitor.

She avoided his eyes. Her face reddened.

Ach. It was a personal reason. A shameful reason. Had to be.

He went back to work, but he wanted to throttle Hen. How could he treat Bethany like that? Dear, sweet, innocent Bethany. Nein wonder she wanted to escape this place and the memories associated with it.

"He doesn't deserve you," he muttered.

"Nobody deserves me, wreck that I am."

"You're not a wreck." Silas turned to pick up a log, and noticed a horse and wagon in the distance. Preacher Samuel and Sam were on their way. "You could, uh, tell Preacher Samuel that Hen dishonored you."

"Then they'll only force him to marry me. Not what I want."

"It has nothing to do with marriage. My parents always told us buwe not to touch a woman until we were married. Not even casually. But I expect that rule had to do with many things." Not just sex, but maybe also the anger issues that had compelled the family to flee the community in shame. After Henry had beaten his old girlfriend Esther, the preachers had spotted Henry's frau, Lily, with an unexplained broken arm. Behavior learned from their daed. Silas realized that the unexplained broken bones and bruises his brothers and sisters had gone to school or to church with were actually easier to explain than people thought.

Silas had touched Bethany. He'd run his hands over the soft curves of her body after she fell from the loft. Touched her shoulder on the way out of the haus last night.

She'd seen him wearing only his long johns.

But he never would have attempted anything inappropriate. And Hen needed to be held accountable for his actions.

Bethany turned and looked at him with wide eyes. "What?"

Silas stared at her in disbelief. Had he spoken his thoughts out loud?

Chapter 9

S o, the rumors were true," Bethany said softly. She lowered her gaze and kicked at a log. "You were abused."

An ugly scowl appeared on Silas's face. He picked up a log and hurled it into the wagon. It bounced against the front and flew over the edge, hitting the ground on the opposite side. Then he took a deep breath, seeming to have regained composure. "Not just me. All of us. But not all the time, just when tempers raged. Which was entirely too often in our overcrowded haus."

Bethany walked around to the front of the wagon, retrieved the wayward log, and tossed it in the back. "Your aim is bad when you're angry."

He didn't crack a smile.

"I'm sorry for sticking my nose where it didn't belong. I'm gut at doing that." She glanced at the approaching wagon, driven by Preacher Samuel. "I should probably get back to the haus." Before she opened her mouth again and made another not-thought-out remark. That would be totally inappropriate.

As if his earlier comment was appropriate, reminding her of his gentle touches when she'd fallen from the hayloft ladder. Reminding her of the desire that ignited briefly within before she snuffed it out. The dwindling hope that maybe things would be different with Silas. That maybe he was the *one* who would be special.

She knew better. Silas was a man. And she didn't want *that* again. Ever.

Even if he hadn't known what he was saying, it was nice to know he would never force her to do what Hen had. But the fact that he had guessed the truth about what Hen did to her....

Her face burned with embarrassment.

"Wait." Silas reached out and wrapped his gloved hand around hers.

She gazed up at him, imagining she could feel his heat through the thick fabric. She struggled for breath. *Why, Gott? Why can't I have a man like Silas? Why couldn't I be gut enough for him?*

"Look, I'm trying to move past my history. That's why I'm here. Well, not exactly. I mean, I'm here because I'm on my way to Pennsylvania. But I'm going there because it was time to go. To, uh, leave home." He let out a harsh-sounding laugh.

"I knew what you meant."

He pulled his hand away. Strange how much she immediately missed it.

"I...I called the police about my family the last nacht I was there. Daed was furious with me. Said I overstepped my boundaries. Maybe I did, but I'd decided enough was enough. Just because I'm a grown man, and my days of being beaten into submission are past, doesn't mean I should just look the other way when I see my brother knocking his frau around for not keeping the boppli quiet when my brother wants to sleep."

"Ach, Silas." She reached out to him.

He evaded her and picked up another log, then placed it neatly in the wagon. "I didn't mean to dump all that on you. It's just...I'm not perfect, okay? I don't have all the answers. I wish I did, but I'm still struggling to find the answers to my own questions." He turned as Preacher Samuel's wagon pulled into the driveway and slowed to a stop.

"I didn't mean to pry." Bethany took a couple of steps backward toward the haus.

Silas shook his head as Sammy hopped down and secured the horse's reins to a fence post. "We'll talk later." He lowered his voice to add, "Maybe we can go for a walk after dark? I could, uh, toss pebbles at your window. If you want."

Bethany's heart rate increased. At the same time, her stomach lurched. Not a pleasant combination. What, now that Silas knew the truth about Hen, did he think he could enjoy the same?

She shook her head. Hard. "Look, I'm sorry for asking you to be my date at Sammy's wedding. I may flirt, but it doesn't necessarily mean I'm interested. I'm *not* desperate. I'm not a—" Her gaze shot past Silas to Sammy and Preacher Samuel, their gazes fixed on her.

Curse her runaway tongue! Her face burned. Bile clogged her throat.

She clamped her hands over her mouth and ran.

~

Silas watched Bethany's hasty retreat to the haus, then pivoted to face Preacher Samuel and his former friend Sam.

Sam delivered a playful punch to Silas's arm. "Welkum back. And you *are* invited to the wedding, Bethany's date or not." He grinned.

Silas glanced at the fleeing figure of Bethany, now scaling the porch steps to the rarely used front door. He looked back at Sam. "I wouldn't miss it. Who's the lucky girl?"

"Her name's Abigail." Sam's voice had softened. Taken on a wistful tone. "She's new to the area, from Sugarcreek, Ohio. Came here recently to live with relatives."

"And you were quick to claim her, jah?" Silas teased.

Sam's smile grew. "Let's just say Gott planned it that way."

Silas looked at the scattered logs on the ground. If only he could count on Gott to plan a relationship for him. He risked another glance toward the haus, but Bethany was nowhere in sight.

"If you want to get the two-man crosscut saw, we can help Silas," Preacher Samuel told his sohn.

"Looks like you're getting the easy way out, with the chainsaw," Sam said with a smirk at Silas.

Silas chuckled. "I'm not afraid of hard work. You can use it if you want."

"Given that you're coming to the wedding nein matter what, maybe you'd like to be my side-sitter? I asked Caleb, but he had to go out of state to a funeral and won't be back in time. He was to accompany Bethany. She's Abigail's side-sitter." Sam's smirk widened into a knowing grin.

Perfect. Just perfect.

Or not. It'd be much better not to pair up with one particular girl. Especially with one he was so interested in.

"Jah, danki." Obviously, his mouth had a mind of its own.

"Great. I'll go grab the crosscut saw." Sam headed for the wagon.

"So, you're giving some thought to staying around here, jah?" Preacher Samuel adjusted his hat to shade his eyes from the sun, which had peeked out from behind the clouds.

Silas shrugged. "What makes you think that?"

The preacher smiled. "Your gaze as it followed her. Bethany's a sweet girl. She has the gift of service, of mercy, and really goes out of her way to take care of people. A bit confused at times, but it's nothing a dose of Gott's healing love can't cure. Of course, that could be said of most of us, ain't so?"

His comments were a bit cryptic, but Silas wouldn't ask him to clarify.

Had Bethany shared her secrets with Preacher Samuel? Or had he read between the lines?

If the latter were true, how much of Silas's hidden past did he know?

❧

Bethany tiptoed into the all-season porch and, as silently as she could, hooked up the water to the wringer washer. She didn't want Rosemary to know she'd snuck outside to talk to Silas.

At least he hadn't flirted with her this time. Had she been flirtatious with him? She tried to remember. He had asked her to go for a walk later. Offered to toss pebbles at her window. She'd declined. She should get points for that, as well as for her apology for asking him to be her date to the post-wedding singing.

While the machine filled with water, Bethany folded the clothes that had dried on the indoor line over-nacht, laying them in neat piles on the round plastic table where they put the starter plants in the springtime.

Maybe she would hang today's laundry outside and let the wind whip the clothes dry, so they would soften more. Silas's jeans were rather stiff. As she forced the unyielding fabric into a fold, she was thankful that it wasn't possible to break denim.

She checked the machine. Full. She turned the water off, and reached for the closest basket. It overflowed with bath towels, dish towels, and rags. The wind would definitely soften those.

She tried to ignore the lure of the chainsaw as it rumbled in the distance. Maybe she would deliver three bottles of water and some cookies to the men as soon as she finished the laundry. That wouldn't be construed as an act of desperation or flirtation.

Or would it? Deliberately seeking Silas out, and with the preacher present....

Well, she was desperate. Desperate to escape Hen.

Rosemary opened the kitchen door and peeked out. "There you are. You were being so quiet, I thought you might've fallen asleep on the job."

Bethany smiled and shrugged. "Just thinking."

"About?"

"Something Timothy said." She hesitated. "Do you think I kum across as desperate?"

Rosemary blinked. "I don't know. At singings, you mean? I've never been to one, since I'm not sixteen. Only a few days to go, now. Do you think Mamm will let us have a party? We had one for you. But not for Emma. That was kind of unfair."

But as she watched the expectant light die in her sister's eyes, Bethany averted her gaze, pained by the expectant light in her sister's eyes. Maybe one of Rosemary's friends would allow Bethany to organize a surprise party at her haus. Mamm wouldn't have to attend. She wouldn't even have to know about it. And Rosemary could have her party.

"I'll take Silas's things out to the barn when I finish." Bethany nodded at the stack of clothes on the table. "Do you mind delivering the rest of the laundry to where it belongs?"

Rosemary slumped. "Jah." She probably took Bethany's change of subject as a negative answer to her question.

"I, um, need to go out as soon as I hang up the laundry. I forgot, I need to...." Ach. She actually had forgotten. "Sammy and Abigail are getting married tomorrow, and I need to, um, help Abigail with some of the preparations. Setting up...you know."

Rosemary nodded. "I need to finish the cheese, but once I'm done, I'll stop by, too, and see how I can help."

"They'll appreciate that." Bethany watched her sister disappear inside the kitchen, and then she returned to the laundry. The faster she finished, the sooner she could do something more exciting. Like setting up for a wedding and talking to her newest friend, Abigail. And maybe planning a birthday party with Rosemary's best friend, Naomi.

The chainsaw silenced. The quieter sound of men's voices took its place.

Silas might enjoy the party. If Naomi agreed, Bethany would let him know.

If he tossed pebbles at her window.

Chapter 10

Cutting up the tree and hauling the pieces to the woodpile took all morning and a good portion of the afternoon. As Silas unloaded the last of the logs and stacked them between two trees along the exterior wall of the barn, he glanced at the laundry flapping in the wind, then looked at the haus.

It was empty. Earlier that morgen, Bethany had left in a pony cart, giving only a brief wave in his direction. He had nein idea where she'd gone. Rosemary had left about an hour later in another tiny cart.

Preacher Samuel and Sam had left about the time the sun reached its highest point. Right after a wagon loaded with benches for the wedding passed by. At the sight of it, Sam had brightened, blushed, then suggested he and his daed head home.

Silas's stomach grumbled with hunger. What was he supposed to do? It seemed wrong to go inside the haus with nobody home, but his body demanded fuel after the hard work he'd put in. He swallowed. At least the tree project was finished. He pulled the wagon into the shed, then approached the haus and entered the all-purpose porch.

He found a pile of his clothes, neatly folded, on a small table. A gut excuse to delay going the rest of the way into the haus. He selected a change of clothes, carried them into the bathroom, and took a shower.

When he finished, Silas deposited the borrowed shirt and pants in the laundry, and opened the door to the kitchen. Silence greeted him.

Maybe it'd be okay if he made himself a sandwich.

He tiptoed barefoot into the room, cringing when a floorboard squeaked. Silly, really—nobody was home, so there was nein need to sneak. He opened the refrigerator and eyed his options. There was some leftover ham from breakfast, and some lettuce. He could make a sandwich, as long as there was enough bread. He went to check the bread box.

A loud sniffle came from behind him.

His hand froze on the lid of the bread box. He glanced slowly over his shoulder.

Timothy.

Silas closed the refrigerator. "Thought you were in school."

"Teacher sent me home. She said I have a fever." The bu coughed. "I was going to heat some chicken noodle soup." He held up a glass jar of home-canned soup. Big chunks of chicken. Carrots. Celery. Onions. And tiny pasta.

Soup sounded so much better than the sandwich Silas was planning to make. And the quart jar held more than enough to share. His stomach rumbled. Again. "I'll heat it for you. For us, if you're sure you don't mind sharing."

"Appreciate it." Timothy handed him the jar. "Where is everyone? I know Emma and Mamm were going to visit Daed, but Bethany and Rosemary…?"

Silas shrugged. "They both left. Bethany earlier than Rosemary. Don't know where they went."

With a frown, Timothy sat at the table. "They didn't say?"

"Not a word." Silas opened the jar, then emptied the contents into a pot on the stove.

"We don't keep money in the bread box, just so you know." Timothy's raspy voice jarred Silas.

"What?" He turned to look at the bu. His insides seemed to shrivel around the hurt his comment caused. "I wasn't looking for money. I'm not here to rob you."

Timothy's mouth quirked. But instead of commenting, he gave a sharp nod.

Which did nothing to relieve the pain his words had caused.

Just because Silas came from a dysfunctional family didn't mean he was a thief.

Bethany helped Abigail arrange greenery around red candles scented like cinnamon apples. Or maybe the delicious aroma came from the actual apples baking in the oven. One of Bethany's favorite treats, they were for the wedding.

Abigail paused at the sound of a boppli crying, and started for the cradle near the woodstove.

Preacher Samuel's frau, Elsie, swept into the room. "I've got him, Abigail. Dishes are finally done. I'm ready for a break with my gross-sohn."

Not that the three-month-old boppli was technically related. Yet. A formal adoption pended. Abigail was about to become a frau and a new mamm at the same time. The boppli didn't have a name yet, either, as far as Bethany knew. His birth mamm referred to him as "Peanut."

Abigail returned to the table.

"Are you going to name him?" Bethany asked her.

Abigail rolled her eyes. "Sammy wants to call him Peter James—the same initials as his birth mamm's. As long as people don't refer to him as PJ, I'll be happy." Then she smiled. "I'm going for Petey."

"Why not call him Samuel Miller the third?"

"That name's reserved for Sammy's first sohn," Abigail stated.

"Peanut is cute," said Abigail's aenti Ruth. "You know that's going to stick."

Abigail groaned.

Bethany looked around at the throng of women cleaning the haus from top to bottom and cooking up a storm. The benches had arrived earlier and were already set up in the barn, and now some men were unloading the tables. She wanted to find Rosemary's friend Naomi and ask her about the possibility of hosting a birthday party at her place.

A group of giggling girls wandered by outside, their laughter floating in through the open door. It wasn't really all that warm out, but with the wood fire, and with so many women working and cooking, it was hot in the haus.

"I'll be right back," Bethany told Abigail. "Need a little fresh air."

Abigail winked. "And a break from working, ain't so?" She laughed, then gave Bethany a gentle shove toward the door. "Get on with you."

Bethany mumbled her thanks and then slipped outside, following the group of girls around the haus. Naomi was with them. Unfortunately, so was Rosemary. The group stopped, their giggles growing in volume, as they eyed the teenage buwe setting up additional chairs. Amish were coming in from other states for the wedding, Abigail's family among the group from Ohio.

Bethany stepped up beside Naomi and touched her hand. "I need to talk to you privately," she whispered.

Naomi followed her around the side of the barn. "What's up?"

"It's Rosemary's birthday this weekend, but Mamm won't agree to have a party for her. I'd really like to surprise her with one, since she's turning sixteen."

Naomi held up a hand. "Say nein more. I'll arrange a taffy pull. She won't have any idea it's for her birthday."

Bethany breathed a sigh of relief. "Danki, Naomi. I know she'll appreciate this. I do, for sure."

Naomi smiled. "I know how the family has suffered since…well, anyway, I'm glad to help. You'll be there, ain't so?"

"Of course. Be sure to let me know if there's anything I can do."

Naomi started to wave her off. "Ach, I have something for you." She reached inside her pocket. "Rosemary said you were upset you didn't get to read *The Budget*. Here, take our copy. We're done with it."

"Danki, again." Bethany took the newspaper and headed back toward the haus, ready for her next assignment.

Weddings were so much work.

But so much fun.

And maybe, someday, it'd be her turn to plan a wedding. To stand with Silas while the preachers talked to them….

Someone bumped against her in the overly warm kitchen. Bethany turned and met the eyes of Hen's mother, Constance.

"We've saved enough money to get Hen out on bail until the trial," she whispered, though it was more like a hiss. "Maybe this time next year, you'll be my dochter-in-law."

Bethany's stomach lurched. She managed a smile but probably appeared more ill than excited.

She didn't want Hen. Not anymore.

Never did, to be honest. She'd wanted to honor Daed's wishes. And having someone had seemed better than having nobody at all.

Seemed was the key word.

Now, she wanted Silas.

Though, at the rate things were going, that wasn't happening.

⌒

Silas fingered the handful of gravel he'd scooped into his pocket earlier in a moment of bravado. He clutched a dim flashlight in his other hand as he gazed up at the second-floor windows of the farmhaus.

He should've asked Bethany which room was hers. He didn't want to wake her mamm, her brother, or any of her many sisters.

If only he'd remembered to check the haus at dusk, before everyone had gone to bed and turned off all the lights.

If only Bethany had volunteered the information when he'd suggested tossing pebbles at her window, instead of….

Instead of….

He pulled in a deep breath.

Instead of refusing him.

Rejecting him.

He swallowed the lump in his throat, pressed his lips together so tight that they hurt, and pulled the pebbles out of his pocket, letting them sift slowly through his fingers to the ground. With head bowed, he turned and walked away.

At least there wouldn't be any evidence of his foolishness, except for a few stray pebbles buried in the grass or the flower bed, wherever they'd landed.

And the next time, he would listen when she said nein.

Though maybe he had heard her this time, and had simply gotten sidetracked by the knowledge that he would be a side-sitter in the wedding, paired with her…and he wanted to tell her.

He kicked at a clump of grass as he trod across the yard to the barn. He still gripped his flashlight in his hand but had turned it off. Didn't need it, not with the harvest moon overhead. He'd brought it along to shine on his face when Bethany answered his summons to the window.

"Oof!"

He'd plowed into someone. Should've been paying attention to his course instead of gazing at the starlit sky and wishing he were walking down the road with a sweet girl.

"Sorry." He flipped his flashlight on.

Bethany smiled in its glow. "Nein harm done. Where've you been? I was just looking for you in the barn."

He chuckled. "I went to toss pebbles at your window, but I didn't know which one was yours."

"It's that one in front." She turned and pointed.

He cleared his throat. "I...um, why were you looking for me?"

"Why were *you* looking for *me*?" she countered, her voice flirty. Teasing.

Two could play that game.

He grinned. Reached for her hand. "Ready for that walk?"

Chapter 11

Bethany's pulse accelerated into overdrive as Silas's hand closed around one of hers. Sparks shot up her arm as his callused fingers slid over her skin. She trembled when he pulled her closer, so that their shoulders touched. She tried to conceal her reaction by adjusting her coat.

"Cold?" His murmured question caused another round of shivers to work through her.

"Nein." Not really. Just overwhelmed by attraction. Something she really needed to control, especially with the unwelkum news that Hen would soon be free on bail. As far as she knew, Daed still expected her to marry Hen. Of course, Daed wasn't in his right mind. Maybe if he regained his senses, and if he found out Silas had returned, as well as learned the truth about Hen, things would change.

She could only hope. Trust. Believe.

Pray?

Nein. To pray would be to acknowledge her dependence on a Gott who heard and answered her prayers. And He'd already proven, beyond a shadow of a doubt, that He did neither of the two.

She blew out a frustrated breath.

Silas released her hand and shifted sideways, separating himself a respectable distance from her—at least a Bible's width apart. "If you don't want to go for a walk, you should just say so. Why were you looking for me, really?"

"I'd like to go for a walk." She wanted more than a mere stroll. She wanted a walk that would turn into a hike. A trek that took her out of the community, out of the nearby town, out of the state, and as far away as she could get from her current situation.

She didn't look at him. Hopefully, he wouldn't be able to discern her true feelings.

"Then was ist letz?" Concern colored Silas's voice.

More than words could say. It was easier to flirt than to get sucked into the whirlpool of regret and unhappiness that swirled around her.

"What could possibly be wrong when you're by my side?" She was disgusted with her own coquettishness.

"Be serious." He shook his head and flicked off the flashlight, leaving her blinded by darkness. She shut her eyes so her vision would adjust quicker.

She could hear his tennis shoes rearranging bits of gravel as he walked away. Without her.

She opened her eyes and scurried after his dim silhouette. "Nein, wait. Nothing's wrong." *Liar, liar.* What was wrong with her? Flirting didn't work. Not with Silas. It didn't work well with anyone else, either. So why did she keep trying?

"I...." He sighed. "Sam asked me to be his side-sitter tomorrow. He said Caleb had to go out of town for a funeral." He lengthened his strides as he neared the road.

Bethany stumbled, causing an avalanche of dirt that would have terrorized an ant colony. Silas immediately spun around, backtracked, and reached out to help her up. A current like electricity shot up her arm from the light contact.

"You'll be with me." She struggled to catch her breath.

"Jah. Sam told me."

She smiled.

"And maybe, if you're nice, I'll ask you to go with me to the singing."

"If I'm nice, huh?" She knew what that would've meant, coming from Hen. Shut up and let him—

Her stomach roiled.

"Maybe a walk isn't such a gut idea after all." She stopped and pulled away from Silas.

Silas turned to face her. "Is it okay if I ask you to be my date at the singing?" He sounded worried once again.

She cleared her throat. "Jah, it's fine. But I'm not that kind of girl." At least, she didn't want to be.

There was a hesitation on his part. "You're not the kind of girl who goes to singings? Because I distinctly remember you asking me if I wanted to go."

She decided to ignore his teasing. "Nein, not the kind of girl who—"

His hand closed over hers again, stunning her into silence.

"I know, Bethany. We've already had this conversation, ain't so?" He let out a soft breath and trailed his fingers slowly down her arm as he stepped away. "Why were you looking for me?"

Her reason sounded stupid now. "Naomi—she's Rosemary's best friend—said I could have Rosemary's birthday party at her farm sometime. I still have to plan it. Mamm said she doesn't want to deal with it. This way, she won't have to. She won't even have to know."

There was a beat of silence. Two. "And you wanted to tell me because…?"

"It's going to be a taffy pull. I thought you might like to go."

"I like taffy pulls." Another moment of silence. "You'll be my partner, of course—as friends, jah? I'll go to the birthday party, whenever it is, and if you're so inclined, you can go to the singing with me."

"Friends," she whispered. "Just friends."

But she wanted it to be as so much more.

⌒

Silas swallowed a lump in his throat. If only they could be more than friends. But even if they weren't, the pain in her voice nearly broke his heart. He nodded toward the road. "So, do you want to go for a walk, or not? I'm sorry. I'm confused."

"I'm afraid."

Silas raised his eyebrows. "Of what? Walking?"

She shook her head. "Of you. Of me. Of what Hen will do. He's getting out of jail on bond. His mamm told me today. I'm afraid Daed will still force me to marry him. I'm afraid that—"

"Back up a second." Silas frowned. "Why are you afraid of me? I've never done anything to hurt you. And I never will. Not deliberately, anyway."

"But you have. You refused to take me with you to Pennsylvania. That hurt, you know."

"Not a gut reason to be afraid of me, schatz. That's a reason to thank me." He grinned, but his smile quickly died. "Are you afraid of me because of my brother? Or because of what you think you know about my family dynamics?"

Bethany gasped. "Ach, nein. Nein. You're a gut man. Really. I used to like…well, I still do like you, really. More than like, actually, but—"

"Okay, so that's settled. You aren't afraid of me."

"Just of your breaking my heart."

And he had nothing to say to that. Because if there was a heart involved—his included—it would be broken.

"Which is why I'm afraid of myself. Curse my tongue! I didn't mean to say that. I don't mean to flirt, but I don't know how to turn off the urge. I don't mean to talk so much, either, but I don't know how to shut up."

He had a gut idea of how to quiet her…but sweeping her into his arms and silencing her with a kiss probably wouldn't be wise.

Especially when they'd just agreed that they were friends.

Only friends.

⌒

If only she knew how to bridle her rambling tongue. But she seemed to have as much control over that as she had over the rest of her life—little to none. Still, maybe she would've had a bit more control if he hadn't called her "schatz." *Sweetheart.* A squeal rose up within her, similar to the one she'd heard an actress unleash when the bu she liked kissed her on her cheek in a verboden movie she'd once seen. Unlike that girl, however, Bethany kept the squeal inside by clamping her lips shut.

It was a miracle, plain and simple. There was nein other way to explain it. Daed had told her once that her tongue was like a runaway horse she needed to tame. He'd made her memorize several passages from Proverbs and Psalms, and verses six and eight from the third chapter of James: *"The tongue is a fire, a world of iniquity. The tongue is so set among our members that it defiles the whole body, and sets on fire the course of nature; and it is set on fire by hell.… No man can tame the tongue. It is an unruly evil, full of deadly poison."* Too bad his prescribed remedy didn't seem to do any gut. Her tongue still ran away on her.

Then again, how much wisdom did Daed have? With his compromised mental state, could she trust or believe anything he said?

She shook her head and looked around. Somehow, at some point, she and Silas had started walking, side by side, down the middle of the dirt road, separated by the distance of about a foot. Going nowhere, really. As far as she knew, there was nothing except for farms—Amish and Englisch alike—along this way.

If they went far enough, they might reach another town. Maybe. Either that or a dead end.

Just like life. You were either on a road to somewhere or on a dead end.

In Bethany's case, it was likely the latter.

She brushed at a tear.

"Was ist letz?" Silas asked again.

"What? Are you really that attuned to my emotions?" She didn't mean to sound so bitter. Hateful.

"Bethany." He spoke her name as a sigh of frustration.

"I'm on the wrong road," she blurted out.

Silas stopped. Looked around. "It's the only one here."

"Nein, not in a literal sense. Just…I'm going to run into another dead end, and I don't know what to do. Where to go."

"Well, if you know you're going the wrong way, you need to change course."

"Jah. So obvious, ain't so?" She shrugged. "I found another copy of *The Budget.*"

He grunted. "So, that widower…."

She nodded. "He's still an option."

"Have you tried praying about it?"

She kicked at a rock. "Gott and I aren't on speaking terms, remember?"

"Still?" Silas shook his head. "How long is this standoff going to last?"

"Until Gott gives in."

"You want Gott to give in to your demands when you aren't prepared to listen to His?"

Bethany scowled. "As if you're any better. Running away from home, because—"

"Watch it. You don't know what drew me away. At least, not the whole story. And what makes you think I didn't pray? How do you know Gott isn't behind this trip to Pennsylvania?"

"Because if He is, it isn't fair. He's allowing you to escape your problems but forcing me to remain in mine."

"What makes you think I'm escaping my problems?"

She ignored him. The answer was too obvious. "How do you know that Gott didn't bring you here so I could join you on the journey?"

Silas chuckled. "Nice try, but nein. You may not use me to get out of whatever lesson it is that Gott wants you to learn."

And that was the problem. Whatever lesson He wanted to teach her scared her, too. Because what if she didn't like it?

What if it involved Hen and not Silas?

What if it involved more pain, either physical or emotional?

Ach, Gott. What is to be my lot in life?

Chapter 12

Silas glanced at Bethany as she trod alongside him with her head lowered, her tennis shoes shuffling through the gravel. He tried to summon the words to reach out and help her through her issues, but they refused to form. He had enough trouble trying to work through his own issues.

But it pained his heart to see her so depressed—the talkative girl who'd never stopped laughing and smiling when they were teenagers. The girl whose grin used to make him go weak in the knees. Had she even smiled during the short time he'd been back? If she had, it had seemed forced. Or sad.

Her considering marrying the widower was a mistake, though. He didn't know the man or the details of his situation, but if he advertised in *The Budget* for a frau, there must be something wrong. Somewhere. Somehow. Bethany wasn't the magic formula to fix the stranger's problems, for sure.

If only he could make her smile again. If he could take away all the hurt, all the pain, all the mistreatment she'd endured. Maybe make a promise—and keep it—that her life would be sunshine and rainbows from here on out.

But he didn't have that authority. Or that ability.

If he did…well, then he'd fix his life, too.

Because even now, in calm, quiet Jamesport, where nothing happened, he had the constant urge to look over his shoulder.

Because *he* would find him if he stuck around too long.

Even Pennsylvania might not be far enough away.

Antarctica, maybe. If there was a human colony coexisting with the penguins.

A car crested the far hill, its bright headlights blinding Silas for a moment. He turned to Bethany, who'd been silent for way too long, and grabbed her hand. "Here. Off the road." He pulled her to the shoulder, through the weedy ditch, and into the woods.

She yanked herself free from him when they were surrounded by darkness. "What are you doing? Ach, nein." Her pitch had risen in panic.

What was the problem?

Ach, nein. He hadn't even thought of *that*.

He'd been more worried about himself. About being found by the wrong people.

⌒

Fear clawed at Bethany's throat as she backed away from Silas, going deeper into the thicket. The calves of her legs collided with the rough bark of a fallen tree, and she tripped backward over it, her bottom hitting the ground on the other side of the trunk. Somehow, she managed not to strike her head.

Her legs were extended over the log, her dress splayed out in the most unladylike manner. Nothing she could do to help that.

The vehicle passed by them, not even pausing. But the driver probably hadn't noticed them, since they both wore dark clothing.

If only they'd been seen. Maybe then she'd be safe.

She couldn't see him. Not from where she lay on the cold ground. She took a moment to assess the damage. She may have scraped her leg, ripped her dress, and bruised her back, but she would live.

And she would fight off this attack with every ounce of energy in her. She should've done so before, instead of giving in when he insisted. This time, Hen wouldn't have it so easy.

A hand landed on her ankle. She screamed, and unleashed the hardest kick she could muster. One that forced him backward when it connected with his chest.

He grunted.

She cringed, waiting for the slap. The punch. The bruising grip. The knee in her belly.

Nothing.

Maybe she'd slowed him down. Some.

Hopefully enough.

She scrambled off the log, rolled to her feet, and screamed again while she tried to decide which direction to run.

The dim beam of a flashlight sliced through the darkness, and she could hear thrashing sounds, as if someone—or more than just someone—were running through the woods toward her. The thrashing continued, growing louder. Coming nearer.

"Easy, there, Bethany. It's me. Me, Silas." He used the flashlight to illuminate his face.

Silas? It couldn't be. But…it was. How could he sound so calm?

She struggled for breath. Struggled to piece together the fragments of thought and memory too horrific to speak aloud.

"I won't hurt you," he said quietly, like he might speak to an injured, frightened animal. He extended his hand as if he expected her to sniff it.

Not happening.

"What got into you?" he asked calmly.

She still struggled to breathe.

The thrashing sounds neared, and two men burst into sight through the trees. One held a flashlight. He shined it directly in Bethany's face, blinding her.

"What's going on?" The voice sounded familiar. "Silas, explain this."

So, they recognized him. Or thought they did. Silas? Hen? Her brain was too scrambled to think. *Ach, Gott.*

"Are you hurt, Bethany?" The man came closer.

Breathe.

Closer….

Closer….

She sucked in a long breath, and released it in the shrillest scream she could manage.

⌒

Silas cringed as Bethany let out another eardrum-shattering scream. Sam stopped in his tracks, and Preacher Samuel looked from Silas to Bethany and back again.

"I think she's having a flashback," Silas said quickly. "Probably about Hen."

He hoped the two men would be able to fill in the blanks regarding what his statement implied—and that they wouldn't demand to know what the two of them were doing in the woods in the first place.

Because if they delved into the underlying reason behind their presence in the woods, Silas would be asked questions for which he had nein gut answers.

Not that the apparent reason was any better. He and Bethany, alone together in the woods, wouldn't be wise—even if she didn't have her past hovering over her. She was a pretty girl. And he, a normal, red-blooded male.

Silas took a step backward as Preacher Samuel closed his eyes and bowed his head, probably praying. Such a wise man. Silas should've thought to do that, too.

Sam didn't stop to pray. Instead, he took another cautious step forward and reached his hand out again to Bethany. "Are you hurt? I have a medical kit at the haus. You know I'm trained." His voice was just as low and soothing as Silas had wanted his to be.

But that hadn't worked. Not the way he'd intended.

He stepped aside to talk to the preacher. "How'd you kum to be here?"

"Sam and I were taking a walk to discuss marriage. Things he should know, like how marriage differs from courtship," Preacher Samuel said. "Things I wish my daed would've thought to tell me."

Silas frowned. That was a conversation he would never have with his daed. If only he had a mentor to talk him through these types of things. A role model to show him how marriage—and life—were supposed to be done.

Preacher Samuel looked up. "Sounds as if I should address some issues with the youth. Nein means nein. It doesn't mean anything else. And I'm also curious if Bethany filed charges against Hen. Though, knowing Bethany and the situation with her daed, I really don't think she would have."

Silas exhaled. "That's probably a gut guess."

Preacher Samuel nodded somberly. "And he's supposed to be getting out on bail. Or so his mamm says."

Silas's frown deepened. Bethany had mentioned that. He'd forgotten.

She whimpered, and he glanced in her direction. Sam had talked her into stepping over the log, at least enough for her to sit down. Her face was buried in her hands. Her shoulders shook. Crying was better than screaming, at any rate.

Maybe. Silas still wasn't sure what he'd done wrong, or what he'd done to remind her of Hen. Guilt oppressed him.

"I'm not exactly sure what happened with Hen, Preacher Samuel." Silas wanted to make that clear. "I'm guessing. She's made hints, but maybe I misunderstood them."

Preacher Samuel shook his head as he surveyed his sohn kneeling beside Bethany, speaking gently to her while she cried. "I'm going to send my dochter Rachel and a few other ladies over to talk to her. Maybe she'll open up to them."

Or maybe she wouldn't. Silas didn't know. This whole thing sickened him. If Hen did get out of jail while Silas was still in the area, Silas would have a hard time resisting the urge to take revenge on him for hurting Bethany.

And the rage that rose inside him, watching Bethany to-nacht, scared him more than anything.

Chapter 13

Tears flowed unrestrained down Bethany's cheeks. They dripped off her chin. Trickled down the sides of her nose and slipped inside her nostrils and mouth when she tried to breathe. Sammy Miller knelt beside her, speaking in a low voice, but she didn't understand anything he said.

What had gotten into her? It was Silas, for pity's sake. *Not* Hen. Silas, who'd said he would never hurt her intentionally. And yet, he had dragged her into the woods. Did he think she'd be easy, since Hen had already gone before him?

Or had she completely misunderstood the situation? He'd grabbed her ankle—kind of an odd place for a man to grab if he had designs on her.

Her breaths still came in shallow spurts. The bad memories hurt. She had to focus on an activity that should be natural. Breathing.

She wiped at her tears, then caught a glimpse of Silas and Preacher Samuel. They both stared at her, probably thinking, *jah*, she was just as off in den kopf as Daed. Soon, someone would kum and take her away to join Daed in the same hospital where he'd undergone multiple brain surgeries and treatments, like radiation and chemotherapy, and who knew what else—with a guard stationed in his room the whole time. Daed was still an alleged convict, after all.

Sammy clasped her hands and gently tugged them away from her face. "Kum, Bethany. We'll see about getting your wounds treated." He stood, gave her hands a gentle squeeze, and pulled her to her feet. "It's okay. My mamm will be there. You'll be perfectly safe."

"I'm fine." Bethany somehow found her voice. "I just want to go home." As long as nobody saw her and started asking questions.

But she didn't want Silas to go with her. She didn't even want Sammy and Preacher Samuel. She wanted to be alone.

Completely, totally alone.

More tears escaped her eyes, chasing the prior ones down the same trails.

"Bethany, you're hurt. Your palms are bleeding." Sammy released her sore hands and grasped her elbow. "Kum. Silas will be with us. He'll see you home."

"Nein." She wanted to stomp her foot like a spoiled child. But that would probably do her as much gut as it had the Englisch toddler she'd babysat recently. She hadn't given in to his demands. And nobody would give into hers, either. She was expected to bow her head in submission. And it'd go easier on her if she did. It might be against her will, but at least she wouldn't get hurt.

That's what Hen always told her, in a menacing tone: "Submit! You might enjoy it. Stop fighting. You won't get hurt if you cooperate."

Bile filled her throat. She jerked out of Sammy's grasp, turned away, and lost her supper on the fallen tree. Which prompted another round of tears to course down her cheeks. How many teardrops did a person have on hand at a given time? Seemed she should've exhausted her supply by now.

A hand rested on her upper back, gently rubbing. "Shhh. It's okay, Bethany. It's okay. Calm down. Nobody here will hurt you."

She wanted to turn into Silas's arms, bury her face against his chest, and breathe in his soapy clean scent. Feel his comforting embrace. And only moments ago, she'd been scared of him. Screaming like a fool. *Why, why, why?*

Instead, she sighed, forced a smile, and dipped her head with a nod to Sammy. "Okay. I'll go." Submissive enough?

Sammy rewarded her with a grin. "Gut girl. We'll get you checked out. Silas can borrow a buggy to take you home. Or we'll call a driver."

As if she couldn't walk herself. She tried to take a step. And stumbled. Maybe she had injured her legs, after all.

Sammy gripped her elbow again. "Careful, now."

Silas's strong hand curved around her other elbow. Sparks shot up her arm. She wobbled. His hand loosened, slipped away, and held her at the waist. His touch sent a sensation like a bolt of lightning pulsing through her body.

These seemed more like the wunderbaar touches her friends giggled and gushed about.

"I've got her," Silas's voice rumbled close to her ear. She couldn't help the shiver that worked through her. She burrowed closer to his side, ignoring the mental alarms that sounded. He was safe. Right now, at least, with Sammy and the preacher both present.

Sammy released her arm. "Gut. I'll just go on ahead and get the first aid kit." He jogged off, leaving Bethany and Silas alone, except for Preacher Samuel trailing along just ahead of them, a calm, comfortable chaperone, his lantern lighting the way.

Bethany tripped again, and Silas tightened his grip on her waist. "Easy, now. Maybe you should hold on to me, too."

Her face heated. But she obediently wrapped her arm around him, acutely aware of his thigh brushing against hers with every step they took. Of his warm hand burning through the fabric of her coat and dress.

This, she could get used to. Could even write about it in her journal, along with her hopes and dreams. Not something she was ashamed of, or that she had to hide, like the pain, horror, and disgrace Hen had caused.

There would be questions about her actions to-nacht that she didn't know how to answer, but she'd deal with those later. For now, all was right in her world.

⁓

Wrapping his arms around her was a mistake, plain and simple.

Silas hadn't expected the fireworks that shot through him, heating every part of his body. Nor had he anticipated she'd actually wrap her arm around him and curl into his side. Nein, he'd thought she would wave him off. Keep her distance.

He wanted to ditch their silent chaperone, pull her into his arms, and claim a kiss—the one he'd dreamed of all summer when she was sweet sixteen, and he'd brought her glasses of ice-cold lemonade during the frolics.

Those were the days. A slight smile curved his lips.

She'd welcomed his attention then. Even so, it had taken him a long time to work up the courage to give her that one single buggy ride home.

And then everything had fallen apart. His life, his plans, his hopes, his dreams—they were all replaced by resignation, and the realization he would never deserve Bethany.

Well, he would never deserve the grace of Gott, either. But—despite himself, despite his family, his past, and his many bad decisions—Gott had taken mercy on him, a sinner. It was enough to make his eyes burn and his throat close up. He wanted to fall on his knees right then and there, and give thanks to Gott.

Now was hardly the time. He needed to escort Bethany to Preacher Samuel's haus.

If only people would extend the same mercy to him that Gott did. If they'd offer complete and total forgiveness.

Well, they probably would, if he knelt and confessed his sins. But what about the sins he couldn't confess? And what about his family? Gott saw fit to put him there. He'd given Silas the same anger his family couldn't seem to control. He'd given Silas the same curse to battle.

And what of the "sins" nobody knew about? The ones that would probably prevent him from staying in Jamesport, and might even follow him all the way to Pennsylvania? The ones that kept him turning away whenever an unidentified motor vehicle approached, until he knew it was safe to show his face to the driver?

He wasn't gut enough for the woman huddled against his side. The woman who trembled, even though she wore a heavy black coat over her dark green dress.

It was probably due to shock. Nerves.

Still, he held her closer as they made their way over the rough terrain.

Finally, Preacher Samuel's farm came into view. The haus and barn were different from the way Silas remembered them, even though they were in the same locations.

"Had to rebuild after we lost the haus to lightning, and the barn to arsonists." The preacher answered his unasked questions.

Had Hen been the arsonist behind the barn fire? Silas fisted his free hand.

Preacher Samuel waved at the haus. "Go on inside. I'll call for a driver so Bethany won't have to walk home with her injuries."

Silas smiled to himself. *Danki, Gott, for supplying our needs.*

❧

When they reached the porch steps at the Millers' haus, Bethany untwined herself from Silas and stepped away.

The door swung open, and Sammy greeted them with a grin. He must've seen them coming. "Took you long enough." His smile widened as he winked at Bethany. "Of course, I'd take my sweet time, too, if I had a pretty girl on my arm."

"Does Abigail know you're such a flirt?" Bethany hadn't meant to sound so cross.

Sammy chuckled. "Uh, yep."

At least he didn't counter with, "Takes one to know one." Or, "Aren't you the pot calling the kettle black." Because confronting her with the truth like that probably would've turned on the waterworks again.

Sammy shut the door behind them. "Have a seat."

His mamm set a plate of molasses cookies on the table, then pulled out a chair for Bethany. "Poor thing. Fell over a log, did you?"

Sammy hadn't told his mamm about Bethany's meltdown? Interesting. Bethany lowered herself into the chair. Hopefully, Elsie would attribute her tearstained face to her fall.

"Might want to wash up, Silas." Sammy pointed to the sink. "Soap your hands up gut."

Silas frowned but followed Sammy's suggestion.

Sammy opened the first aid kit that sat on the kitchen table. "I already washed up." He lifted some disposable gloves out of a box and stretched them out. "Want me to clean up those scrapes? Or Silas?"

"I can do it myself," she said curtly, then softened her voice to add, "Danki."

"Of course, you can. But this is your chance to have a handsome single man kneeling at your feet," Sammy teased. "I think I'll let Silas do the honors."

Silas frowned and shook his head.

Bethany felt a twinge of rejection. Didn't he want to touch her anymore? He'd seemed to enjoy helping her walk here.

"Don't worry," Sammy assured him. "I'll tell you what to do. I'm not taking nein for an answer. Now, dry your hands and put these gloves on."

Silas snapped the gloves into place, then accepted the alcohol wipes Sammy handed him. His frown deepened as he knelt before Bethany and gently took her hand in his. "This might sting."

It did.

Another round of tears burned Bethany's eyes. But not because of the pain.

It was because of the tenderness in Silas's touch as he cradled her hand and gently treated her wounds.

Something shifted inside her.

Gott, help me to be worthy of him.

She wanted to ask Gott to help make Silas attracted to her, too. But that would be beyond selfish. Even for her.

Not to mention, Gott didn't listen to her. Didn't hear her. Didn't care.

Because if He did, He'd fix everything. Absolutely everything, from the day her brother died to the present.

But would He? Nein. Even though He was more than capable.

Besides, Hen was getting out of jail. On bail. And if she was still around, she would be forced to submit to him again.

Whether Silas liked her or not would be a nonissue.

Because before Hen came home, she'd be gone.

One way or another.

Chapter 14

Butterflies still danced in Silas's stomach long after he'd seen Bethany safely inside her haus. He paid the driver with the money Preacher Samuel had slipped him, then entered the barn and crawled into the loft, his mind replaying the events of the evening. Wondering what he'd walked into.

Jamesport was supposed to be a temporary stop. A gut nacht's sleep, maybe even a hearty breakfast—if he were lucky—and then he'd be on his way. He hadn't expected the much-needed temporary job to land in his outstretched hands. Or his ancient attraction to Bethany to spring to life again with nein effort at all.

He should pack his bag and leave town to-nacht. Before it got any colder. Before he dug himself in any deeper. Before he gave in to the temptation to stay.

But what about Bethany? Whatever Hen did to her—if it was anything like Silas imagined—was too awful for words. Considering her extreme reaction to his own innocent mistake, and the comments she'd made earlier, it appeared her desire to leave with Silas was based more on survival instincts than on shame. Though there still might be a considerable amount of shame mixed in.

Silas's stomach churned. In spite of what Hen had done to her, Silas still had the gall to be physically attracted to her. To relish the sparks he felt when he touched her. To want to kiss her.

When the memory surfaced of running his hands over her body after her fall from the hayloft ladder, he dropped to his knees. He may not be in possession of his Bible anymore, but that didn't keep him from recognizing the lust of the flesh. Or from remembering the gist of the Scriptures that spoke of the consequences of looking upon a woman with lust. And he had done that. Did that. Would do that.

He was a sinner, plain and simple.

Gott..... He didn't know what to say. What to pray.

All he knew was, Bethany had suffered enough at the hands of a man.

She didn't need him—and his past—in her life.

～

After the wedding ceremony, Bethany filed out of the barn with the other unmarried maidals at Abigail's grossmammi's haus. She envied Abigail. Sammy was a gut man. Like Silas. He would make Abigail so happy.

But now…now came the hour of reckoning. And it would probably go the same way as all the other post-wedding singings she'd attended since she turned sixteen: Waiting expectantly in the cold back bedroom of the haus for that one special man to knock on the door and ask, specifically, for her.

Nobody ever had.

Not even Hen.

Nein reason to think this nacht would be any different.

She worked her way to the far corner of the room, greeting and talking with the other girls as she went. All of them were giggling and peering into tiny handheld mirrors, making sure every single strand of hair was tucked in place. The room smelled of lilac, but whether it was from flowers pressed into the dresser drawers or the verboden body spray someone wore, she didn't know.

Some of the braver ones lightly applied makeup, even though it was against the Ordnung. Bethany pretended not to notice. But she did. She even saw the tiny silver chain of a necklace peeking out from the collar of a girl's dress—another verboden item. And it was the girls who broke the rules and wore makeup, perfume, and jewelry who were usually among the first to be called on.

Maybe Silas would kum for her. Maybe she would be called first, instead of left for last. Unmatched. Solo. A tiny flicker of hope ignited inside her.

The first knock sounded. The giggling came to a complete and utter stop, as all the girls peered around at one another. Martha spritzed herself with some body spray, handed the bottle to another girl, then opened the door. The giggling and whispers started again.

"Naomi."

"Martha."

"Tabitha."

"Dorcas."

The requests kept coming. One by one, the girls left the room.

The tiny flame of hope flickered and died as Bethany became one of three maidals left. And, as far as she knew, only unattached male had yet to claim a date. Silas.

Bethany eyed the other two girls: Susanna King and Lydia Hershberger. Lydia didn't live in Jamesport, and was already betrothed, to someone in Ohio. She was Abigail's best friend—and her other side-sitter at the wedding.

Silence stretched. Long minutes passed.

Bethany approached the window and gazed outside. Tomorrow morgen, she would write the widower in southern Missouri. Let him know she was coming. She would work as a haus-keeper, if necessary. Anything. She'd do anything.

A hard knot formed in her stomach.

And then, another knock. Quiet. Timid. As if the man wasn't sure of himself.

Her stubborn hope flared. She forced herself to remain standing at the window, but she watched the reflection in the glass of Susanna opening the door. She couldn't see who stood there.

Nor could she hear the name that was spoken. It got lost in the rush of worry roaring through her.

She squeezed her eyes shut, waiting for the chosen girl to let out a tiny sigh of relief as she went for the door.

Long seconds passed. Then somebody touched Bethany's arm. Bethany jumped, startled.

"He asked for you," Susanna said softly.

Bethany glanced at Susanna, her face a blur because of Bethany's unshed tears. Bethany swallowed. "Really?" It was hard to get that single word past the lump in her throat.

"For sure." Susanna squeezed Bethany's hand, then gave it a tiny tug.

Bethany turned.

Silas leaned against the doorframe, his lips curved in a half smile, his gaze dark and dangerous. He looked so handsome. So strong.

Her heart lurched.

⁓

Silas might've made a mistake. He wiped his sweaty palms on his pants as Bethany stood before him, trembling.

Or maybe that was him, shaking in his shoes.

He should've followed his first instinct and headed for the bishop's farm to collect his things before hitting the road.

But here he was, like a fool. Taking that second "date" with the girl he'd always wanted but would never have.

He'd wanted to be first in line. To claim Bethany before any of the other girls was called. Instead, he'd forced himself to hang back and watch, his heart in his throat, as the other young men took turns going to the back bedroom. He was afraid someone else would ask for her. And he'd breathed a sigh of relief as the men had returned, one by one, with a blushing girl other than Bethany by their side.

When the other two unclaimed girls clustered around Silas and Bethany, he forced a smile. "The benefit of being late—I get three beautiful girls."

Unlike an Englisch man he'd once known who seemed to have a girl hanging on each arm at all times, Silas wanted just one girl. How could he reveal his intentions without drawing attention to himself?

But then, he already had drawn attention to himself, by returning to the scene of the crime, so to speak. A community where his family had lived but not exactly prospered. An area where their behavior had gotten them thrown out of town—and not for the first time.

Silas wanted to undo the damage. Start over with a clean slate. Marry and settle down. Earn a reputation as an upstanding member of the community.

He'd begun with a black mark against him. Maybe more than one.

You're not gut enough. You'll never be gut enough.

A gentle whisper followed: *You are accepted in the Beloved.*

If only that wasn't so hard to believe. The other voice was louder. Stronger. Turning into a refrain. *Not gut enough. Not gut enough. Not gut enough.*

None of the three girls in the bedroom seemed to know he wasn't gut enough. They closed in around him, leaving anyone to guess which one he'd actually chosen.

He wanted to make it clear.

But maybe it was better this way.

Except that he didn't know the names of the other two girls. Didn't have any desire to, either.

He led his entourage into the barn, where the singing was already under way, and the four of them found seats at the end of one of the long tables.

Bethany sat on Silas's left.

He wanted to be gut enough for her. Under the table, he reached out and gently took her injured hand in his, entwining their fingers.

She stiffened...then relaxed.

A soft smile curved her lips.

And she didn't pull away.

Chapter 15

Shivers worked through Bethany as Silas slid his thumb lightly over the top of her hand, making tiny circles. Her heart rate stuttered and broke into a gallop. This would definitely go into her journal. *Sweetest moment ever.*

The barn door opened, and a man entered with his hat pulled low over his eyes, his thumbs hooked in his suspenders. He surveyed the crowd, then strode toward the back of the room, where she sat with Silas.

Hen? Bethany's breath caught in her throat. But as he neared, the air whooshed out of her lungs with relief. It was Caleb Bontrager. He made his way to the end of the table. His gaze skimmed over Lydia and Susanna, then shot back to Lydia and lingered there. He frowned as he pulled up a chair between Bethany and Susanna.

Bethany leaned closer to him as he sat. "Back from the funeral?"

"Jah, just a bit ago. Stopped by to give Sam some well wishes and thought I'd stay for the singing. At least some of it." He accepted the copy of the Ausbund that the bu across the table handed him. Bethany slid her copy toward him so he could see the page number.

"Who's the girl?" Caleb tilted his head toward Susanna.

Silas withdrew his hand, leaving Bethany's cold. She glanced at him. He glared at Caleb.

Bethany looked back at Caleb. "You know Sus—"

"Next to her." Caleb's voice was brusque.

"Ach. That's Lydia. She's from Ohio."

"Not here, then. Gut." Caleb thumbed through the pages of the Ausbund. "Who's your date?" Now he nodded toward Silas.

"Silas Beiler. He used to live here, remember?"

Caleb grinned at Silas, then turned his attention to the song.

Silas didn't smile back. Instead, his frown deepened.

Bethany glanced down at the page but had lost her desire to sing. She listened to two or three of the verses before she pushed out her chair and walked over to one of the big picnic jugs set up on a table outside the barn. She grabbed a plastic cup and studied the jugs. Looked like her options were water or tea.

Tea it was. She held the cup under the spigot and pressed the knob. A thin dribble of tan liquid emerged. She tilted the container, prayed she wouldn't get bathed in tea, and tried again.

"Let me." Silas stepped up behind her and grabbed a cup.

Bethany looked at him as she lowered the bottom of the jug to the table. "Do you want to tip the container or hold the cup?" Her heart pounded.

"I'll tip." He tilted the jug forward and waited while she filled two cups—one for her, one for him.

"They probably have another picnic jug in the haus," Bethany said. "They'll need it when everybody takes a break from singing. I'll go see."

"I'll go with you. You'll need me to carry it out, ain't so?" Silas fell into step beside her. After a moment, he sighed. "Look. Would you like me to withdraw my offer to take you home, so you can ride with that other guy?"

"Caleb?" Bethany frowned. "Nein. He's my cousin. He was to be the other side-sitter, but he had to go to a funeral."

"Cousin, eh?" Now there was a smile in Silas's voice. His hand brushed hers, then caught it.

"Are you jealous?" Then she winced. Flirting again.

Silas tightened his grip. "I was worried he might be Hen."

Just as she had, at first.

Right now, she was more focused on the man next to her. The one causing her pulse to race like a runaway horse.

She couldn't wait to ride home with him.

Silas held Bethany's hand all the way to the haus. He released it when they climbed the porch stairs, and he noticed a picnic jug waiting beside the door. "Is that one ready to be delivered to the drink table, you think?"

Bethany nodded. "Likely so." She gave it a nudge. "It's full. Abigail's aenti set all the jugs out here so the old mauds wouldn't have to worry about them. Though I'm sure Preacher Samuel or Abigail's onkel are still around, somewhere."

"Chaperoning." Silas had seen the preacher in the barn, as well as his dochter Rachel, and a few others he didn't remember.

Bethany muttered something else, but he didn't catch it because of a loud clatter that came from inside the haus. Bethany spun around and jerked the door open. A screeching cat streaked past, its back arched, its tail erect.

Bethany's squeal matched the cat's in volume, and she jumped back. Silas wrapped his arms around her, enjoying the feel of her body pressed against his. He inhaled a shuddery breath as his arms touched her soft curves.

An old lady came to the door, laughing so hard that tears streamed from her eyes. "Did you see that, Bethany? That silly cat scared herself. She jumped up on the kitchen counter and knocked the cake pans off it." Her gaze lowered to Silas's arms, still wrapped tightly around Bethany's waist. The old lady fanned herself with her apron.

Silas reluctantly released Bethany and took a step away from her. His feet tottered for a second on the edge of the porch, and then he fell backward, landing in a prickly garden of holly bushes. At least the shrubs had broken his fall. He now lay rather awkwardly on his back, with his legs against the side of the porch.

The old lady's laughter turned into a full-fledged guffaw as she peered down at him. "Are…are you…all right?"

In the next second, Bethany was kneeling by his head. With one hand, she snatched his black hat up off the ground; with the other hand, she smoothed his hair out of his face. "Are you hurt?"

His back was sore, his face and hands had been scratched. But he didn't seem to have broken anything, and her hand in his hair was a wunderbaar surprise. He carefully rolled over and crawled out of the bushes "I think I'm fine."

"Just considerably rumpled up in spirit?" Bethany's lips curved in a slight smile. "*Anne of Green Gables*. I loved those books as a child."

He didn't know what she was talking about. But he wouldn't ask. Instead, he stood, stretched, and looked up at the gray-haired lady who hadn't stopped chuckling.

"Why don't you two kum on in and sit a spell? Or perhaps you're in a hurry to get back to the singing." She glanced at Bethany. "I don't think I know your beau."

Silas squirmed. "I, uh, need to take that picnic jug to the table, and then I should probably head home." To the Weisses' barn. Silas hesitated a moment. He looked at Bethany. "If you can find another ride."

"I'll kum with you, I just need to say gut-bye to Abigail and Sammy." Bethany smiled at the old lady. "This is Silas Beiler. He used to live here, Zelda. I'm sure you remember him."

Zelda. Silas frowned. She was an old maud, if he remembered right.

Zelda shook her head. "Can't say I do. But I often struggle to recall as recent as yesterday."

Silas grinned. Finally, someone who wouldn't judge him by his family or his past.

⌒

Bethany hugged Abigail, then turned to Sammy. He hadn't left his bride's side at all since the ceremony, as far as Bethany knew. Even now, his gaze was fixed on Abigail with a look of admiration and love. Bethany held back a sigh. If only someone would look at her that way. With love, not lust.

Sammy accepted her congratulations with a smile. "Danki for coming, Bethany, and for being a side-sitter." He grinned at Silas. "Danki to you, too. Really nice to have you back in the area."

"For now." Silas's voice was rough.

Bethany stiffened. Did he have to remind everyone that he was just passing through? They might plead with him to stick around, and Bethany wanted—needed—him to go away, and take her with him. On the other hand, if he was serious about refusing to take her along, she was fine with him staying as many days as it took for her to convince him to change his mind.

Sammy's gaze flickered to Bethany and back to Silas. "Maybe you'll find a reason to stay."

"Maybe." Silas flexed his fingers, then entwined them with Bethany's. "Congratulations to both of you." Then, grinning, he led the way out of the barn. They walked slowly toward the field where all the buggies were parked in nice, orderly rows. "Which one is yours?"

"Chocolate Chip." Bethany whistled, and a horse whinnied in response.

"My mamm always said, 'A whistling woman and a crowing hen always kum to some bad end.'" He laughed. "I thought your brother called the horse Cookie."

She shrugged. "Her official, papered, racing name is Chocolate Chip Cookie Dough. Daed calls her Cookie. But he's not here to correct me, and I like Chocolate Chip better."

He raised his eyebrows. "A rebel, huh?"

She knew he was teasing, but the comment hurt just the same. It made her think of the Scripture verse that equated rebellion with the sin of witchcraft, and left her feeling that she deserved all the evil ever done to her—past, present, and future—because of her failure to submit to authority. She swallowed the hard lump in her throat. Gott was a harsh judge, just like Daed. Why couldn't He be more like Sammy's daed? Kind. Accepting. Loving. Offering gentle correction rather than quick condemnation.

And Silas wondered why she wasn't on speaking terms with Gott. She snorted.

"What?" He approached Chocolate Chip and pulled something out of his pocket. "Sugar cube. They had them on the tables at the wedding."

Bethany knew that. She just hadn't seen Silas take one.

The horse accepted the treat, then nosed Silas's pocket. Silas chuckled, pulling out another cube.

So, he'd taken more than one.

He eyed Bethany. "Would you kiss me for a sugar cube?"

A surge of unexpected excitement shot through her. Of anticipation. Willingness. Want. Need. Sparks hovered in hopes of a new memory to erase the mental scars of yesterday.

But then he released her hand and lowered his head. "Forget it. I shouldn't have asked."

Actually, his asking spoke volumes about him as a man.

Bethany clamped her teeth down on her lower lip. He was probably recalling her reaction when he'd pulled her into the woods last nacht. Unadulterated terror. Screaming. Kicking. He'd have nein reason to believe she'd be more welcoming now.

Tears burned her eyes. Would she never escape her history? Not that she would have wished it on anyone else, but it would be nice not being expected to fear a man's touch. To look forward to it with the same sort of blushing anticipation she'd seen on Abigail's face at the wedding celebration.

But then, Silas hadn't asked last nacht. Maybe if he had, instead of grabbing her by the hand and yanking her through a weedy ditch into the darkness of the woods, she would've reacted differently.

"Why did you take me into the woods last nacht?"

He grunted with a nod at the buggy. "Need help getting in?"

So, he wouldn't answer. Her wariness of him was justified. He was a man, and men were as trustworthy as Gott.

Not at all.

She could get into the buggy just fine, all by herself. Even so, she nodded. He would have to touch her in order to assist her, and she wasn't ready to relinquish the guilty pleasure.

One of his hands clasped hers again, while his other hand rested on her lower back. Once she had settled in the seat, he climbed up beside her and released the brake. He clicked his tongue at the horse, then drove out of the field in silence.

About a quarter mile down the road, Silas cleared his throat. "The woods last nacht…I…it wasn't what you think. I, um, there was a car coming, and…well, suffice it to say I left some enemies here, and they might have reason to…." He sighed. "They might be keeping an eye out for me."

Bethany eyed him with alarm. "Why?"

He shook his head. "I really can't say."

"Can't? Or won't?"

"Won't. Your knowing might put you in danger, too."

Chapter 16

Ten minutes of silence. Silas hadn't known it was possible. Not for Bethany. He liked the peace and quiet, at first. But after a while, it began to worry him. He actually missed her happy, rambling chatter. He glanced over at her, to see whether she'd fallen asleep. Nein, she only stared out at the darkness with a serious expression on her face. If only he could read her thoughts. "Cat got your tongue?"

She startled, then straightened and turned toward him. "How could *I* be endangered by the knowledge of whatever it was that you did? What'd you do? I've been puzzling over the possibilities, and I can't think of anything you might've done that might put me at risk."

Ah, there was the Bethany he knew. He almost regretted opening the barn door wide. "You don't want to know."

She heaved a sigh of impatience. "Then why'd you bring it up?" She bounced her knees.

"You're the one who wanted to know why I took you into the woods," Silas reminded her.

"*Needed* to know. Are you saying you run from every car you see?"

His breath stalled. "Um, nein. Just the potentially dangerous ones."

"The potentially dangerous cars? Or the potentially dangerous people driving them?"

Could she sound any more sarcastic?

"And just how do you know which cars are 'potentially dangerous'? You'd have to run from all of them, ain't so?"

"Not exactly true. I didn't run from the farmer when we rounded up the cows. Or the cheese-buying tourists."

She snorted as they turned into her family's driveway. Surprisingly, the haus was dark. Not even a lone lantern flickered in a window.

Bethany scooted to the edge of the buggy seat. "I wonder where everyone is."

At least the topic had changed. Silas pulled the buggy to a stop at the foot of the porch steps. "Why don't you go inside and find out what's happening? I'll take care of Cookie—er, Chocolate Chip."

Bethany sat still. Frozen. And stared at the haus. "Wh...wh... what if...?"

Silas frowned as he studied her. What was her problem?

Ach. He swallowed. "I'll go inside and check things out. Then I'll take care of the horse." Not that he was in a huge hurry to meet this infamous Hen. "Stay here." He handed Bethany the reins, then climbed out of the buggy and climbed the porch steps. He opened the door to the laundry room and stepped into the darkness. The washing machine loomed before him, large and scary-looking. He reached for the flashlight Bethany said was kept on the shelf, and knocked something off. It fell to the floor with a clatter.

"Here." Bethany's voice sounded close behind him. Why hadn't she stayed in the buggy?

Silas glanced over his shoulder. "You don't listen so well."

She fingered his back muscles, sending shivers through him. Then she gripped one of his suspenders' straps.

Ach, Bethany.

With her other hand, she pushed the flashlight forward, into his grip. He flicked it on, and its brightness sent the darkness scurrying into the far corners of the room.

The haus remained silent. Nobody came to investigate the crash. Even so, Silas whispered, "I don't think anybody's here."

"That can't be. Where would they go? Mamm didn't say anything. And she was at the wedding. I think." Her voice was just as hushed.

Silas didn't remember seeing any of Bethany's family members at the ceremony. But there had been a crush of people there—Amish from nearby and from other states, and Englisch friends and coworkers of Sam's.

Not to mention, Silas had kept his attention on Bethany the entire time. Hopefully, nobody had noticed him gawking at her. She'd grown up to be a beautiful girl. Woman. And he wanted her with every fiber of his body.

Especially now, with her softness pressed up against his back. If the situation were different, he could have simply turned around and....

And she would scream.

Scratch that idea.

Silas edged forward, Bethany still gripping his suspenders, and peeked into the kitchen. The room smelled faintly of the bread someone had baked that morgen.

Bethany's breath hitched. "There's a note."

Silas looked where she pointed, at the table. A piece of paper lay there, folded partially, with a pen beside it.

Bethany released him and lit the nearby lantern.

Silas moved away, though he wanted to stay and see what the note said. "I'll check the rest of the haus."

Maybe she would ask him to stay with her.

Silence.

He headed for the stairs.

Bethany sank into a kitchen chair and picked up the note with clammy hands. Her heart pounded. The paper shook and trembled in her grasp.

Calm down. Breathe.

Hen had always folded his notes like that. A trifold, with only the top third creased, the bottom two-thirds unmarred. He said it made it more "mysterious."

He'd even left a note on Bethany's pillow one time. She'd freaked out because he'd been in her bedroom. Violated her personal space.

If this letter was from him....

Bile filled her throat.

But it wasn't in her room.

If only Silas had stayed with her. If only she hadn't let go of him.

She lifted the top third of the paper. Mamm's handwriting peeked out at her.

Her breath let out with a whoosh of relief.

Bethany,

At the wedding this morgen, Preacher Samuel handed me a printed message from the hospital. I went to the shanty and called the hospital in Kansas City. They want me to sign some papers for an emergency surgical procedure your daed needs.

Daed needed emergency surgery? For what? Nein wonder Mamm had taken off in a hurry. She'd probably hardly finished writing a note when the driver arrived.

I didn't understand what they were saying, but I was a bit stressed and probably not listening too clearly. Timothy, Sarah, and Carrie are staying at Onkel Ducky's for the rest of the week. They'll enjoy being with their cousins. They'll kum home Sunday, unless something changes and I need to be gone longer. I took Rosemary with me.

So much for Rosemary's birthday party. It seemed Mamm had the ability to cancel it even without knowing about it. Now Bethany needed to notify Naomi, so she wouldn't plan a party for a no-show birthday girl.

Where was Emma? Probably still at the singing with Roman. She would be home eventually. When Roman drove her, he liked to stop on a back road so the two could talk and dream about their future together. There were likely a few kisses mixed in with their conversation.

I left enough money to pay Silas if he needs to leave before I get home. It's in an envelope in the top drawer under the silverware tray. If Silas leaves, let Onkel Ducky know, and he and Timothy can do the chores. You'll be fine, but contact Onkel Ducky if you need anything. You might want to take down the "Cheese for Sale" sign, unless you think you can keep up with the orders.

I'll keep you updated as I find out more.

Mamm

Silas came back into the room. "The haus is empty."

Bethany slid the note across the table toward him. "Jah." Nothing else to say. She was alone. *Alone.*

Until Emma got home.

She hated being home alone.

At least Hen was still in jail. Maybe. Bethany hadn't seen his mamm at the wedding today. What if she'd gone along to pay his bail and pick him up? Fear pricked Bethany, and her hands shook more violently than before. How long would it be before he showed, expecting to pick up where they'd left off?

And with Mamm and her siblings gone?

Alone. She was alone.

Somewhere in the house, a board creaked.

Bethany's heart pounded. She bit her lip to keep from screaming. She *had* to get out of town, now.

She glanced at Silas and willed herself to calm down. She wasn't alone. Silas was with her. A comforting presence. If only she could grab hold of his suspenders again and not let go. "Mamm left money for your pay. Maybe there's enough for two bus tickets. To your onkel's."

"Bethany." Silas dropped into the chair beside her. "Nothing has changed. I still can't take you with me."

Tears burned her eyes. "But Mamm's gone. And Hen might be free on bond. And…."

He reached out his hand, then pulled it back without touching her. "Preacher Samuel would've said something if Hen was free."

Unless Preacher Samuel hadn't heard. Or didn't want to share bad news at the wedding of his sohn.

Bethany bit her lip and shook her head. A single tear escaped her eye and trailed down her cheek. "Stay with me to-nacht?"

"What?" Silas's eyes went wide with a look of horror. "Nein, Bethany!"

Oops. She hadn't mean it *that* way. "Not *with me* with me. Just in the haus. On the couch, or in Timothy's bed. While my family is gone. At least until Emma gets home."

"Jah." His brow furrowed. "Jah, I can do that."

"Gut. Danki." Silas would protect her. Surely, Hen wouldn't kum if Silas was here.

"Except...Emma won't be home. She told your mamm at breakfast this morgen she was hired on as a mother's helper, and that Roman was taking her to the family's haus to-nacht. Remember?"

Bethany shook her head. "I forgot." A wail rose inside her.

She bit it back. Silas would be there.

She would spend the rest of the nacht plotting her escape. Where she would go. How she would pay for it.

She glanced at the cupboard where Mamm always kept a canning jar full of cash.

Mamm had left money for Silas's pay. That alone would be enough for one bus ticket to...somewhere.

But stealing? She hesitated as guilt filled her. Desperate times called for desperate measures. Hadn't Daed said that once? Daed, who, for all she knew, was dying in an Englisch hospital...what kind of emergency procedure did he need, anyway?

This was definitely a desperate time.

Maybe she could visit her second cousin Rebecca in Montana, where she'd just moved with her family. Bethany could write the widower in southern Missouri from there. If she could find that spare copy of *The Budget*. It'd gone missing again. If she didn't know better, she'd think Gott didn't want her to contact the man.

She would leave for Montana first thing in the morgen.

⁓

Silas glanced at Bethany. It would be so easy to pretend they were married. He slowly reached for her hand. She wrapped her fingers around his and clung. Her palms were clammy.

Poor thing. She was terrified enough as it was, in the wake of her flashback last nacht. The painful memories must be close to the surface. And here he was, dreaming of marriage. Wanting to draw every bit of enjoyment out of this situation.

He sighed, forcing his thoughts away from *that* direction. His role was protector and comforter. Not would-be lover.

"I'm scared."

"Jah, I…I know." His hand tightened around hers. "Lord Gott, please put Your hedge of protection around Bethany. Help her to know that You're here, and that You hear her prayers and will answer them. Danki for Your love and mercy. In Jesus' name, amen."

Her eyes were wide when she glanced at him. "You talk to Gott out loud?"

Uh. "I heard Preacher Samuel do it once. He said Gott hears prayers, nein matter how they're spoken, and sometimes it helps the one who's being prayed for to hear the prayer, as well. It imparts peace." It truly did. He knew, because the person Preacher Samuel had prayed aloud for had been Silas. He shut his eyes. Even now, years later, he remembered. *Bless Silas, Lord. Go with him and his family in their new home, but let Silas know he's not abandoned. That You hear him and will remember him.*

Something pressed against his cheek. Moved. Warmth spread through him as he turned his head slightly.

Bethany, kissing him on the cheek.

He shifted more, his hand sliding up to enfold the back of her neck, drawing her gently toward him. He opened his eyes, his gaze focused on her mouth.

Giving her plenty of time to pull away, he lowered his lips to hers.

Chapter 17

Tears filled Bethany's eyes as Silas's lips lightly brushed against hers. The kiss was so sweet, so tender, so gentle. Feelings she'd never experienced before rocked her to the core.

After a few moments, Silas pulled away, his gaze meeting hers, probing, gauging, before his eyes lowered to her lips again. "I've dreamed of kissing you since…since before I left. Since that summer so long ago." His whispered words were just as sweet as his kiss.

Bethany allowed herself to be drawn nearer, nearer, as he came back to claim her lips more fully. He tasted sweet, as if he'd eaten some of the stash of sugar cubes he'd shared with Chocolate Chip.

As Bethany leaned into him, her eyelids fluttered shut, to focus on the sweetness of the kiss and the new sensations it awakened. His hand tightened around the back of her neck, while his other hand touched her waist, then slid around to her lower back, urging her closer, closer, closer….

She shivered.

He hesitated, then started to pull away. "Sorry."

Nein. She didn't want it to end. She raised her hands, putting one on each side of his face. She wanted to be closer than they could get, awkwardly leaning toward each other as they were from the separate chairs where they sat. She wanted his body against hers. Touching.

She scooted forward, rose, and settled down—sideways—on his lap.

⤳

Silas's eyes snapped open, his hands splayed on the far side of her waist, and his mouth gaped as he sucked in breaths of air. "Beth—"

She wrapped her arms around his neck, and…*wow.* He'd thought he kissed her.

He groaned deep in his throat as he tightened his arms around her.

Time passed in heart-pounding moments, one kiss morphing into two, ten, fifteen. She whimpered and squirmed closer, as if that were possible.

His body jumped, heated, came to life.

And he....

What was he doing? What...? He wrenched away, gently pushing her head down to rest against his shoulder. "Nein. We must stop."

She moaned, her finger trailed down his cheek, then a second later, she shoved herself off his lap. She stood, wobbling in front of him, staring down at him. Her chest heaved as she fought for air.

He experienced the same problem. In fact, he was fairly certain that if he tried to stand on his shaky legs, he would collapse from lack of oxygen.

"How dare you? I trusted you." She spun around and ran from the room. Her feet pounded the steps on the way up to the second floor. A door slammed.

How dare he? "Hold it. Who sat on whose lap? Who kissed whom?" He didn't exactly shout the questions, but they were louder than whispers. Not that anyone was around to answer.

Did he really owe her an apology?

She'd trusted him, and he blew it. Okay. But it seemed she was just as involved as he. He would've stopped if she'd asked. Wouldn't have started in the first place if she had pulled away. And....

Okay, jah, he was sorry.

Sort of.

Not really.

He grimaced. Sorry that it had blown up in his face. Not sorry it had happened.

Kissing her had been just as amazing—even more so—than he'd imagined.

A horse snorted.

Silas shook his head to bring his mind back to the present. Chocolate Chip still waited in the yard.

He'd figure out Bethany later. Right now, her horse needed his attention. And maybe a sugar cube or two as an apology for the delay.

⌒

Bethany threw herself on her bed, tears streaming down her face. She hated what had happened with Hen—and yet she'd turned around and thrown herself at Silas. Her brother was right. She was a flirt and probably deserved the reputation of being desperate. And now, Silas would avoid her, like a gut Amish bu.

Nein doubt she'd shocked him—first, with her forward behavior, and then by turning around and blaming him. All because he'd stirred those feeling inside her until she didn't want to hold them in anymore. She'd wanted to give in to the desire.

Hen might have been right when he said she'd asked for it the first time he violated her. He'd called her a little tramp. Told her she deserved it. Told her…. She swallowed. Hard.

Well, he'd also told her that Daed said she was to marry him. Said they were destined to be together and, in the eyes of Gott, were already married. That was before he….

She swiped her fists angrily across her eyes.

Why couldn't she be normal? Why had she gone and attacked Silas when he'd been so amazing? Beyond amazing, actually. Kind. Loving. Gentle. And he hadn't forced her. He hadn't chased her, like Hen had. She'd run from Hen, scurrying up into the highest parts of the loft, and then….

Ugh.

Would the memories follow her to Montana? Would the shame? Or could she face her second cousin and hold her head high, pretending she was just as innocent, just as normal, as…well, as any of the other girls in her community.

And she thought she'd be able to marry that widower in Seymour who'd advertised for a frau. She'd probably freak out, like she'd just done with Silas. And he would call her a tease. And then….

She would never marry. Never.

She would call for a driver to-nacht. Arrange to be picked up first thing in the morgen. And then she would pack. If she saw Silas, she'd apologize for overreacting.

Then, if she got a job in Montana, she'd reimburse her mamm for the money she'd stolen to make her escape.

She rolled over, sat up, and dried her face with her apron. Then she stood, smoothed her clothes, and splashed water on her face before heading back downstairs.

The man standing in the kitchen doorway wasn't Silas.

Her stomach knotted in terror.

"'Bout time you make an appearance."

Chapter 18

Silas finished brushing Chocolate Chip, then gave her a few sugar cubes, along with a carrot he'd snagged from the kitchen on his way out. If only it were as easy to pacify Bethany. He didn't know how to fix whatever it was he'd done wrong. Had he erred by kissing her in the first place? Or was it his response when she climbed into his lap, and they...well, indulged in a few moments of verboden passion.

He hadn't done anything beyond kissing. Her hair was still pinned, her kapp in place, and her virtue intact, as far as he was concerned.

He gave the horse some fresh water, then climbed up into the loft to exchange his gut church clothes for an outfit better suited for farm work.

His freshly washed clothes, clean-smelling and neatly folded, were stacked on his pillow. Bethany must've delivered them when she'd taken the laundry down earlier. Wearing garments Bethany had laundered and brought to his temporary bedroom....

And he couldn't stop thinking about her as it was.

If only he could do it over again. Except, this time, he wouldn't have kissed her. Wouldn't have started it in the first place. Nein matter how much he'd wanted to. Had wanted to, since he'd first sat beside her in an open buggy, his palms sweating, his heart pounding, his mind daring to dream of a future that would never be his. Theirs.

Never.

He frowned and kicked at a pile of straw.

He was going to Pennsylvania. Embracing the Mennonite faith. Getting a college education, and....

And she planned to write to and marry a widower in southern Missouri? Silas didn't see that working out very well.

Besides, he wanted her for himself. But, with the way things were, it'd be an interesting wedding nacht, for sure.

He slammed his fist into his pillow, as if that would do any gut.

If only he could figure out how to help her to heal.

Maybe Preacher Samuel would have some ideas. Or…. Silas knelt beside his cot and bowed his head. *Lord Gott, I….* Why was it that sometimes, when you needed to pray, the words wouldn't kum? The right words, at least. Should he pray for healing? For comfort? For acceptance? For wisdom? For patience? Maybe all of the above.

Lord Gott, I know You love Bethany. I don't have any idea how to begin to help her. She's scared, Lord. And I just messed things up by kissing her. Or by allowing her to kiss me. Something. Just…protect her. Watch over her. Guide me and my words and actions as I attempt to take care of her. In Jesus' name, amen.

He stood, and had the impression that he ought to go check on Bethany.

He considered it a moment, then shook his head. She'd gone to her bedroom. She would be fine.

He climbed back down the ladder, pulled the buggy into the shed, and then began the evening chores.

～

Bethany's breath caught in her throat as she stared at Hen. Her heart jumped, stuttered, then raced. She fought to put forth a calm, collected demeanor, though everything inside her wanted to scream. Where was Silas when she needed him?

Oh, jah. She'd sent him away.

She was on her own.

"What are you doing here?"

Hen sneered. "Nice to see you, too, Bethany. I missed you." His smug expression twisted into a cruel grin as he moved toward her.

It wouldn't do her any gut to run, as much as she wanted to. Where would she go, anyway, in the unlikely event she made it out of the haus? To the barn? To Silas?

To the hayloft…the scene of the first vicious attack?

Nein, nein, nein.

Hen had moved the lantern off the table. Or maybe Silas had. It sat, still flickering, on the counter.

"Your turn to tell me you missed me." He steadily moved closer. "Your mamm said you'd be happy to see me. She said you'd be alone, that she was going to Kansas City to visit Bishop Joe. And it'd be so nice if I stopped in and spent some time with you."

Mamm had said that? Mamm had betrayed her? Bethany's lips parted, and she struggled to keep calm, even though her pulse galloped. She couldn't find enough air to fill one thimble, let alone both her lungs.

"And so I'm here. Kum give me a hug, Bethany. Welkum me the way you know you want to."

Somehow she managed to shake her head. "You need to go. I'm... I'm not alone." *Where is Silas, Gott? If You are there, if You hear me—*

"I know better, Bethany. I know better." Hen moved closer still.

She edged sideways and grabbed the metal canister of cooking spray from the counter. Aimed the spray nozzle at his eyes. Pressed down.

The nozzle gave a sick-sounding little hiss.

Empty? It figures. As usual, Gott had abandoned her.

And Silas had prayed for a hedge of protection around her. Proof positive that Gott didn't hear her, or anyone praying for her.

She threw the spray canister at Hen, but he didn't even flinch. "Wanna play rough, huh? The guys in prison said that's a turn-on for some girls. Guess you're one of them." He grabbed her hands and twisted her arms behind her back. Then, still gripping them with one hand, he ran the fingers of his other hand from her neck down to her hips. "I know you want me, Bethany. I know I've spent the last ten months thinking about how it used to be between us. How it'll be again."

Screaming had brought Preacher Samuel and Sammy running last nacht. Would it work now? She opened her mouth, but all that came out was a tiny yelp as his lips closed over hers in a bruising kiss that ground her skin against her teeth. She tasted blood. And then he bent her backward, backward, backward, until she landed on the floor, his body on hers, his free hand yanking at the pins holding her dress together. His other hand still gripped her wrists together behind her back. It hurt.

"Nein! Please, nein." She hated the way her voice quivered. She attempted to bring her knee against her chest, but he slapped her, hard enough to provoke a rush of tears to her eyes.

Blinking against the burn, she turned her head away from his mouth, not that it mattered. He concentrated on her neck, working his way down to the skin he'd bared.

Lord, nein.... But then, Gott had abandoned her to a life of perpetual shame, and there was nothing she could do to change that.

"Stop resisting, Bethany. You know you've been dreaming of this moment."

In her nightmares, maybe.

"But I forget—you like it rough." His voice grated. "Which will it be? A punch? Another slap? Or...." His knee forced her legs apart and rammed upward.

She whimpered and wiggled, trying to get free. His hand tightened around her wrists and twisted them into another unnatural position. Any attempt to escape only made things worse. He yanked on her arms, and a shooting pain sliced through her shoulder. She didn't want a dislocated joint to deal with, too.

She shuddered as his hand ran over her body. "You like that, Bethany?" The material of her dress ripped. Cool air hit her, down to her belly button. Below.

Something metallic flashed in front of her eyes. Hen ran the cold blade of a knife down her check to her throat. "You'll like this, too." He pressed the metal against her throat.

Pain....

He emitted a deep, sinister-sounding chuckle. "I like it when you fight back, Bethie. Makes it more fun."

Even if she could have collected enough air to scream, she didn't dare. The one time she had managed to yell, he'd punched her so hard, she'd seen stars. And by the time her vision had cleared, it'd been almost over.

And nobody had kum, anyway.

She clamped her teeth upon her lower lip. *More fun? It made it more fun?* She wouldn't give him the satisfaction of screaming.

Besides, it was over faster when she submitted.

Ach, Gott....

A pair of tennis shoes came into focus. Jeans above them. A T-shirt. *Silas.*

He stared down at her. At them.

A little late. Tears escaped out of the corners of her eyes as the knife pressed harder against her throat.

She shook her head. *Go, just go. Don't witness my shame.*

There was nothing Silas could do. Would do.

The Gott who he claimed loved and heard her forbade him to help.

Pacifism.

The knife bit into her skin.

⌒

White, blinding rage hit Silas. He clenched his fists at his side. But something—Gott, maybe—kept him from lunging at the man holding a knife to Bethany's neck. Her arms were twisted behind her, and her breathing was shallow. Irregular. Barely under control.

Silas didn't know what to do, how to act. He didn't want her getting killed due to his rash actions. *Gott, help!* He looked around for something, anything, to use. If only he had a cell phone for calling 9-1-1.

He must've made some noise, because the man turned his head and peered up at Silas with cold snake eyes. "Get lost, kid." The voice was as icy as his eyes. Dangerous.

Silas didn't move.

"Don't make me get up." The man's knife wavered, slicing Bethany's chest. He ignored her gasp of pain and rose up on one knee, releasing her arms as he did. "If you know what's gut for you, leave *now*. And don't kum back."

Obviously, Silas didn't know what was gut for him. Bethany was more important. *Gott, help.*

The other man stood to his full height. "I warned you."

Silas braced himself, in case the other guy started swinging. He tried not to look at Bethany, at her bared upper body, at the thin lines of blood trickling over her chest and throat.

She jerked the folds of her dress together and rolled in the opposite direction.

The other man lowered his head and charged at Silas, the open blade still in his hand. It was a long knife, for hunting.

Silas was permitted to wrestle. Buwe did it all the time, to prove their strength. Gut, honest fun.

Never had Silas wrestled a man with a knife.

There wasn't any choice.

Gott, give me strength and dexterity.

The hand holding the knife was aimed at Silas's heart. The man drew nearer as if in slow motion, allowing Silas to notice every detail— or maybe it was due to the adrenaline that had awakened his senses.

The knife clattered to the floor only inches away. The man crumpled into Silas's arms.

Behind him stood Bethany, an iron skillet clutched in her hands.

Chapter 19

Bethany's breath hitched, and she dropped the skillet at her feet. The pan landed with a horrible crash. Blood gushed from Hen's head and flowed down his neck. Ran over Silas's arm, soaking his shirt.

Silas lowered him to the floor. "I think you...."

The rest of his words were lost in a tidal wave of fear. Plain, unadulterated terror.

Groaning, Bethany collapsed beside Hen, somehow avoiding the blood that pooled around his head. "I *killed* him! I'm a *murderer*! I'm going to *hell*."

Silas knelt next to her and pressed his fingers against Hen's neck. Silas's lips moved, but she couldn't hear what he said.

Tears burned her eyes and spilled over onto her cheeks. She hugged her knees to her chest and rocked back and forth, staring at the unmoving body. "I didn't mean to kill him. I just wanted to stop him. That's all. Just stop him. Ach, this is terrible. Beyond terrible."

Silas rose, touched her kapp with his hand, and then disappeared somewhere behind her. The door slammed.

Leaving her alone with the body. With her sin. With her shame.

Gott would never forgive her for this. Never.

Murderer.

She would end up shunned. Bear the mark of Cain.

Nausea rose in her throat, threatening to choke her. She tried to rise so she could run to the bathroom, but she couldn't find the strength to stand. Instead, she threw up all over the floor, herself, and Hen.

That just seemed to make it worse. Adding insult to injury.

The peal of the emergency bell outside the haus broke into her scrambled thoughts. Was there a fire, too?

She still couldn't make herself move.

The door slammed again.

A hand rested on her shoulder. "Shh, Bethany. Pull yourself together. It's over. You're safe."

Safe? She would never be safe.

Silas stooped down and lifted her in his arms, one hand behind her knees. Her dress fell open. She hadn't even looked for the pins. It hadn't mattered.

Now, it did, but not as much as distancing herself from her bloody deed. She grabbed a fistful of fabric and yanked it over as much of herself as she could.

The door opened. "Call nine-one-one," Silas shouted over his shoulder.

Bethany didn't want to know who had entered. She squeezed her eyes shut. Like a child who believed that nobody could see her if she couldn't see anyone else.

Silas carried her upstairs and gently laid her on a bed. "I'll send the first woman to arrive up to help you."

A bath would be in order. She shivered as she curled up in a ball. *Ach, Gott. I didn't mean to kill him. I'm sorry. So sorry.*

⌒

Silas ran downstairs to find the man who'd responded. He hadn't even seen his face. Caleb Bontrager stood by an open window, talking on a cell phone. He turned as Silas came into the room. "I was passing by when I heard the emergency bell."

Silas nodded, though he wasn't sure if Caleb had been addressing to him or whoever was on the phone. The metallic odor of blood and the putrid smell of vomit still hung in the air. "He's still alive, but head injuries bleed a lot, so it's hard to tell the severity of the wound. I don't know. She...she's in shock."

"They're going to send an ambulance and the police." Caleb still held the phone to his ear as he nudged Hen's leg with his shoe. "They told me to stay on the line. Did he...violate her?" A look of concern mixed with disgust crossed his face.

Technically, *jah*, plenty of times. But today? Enough, but not as much as he had in the past. Silas frowned. Bethany probably wouldn't want so much information shared, even if Caleb was her cousin. "He was stopped in time, on this occasion." And would've been stopped even sooner if Silas had listened to the still, small voice urging him to check on her.

"On this occasion?" Caleb shook his head. "We've wondered if... *jah*, that explains much. Who hit him?"

Silas cleared his throat. "Bethany. He would've killed me otherwise. I'm the one who found them." Silas looked around for the knife. There, under the counter. He pointed to it. The blade looked just as long and wicked as it had before, even from this distance.

Caleb glanced at the weapon, and his eyes widened. "Gizelle Miller is out in my buggy. Should I send her in to sit with Bethany? Or should I send her to summon one of the preachers?"

If only Gizelle could be in two places at once. Silas didn't know which task was more important.

Caleb shrugged. "I told the dispatcher the location, so I suppose I could go for a preacher while Gizelle sits with Bethany. She shouldn't be alone right now." He handed the phone to Silas. "Here, take this. I'll hurry."

"*Danki*. Get Preacher Samuel, if you can." That would be perfect. "Though he might not be able to *kum*, since Sam's wedding was today." Silas stared at the phone, then brought it to his ear. Did he need to say hello?

"Preacher David is closer. I'll see who's home and available." The door closed behind Caleb.

Moments later, the door opened again, and a woman entered. Gizelle, presumably.

Through the phone, Silas heard a female voice: "Sir? An ambulance has been dispatched. ETA of ten minutes from now. First responders have been alerted and are on their way. Is he still breathing?"

Gizelle glanced at Hen, paled, and turned away, clutching her stomach.

Silas pointed upward. "Bethany's upstairs," he whispered. "Bedroom." As she hurried out of the room, he glanced at Hen. His chest rose and then fell. "Yes, still breathing," he affirmed.

Should he start to clean up the scene? Or leave it and wait for the first responders?

Vehicle headlights flashed in the window.

For the first time in a while, Silas didn't fear them but eagerly opened the door for whoever it was that had just arrived.

⁓

"Bethany." A female voice intruded on her thoughts. A pair of hands caressed her back.

Bethany pulled her legs closer against her chest and made a moaning sound. Not on purpose. She'd meant to say, "Get lost. Leave me alone."

"The police are on their way. And the ambulance. We need to get you cleaned up." The hands continued with the rubbing motion. "Or maybe it'd be better for the police to see you like this."

With her dress ripped open? Nein. If word got out that men had seen her partially dressed, her reputation would be left in shreds. Bethany eyed Gizelle with distrust. Would she talk?

"They need to know, Bethany."

"Are you saying that because I...I killed him?" She would need all the help she could get making herself sympathetic.

Gizelle frowned. "Silas says he's still breathing."

She hadn't killed him? A wave of relief washed over her, followed by a fresh surge of dread. That meant her nightmare wasn't over. She'd still have Hen's visits to dread. And when word got out to the preachers that she—they—had been intimate, albeit not by her consent, they would likely be forced to marry. Daed had been known to enforce that rule.

She whimpered again.

But then, Preacher Samuel probably already knew. He'd found her screaming in the woods last nacht.

The mattress sagged as Gizelle sat beside her. She didn't speak. Had probably run out of words to say to reassure Bethany. She also didn't touch Bethany any longer. As if she'd be defiled by association? Amazing she didn't run screaming from the room.

"Someone else just got here." Gizelle glanced over Bethany's head and out the window. "Looks like the first responders have arrived."

They had? And nobody cared enough to check on her?

Figured.

Though, if Hen really was still alive, he required more urgent attention.

As always.

Chapter 20

Silas watched as the EMTs strapped Hen to a stretcher. He'd begun to regain consciousness and now groaned, as if someone had beaten the stuffing out of him.

Someone had.

Bethany.

The officer who'd been questioning Silas clicked his pen shut. "Where's the girl?"

"Upstairs. In her room." Silas looked down at his bloodstained shirt. He plucked the wet, sticky fabric away from his body. He couldn't wait to shower and change clothes.

"Can you bring her down here?"

"She's in shock." Maybe Silas had done the wrong thing by carrying her upstairs, but protecting her the only way he knew how had been foremost on his mind.

Just then, the kitchen door opened, and Preacher Samuel entered, Caleb on his heels. Preacher Samuel scanned the room: Hen on the gurney. The mess. The police officers and EMTs. His gaze finally rested on Silas, and he hitched an eyebrow. "What happened?"

As if Silas alone held the answers.

"You didn't tell her Hen had been released. Didn't you think she should know?" Silas hadn't meant to sound so accusatory.

Preacher Samuel frowned. "We knew his mamm had earned the money. Nobody expected her to go up today to post bond for him. I didn't know until just now. Nor am I aware how Hen found out Bethany would be alone."

"So, you knew he was a risk?" The officer clicked the pen open again.

The preacher's frown deepened. He shook his head. "All I know is, he was arrested for arson. As for Bethany, suspicions of abuse have kum out only recently. But nothing has been verified."

"I'll call for backup, then take some photos of the crime scene." The officer pulled a radio out of his belt and turned away as he spoke into the microphone.

Silas turned to Preacher Samuel. "Should I go see if she'll kum down?"

The preacher started to shake his head, then hesitated and began to nod. "That might be best."

Silas took the stairs two at a time. Inside the second room, Bethany lay on the bed, curled up in a shivering ball, still clutching the front of her soiled dress together. Seemed Gizelle should've had the sense to cover her with a blanket. Instead, she stared out the window at the flashing lights of the ambulance.

Silas knocked on the open door. "Bethany's wanted downstairs."

Gizelle turned away from the window and glanced at him. "Gut luck with that." Then she pushed herself to her feet and touched Bethany's shoulder.

"I don't want to go." Bethany's voice sounded raw.

Should he tell her she had to anyway? Would Preacher Samuel and the police officer kum upstairs to talk to her if she refused to go down?

"Preacher Samuel said—"

Bethany sighed loudly, then moved. Sat up. One hand still clutched the front of her dress. She looked down. "I need to shower and change."

"Actually, I think you'd better not," Gizelle murmured.

She was probably right, as much as Silas hated the idea of anyone seeing Bethany like this. He looked around for a robe. Not seeing any, he grabbed a pastel pink blanket from the end of the bed and draped it over her. "Can you walk?"

She huffed indignantly, as if the question offended her in some way. Well, maybe it did. Considering how she'd been hurt, violated, and shamed, her ability to walk was the least of her concerns. And yet her wishes were ignored once again because a church leader told her to kum.

If only Silas dared to stand up for her. To point out that a church leader's ordering her to appear before him was only adding insult to injury. But Silas was in the same position, subject to Preacher Samuel's authority. His ultimate authority, in the bishop's absence.

Silas had once read a well-known quotation about the tendency of power to corrupt, so that great men were nearly always bad men. In the case of Bishop Joe, based on what Silas had heard, it seemed valid.

Bethany wobbled, as if her legs had turned into limp noodles, and Silas automatically reached for her. He tucked his arm under her elbow, since she was using both hands to hold the blanket closed. Gizelle followed them.

Once downstairs, Bethany paused in the kitchen doorway and swayed. Her face paled.

Silas led her to a chair. "Sit. Please."

As she did, she adjusted the blanket. She shivered so violently that her teeth chattered.

The officer approached her, pulled up a chair, and sat down. "Tell me what happened."

Bethany's gaze shifted from the stern-faced officer to Preacher Samuel and Silas, who sat on either side of her, to Caleb and Gizelle, standing near the door, as if unsure whether to stay or go, and finally across the room to the paramedics who worked on Hen. "Aren't they taking him to the hospital?"

"They're waiting for another officer to accompany them." The officer glanced over his shoulder, then looked back at Bethany. "He's going back to jail once he's stitched up."

Bethany swallowed another round of bile. Hen's mother wouldn't be thrilled Bethany had undone all the saving and scrimping she'd done for months to get Hen out of prison. Hopefully, she wouldn't demand payment from Bethany.

"What happened here?" the officer asked again. "Did he violate you?"

The gentleness in the officer's voice was Bethany's undoing. With another round of tears stinging her eyes, she pulled in a breath and then released a flood of words. "He has, in the past…multiple times. But not this time. Silas stopped him. But…."

Silas reached for her. Rested his hand on hers. She grasped it and held on tight. Squeezing.

She shifted the blanket enough for the officer to see the tattered remains of her soiled dress. The bleeding gash on her neck, and the other one on her chest, which throbbed with every beat of her heart.

"A paramedic will need to bandage those cuts." The officer pulled out a cell phone, and something flashed. Had he just taken a picture of her? "I don't think you'll need stitches, but if you do, you'll have to go to the hospital." He nodded to one of the men near Hen, and he approached, carrying a big black bag.

Bethany flinched. Not another man touching her.

"It's okay, Bethany," Preacher Samuel murmured. "Purely professional."

While the paramedic cleaned and bandaged her wounds, three more officers arrived. They congregated near Hen, who had yet to regain full consciousness. Not a moment too soon—yet an eternity too late—they loaded him into the back of the ambulance.

The only ones who remained were one officer, Silas, Preacher Samuel, Caleb, and Gizelle.

"I want to collect your clothing as evidence," the officer told Bethany.

Bethany's face heated. Did he expect her to undress and hand over her clothes right then? She looked at the preacher.

Preacher Samuel nodded at Bethany. "Go ahead and take a shower and change. Put your clothes in a bag. I need to talk to you when you're through." He looked at Caleb. "Take Gizelle home and get my frau, please."

Glad to be excused, Bethany skittered out to the all-purpose porch. Her purple dress still hung on the line. She took it down and stumbled into the small bathroom. She threw her ruined dress into an empty trash bag, followed by her ripped undergarments. Mamm would have called it wasteful, since the dress had been for church Sundays, but Bethany didn't want to see it ever again. Her kapp joined the soiled clothes in the trash. Somehow, it had gotten stained with blood, too.

She stepped into the stinging spray of hot water with her back to the nozzle, in an attempt to protect her bandaged chest. Then she soaped herself and scrubbed her body red, trying to erase the memory of Hen's touch. If only it would disappear as easily as the bubbles swirling down the drain.

If only her insides could be washed as clean as her outsides.

She watched the river of water flow down the drain, and imagined it carrying away every bad thing that had ever happened to her. Making her clean. Sinless. Unviolated. A virgin with her innocence restored.

If only.

Too soon, the water started turning cool. She stepped out of the shower and dried herself with a fuzzy black towel. She dressed, using some of Mamm's sewing pins left lying on the folding table to secure the garment shut. After she'd braided her hair, she grabbed one of Daed's big navy blue handkerchiefs off the clothesline, folded it into a triangle, and covered her hair, tying the knot under her braid.

Bethany cleaned the bathroom and then, unable to find another excuse, carried her bag of ruined clothes into the kitchen.

Preacher Samuel's Elsie stood at the stove, stirring something in a saucepan. Hot cocoa, from the smell of it. Preacher Samuel and Silas sat at the table, a slice of partially eaten pumpkin pie covered with creamy whipped topping in front of each man. They both paused with loaded forks halfway to their mouths when Bethany entered.

The officer accepted the bag of clothes from her and left, carrying a slice of pumpkin pie on a paper plate with his other hand.

The mess on the floor had been cleared away. The only indication that something had happened was the sheen of the freshly cleaned floor in the flickering light of the lantern. The knife was gone. Probably confiscated by the police.

"Sit down, Bethany." Preacher Samuel nudged a chair away from the table with his foot. Elsie brought over two cups of steaming cocoa, and set one in front of Bethany. Two empty dessert plates and a pair of forks sat near the pie tin in the center of the table.

Bethany's stomach churned. Hopefully, Elsie wouldn't make her eat.

Preacher Samuel set his fork on his plate. "Why don't you tell us what happened, starting at the beginning? You and Hen went to school together. Grew up together. When did it become more?"

It hadn't. But then again, it had.

Bethany swallowed. Her throat hurt from all her crying. "He started coming around all the time. I thought...well, I thought he was coming to see me. And I was kind of flattered. Most buwe are afraid of me because of who my daed is. But then...have you ever been the hunter?"

Silas blinked. Preacher Samuel frowned as he glanced at Silas, and then he returned his gaze to Bethany. "Of course, but—"

"Have you ever been the prey?" Bethany looked at the place on the floor where Hen had attacked her.

"Can't say that I have." The preacher bowed his head as Bethany returned her attention to him.

"Hen told me that Daed said I had to marry him. This autumn. That, in God's eyes, we were already married."

Preacher Samuel's head snapped up. "So, you thought...or he thought—"

"He said he had the right. I didn't want to. I tried to fight him, but he's so much stronger. And it seemed better to give in than to get badly hurt. When he was put in jail, I thought I was free. I hoped I was."

"Ach, honey." Elsie scooted her chair closer, then wrapped her arm around Bethany's shoulders and pulled her near, as if Bethany were a frightened child. Her embrace comforted the ache within. Had Mamm ever hugged her like that?

"You're *not* married to Hen." Preacher Samuel slammed his fist on the table hard enough to rattle the dishes. "Did you tell your father?"

"I tried telling Daed and Mamm both. They said I needed to submit to authority. That, just as Daed was given authority over Hen and the community, Hen was given authority over me. That I had to obey. And...and Mamm told him I would be here." Her voice broke. "He said she told him I was alone. Told him to kum see me. That I'd welcome his visit." She shrugged, her shoulders shaking. "I'm not important. My wishes, my concerns, my fears…they don't matter. Just so long as I obey the rules."

"Ach, honey," Elsie said again, as she gently rubbed Bethany's arm.

"Nobody one cares what happens to me. Nobody cares to check up on me. As a woman, I'm considered disposable. But I want to be loved by someone. Cherished, like…." She stopped short of naming several of her married friends. Instead, she shook her head. "Gott doesn't care about me. He's just another harsh, demanding judge, like Hen. Like Daed. If I obey without resistance, it's all gut. It might hurt, but who cares? But what if I don't want to marry Hen?" Bethany swiped at a tear. "Is there really any reason for this game we play?"

Preacher Samuel stared at her, speechless. Elsie didn't pause with her gentle shushing, as if the sound were stuck in gear, but her eyes were wide.

Bethany had said enough. Too much. Curse her tongue.

❧

Silas bowed his head and balled his hands into fists. He wanted revenge brought upon both the bishop and Hen for hurting Bethany in the many ways they had. And on Bethany's mamm, for informing Hen that Bethany would be home alone, when she knew how Hen had hurt her.

But then, Bethany hadn't been home alone. Silas had been with her. Maybe her mamm hadn't expected him to go into the haus. She might've thought Hen would be alone with her.

The possibility sickened him.

Or maybe she'd expected him to intervene and bring the whole painful situation to a head.

"Please, don't make me marry him." Bethany's voice shook.

I'll marry her. Silas bit back the words that sprang to the edge of his tongue. They were better left unsaid.

Chapter 21

Bethany's jaw dropped, and she gawked at Silas, almost afraid to hope she would finally be free from her bondage. "Really? You mean it? You'll marry me? Then you'll take me with you to Pennsylvania, ain't so?"

Silas's eyes widened. "Did I say that out loud?"

Bethany's heart plummeted.

Silas gulped, his Adam's apple bobbing. He looked down at the forkful of pie resting on his plate, then at Preacher Samuel, and finally back at Bethany. This time, there was a glimmer of something—willingness?—in his eyes.

Jah, jah, jah. Her heart started dancing a jig, and a smile began forming somewhere in her soul. *Gott, please let Preacher Samuel see something positive in me and in Silas. Let him know, beyond a shadow of a doubt, that Silas is exactly what I need. And let him say a big, hearty jah—*

"Nein," Preacher Samuel stated.

And her hopes fell crashing to the ground.

Tears burned her eyes. She swallowed a hard lump in her throat, and stared down at the mug in front of her. Untouched.

Seemed her hot chocolate was destined for the drain. Her appetite for it was gone.

Just like her dreams.

Gott cares for you, He hears your prayers.

Jah, right.

Bethany straightened, and Elsie released her. She pushed her chair out. "Am I doomed to marry Hen?" She couldn't help the quaver in her tone. The despair. The barely suppressed anger.

If he said jah....

Bethany squeezed her eyes shut.

"Neither one of you is ready for marriage."

Bethany's eyes popped open.

"Silas needs to face what he is running from, and—"

"What?" Silas jerked upright.

Preacher Samuel frowned at him. "And Bethany needs time to heal from the abuse before she marries."

She glanced at Silas.

He nodded.

She looked back at the preacher and rubbed her fingers over the bandage that covered the wound on her chest. "So, you won't make me marry Hen?" Did she dare hope?

The preacher's frown transferred to her. "Nein. I will allow Silas to court you, if you're both willing. But...."

Jah! Her heat did a happy dance. She wouldn't have to marry Hen, after all. And Silas being permitted to court her meant....

Silas shook his head. "She's already made it clear she doesn't want to marry me."

"What?" Bethany twisted to look at him. "I never said that."

A half smile lifted one side of Silas's well-formed lips. A twinkle appeared in his eyes. "You denied proposing."

She stared at him. "You said you wouldn't take me to Pennsylvania."

"I said I wouldn't take a girl I wasn't married to." His half smile grew as his gaze lowered to her mouth. And lingered.

Desire shot through her, unexpected in its strength. She couldn't keep from leaning toward him, but then she caught herself. They had an audience.

Preacher Samuel chuckled. "Okay. Now that this is settled, it's time for me to take my frau home. Or...." His grin faded into another frown, and he glanced between the two of them, then looked at Elsie. "I think we'll just stay the nacht here."

"I think that would be wise," Elsie agreed, sending Bethany a gentle smile.

Silas quickly finished his pie, then stood. "I'll go on out to the barn. Unless I'm still needed here."

"The haus would be warmer." Preacher Samuel glanced at the woodstove. "Add another log or two, then bank it. You can sleep in Timothy's room, since he's gone. Tomorrow, we'll kum up with another arrangement."

Bethany stood, struggling to steady herself. "I'll get the beds ready." Her hands and knees shook. Her body shivered, despite the hot shower she'd taken, and the warm fire nearby.

Silas would sleep in the room next to hers. She glanced at him, and he met her gaze, a slight smile on his face. Her pulse quickened, first with excitement, then with fear. Would he try anything? But she was safe. Preacher Samuel and Elsie would be right across the hall.

Elsie pressed her hands on Bethany's shoulders. "I'll take care of the beds."

Bethany wanted to lean in for a hug. It'd been so long since she'd been embraced by someone who loved her.

"I guess I'll go to bed." And maybe try to make some sense of what had happened. Because even though she'd sat through the conversation and tried to pay attention, she didn't know what, if anything, had been decided.

Except that she wouldn't have to marry Hen.

A major relief.

And Silas would be allowed to court her.

She forced her eyes away from Silas's warm gaze to the spot where Hen's blood had pooled on the floor. Hen said Mamm had purposely left her there alone. Did Mamm know what Hen would do?

Bethany's knees wobbled as if they were made of Jell-O.

Silas watched Bethany make her exit. She held on to the backs of chairs, the counter, and the wall, as if she didn't have the strength to walk without support. The familiar bounce had disappeared from her step.

When she vanished into the dark hallway, followed several moments later by Elsie, Silas turned his attention to the chores Preacher Samuel had assigned him. He added a couple of logs to the fire and banked it so it wouldn't burn so fast through the nacht.

"Silas."

He turned.

Preacher Samuel stood at the sink, washing the few plates and utensils they'd used. It was an odd sight, since the women always did the dishes. "The most important thing you need to understand is that the ehemann should love his frau as Christ loves the church. Tell me, how does Christ love the church?"

Silas swallowed as he thought back to the events of that evening. He'd been willing to die to save Bethany from further injury. His gaze drifted to the hallway she'd retreated down only minutes ago. "He loves the church so much that He gave His life for it."

"Her. The church always takes a feminine pronoun. She is the bride of Christ. And?"

"He loves her unconditionally."

"Jah. Despite her shortcomings, despite her failures, He loves her. And He loves you, Silas. Nein matter what you did. Nein matter...." Preacher Samuel dried his hands and walked off. Left the room.

That was a strange conversation. Stranger still to leave in the middle of it.

Silas bent and adjusted the vents on the stove, closing them to cut the air flow. Then he straightened.

Preacher Samuel returned to the room carrying the bishop's black leather-bound Bible. Big and imposing, just like Bishop Joe.

Preacher Samuel placed the volume gently on the table and flattened his hand on the cover. "I was going to give you the same talk I gave to Sam last nacht, just before we heard Bethany screaming." He exhaled heavily. "Gott says nein. Not yet. He wants you to hear something else first."

Silas blinked. "You hear from Gott?" He'd never expected blasphemy from Preacher Samuel.

The older man tugged his beard. "We need to talk. Tomorrow nacht. There's a group of men that meet every other week. For accountability, they explained to me when they first started getting together. I went because I feared what it might be. The young men who started it.... That's a story for another day. Really, this is more than an accountability group. Much more. Turned out to be a very gut thing. But to-nacht, I want you to read John chapter three. And I need to spend much time in prayer." His hand remained, firm and flat, on Bishop Joe's German Bible.

"Uh, do you want me to take it?" Silas looked at the thick tome.

"Nein." The preacher released another heavy breath as he reached in his back pocket and pulled out a small, thin Englisch New Testament bound in orange faux leather. "I want you to take this one. You can keep it."

"An Englisch Bible?" Silas's eyebrows shot up. "I thought God's holy Word was to be read only in High German. And only by the preachers, during church services."

"We need to talk," Preacher Samuel repeated. "And I need to pray. John three."

Silas accepted the Englisch New Testament and stared down at it. His stomach churned with nausea, and he fought the urge to look over his shoulder. "This isn't what I've been taught. Is this a test?" And would Preacher Samuel change his mind about allowing him to court Bethany if he gave the wrong answer?

Preacher Samuel released a wry chuckle. "Nein, I'm very serious. We can read it together, if you'd be more comfortable."

Silas considered the proposition. Preacher Samuel would be by his side, encouraging him to study God's Word for himself—something Bishop Joe had always discouraged—and would be available to answer any questions he might have. "Please."

While Preacher Samuel prepared a kettle of hot water, Silas pulled out a chair and dropped into it. He thumbed through the pages of the Bible until he reached the book of John, then located chapter three. This would definitely be easy to read. He'd never been taught to read High German. Only Englisch.

Preacher Samuel poured some hot water into a couple of mugs, then got out some dried leaves and a tea infuser. "Feverfew. I suffered tension headaches for a time, and the local healer suggested this as relief, and to alleviate stress. I'll make a mug for Elsie to deliver to Bethany."

Bethany could probably use it.

For that matter, so could Silas. "Danki."

Preacher Samuel nodded as he lowered himself into the chair next to Silas. He opened Bishop Joe's Bible to the book of John. "Read it, sohn. Out loud, please. And if you have any questions, don't hesitate to ask."

An open door to Gott, through Preacher Samuel?

Silas smiled and started to read.

~

Bethany stood at her bedroom window and gazed out. Stars twinkled in the clear nacht sky, heedless of what was happening here on Earth. It seemed Gott was just as far removed.

She stepped back and fluffed her pillow, though she didn't expect to sleep a wink. She still needed to figure things out. Even if Preacher Samuel had said she didn't have to marry Hen, the fact remained that Hen would get out of jail again, eventually. And then what? He was sure to find her.

There was nein easy way out.

He might even threaten Silas again. Or anyone else who might try to protect her.

There was a soft click, and her door opened. She spun around, clutching the front of her nacht-gown above the stinging wound Hen's knife had inflicted.

Elsie entered, carrying a steaming mug.

Bethany hadn't expected anyone to care enough to check on her. She eyed the mug.

"Feverfew tea," Elsie said, answering Bethany's unasked question. "You need to try to get some sleep."

As if she could.

"Tomorrow's going to be a busy day. Silas needs to take you into Jamesport to press charges and to file a restraining order against Hen."

"Press charges? File a restraining order? What happened to 'Forgive as God has forgiven'? 'Turn the other cheek'?" Bethany didn't mean to sound bitter, but she couldn't help it.

"Jah, and it's biblical, for sure. But this...this is for your protection, Bethany. It has nothing to do with forgiveness or revenge. You still need to forgive Hen, but it will be for your healing. Harboring bitterness toward him will only hurt you."

Bethany sighed, yanked back the covers, and climbed into bed. She sat back against the headboard and accepted the mug of tea Elsie handed her. After taking a sip, she set the drink on the bedside table.

Elsie sat on the edge of the mattress and patted Bethany's hand. "I've been trying to think how I'd handle this situation if you were my dochter…what I would say or do. I can't even begin to imagine the horror. I'm…." She shook her head.

Bethany forced herself to smile, but it probably looked fake. The sip of tea she'd taken churned in her stomach. "Daed would say that Gott willed it, and I should never question der Herr. Besides, he already told me it was my fault. Told me I deliberately teased and tempted buwe, and that it's the duty of the frau to submit to her ehemann."

Elsie shook her head. "Except that you aren't Hen's frau. He isn't your ehemann. What he did was a sin and a crime, Bethany. But right now, I'm not concerned about him. I'm concerned about you. A thing like this—"

"Why doesn't Gott care?" Bethany wailed. "Why doesn't He stop it? I've prayed and prayed, but He doesn't hear me."

Tears glistened in Elsie's eyes. "Gott *does* care. He hears you, and He cares. But we live in a fallen world, Bethany. We aren't puppets or dolls controlled by Gott and His active imagination. He doesn't plot how to hurt Bethany Weiss. He gave all of us free will, to choose whom we shall serve. And, I hate to say this, but Hen—and likely your father—have not chosen Gott. They've chosen to believe the lies of the wicked one. The same one who's lying to you, telling you Gott doesn't care. Gott is working behind the scenes to heal you. The Bible says, in the book of Jeremiah, "'For I know the plans I have for you," declares the LORD, "plans to prosper you and not to harm you, plans to give you hope and a future. Then you will call on me and come and pray to me, and I will listen to you. You will seek me and find me when you seek me with all your heart."'"

If only that were true. "But…."

Elsie reached for Bethany's hand once more, and her thumb began rubbing it. "Believe Him, Bethany. Seek Gott and take Him at His word. He has this. He has you, right in the palm of His hand. He loves you. He cares. And His heart is broken because of how you were treated and because you blame Him."

Bethany fingered the edge of the bedsheet. Could it be true? Did Gott hurt because she blamed Him? But....

"How do you know He has this?" Bethany sniffed. "How do you know He's going to heal me?"

"Because He said He would."

Would. But when? She hadn't seen any evidence to support Elsie's belief. Bethany wrapped a fold of the sheet around one hand, squeezing it in her fist. *Gott, let me know You care. Somehow. If You really do.*

Chapter 22

Early the next morning, Silas shuffled reluctantly out of the warm haus into the frigid outdoors. He hadn't wanted to leave the comfortable bed. Big difference between a hard, narrow cot with mice, cats, and bats as company, and a soft twin-sized mattress with nein roommates. He could get used to it, but he wouldn't permit himself the pleasure.

He slapped the ladder to the loft as he went by, and it creaked. He should look for some spare lumber to replace the weakened boards. He'd hate for Bethany to fall again. Maybe he could do that today. Tomorrow, at the latest.

He fed and watered the chickens, then went into the cow barn and got out a pail and a stool. Preacher Samuel joined him a few minutes later. "Elsie is helping Bethany with breakfast. They were talking about Christmas, and Bethany mentioned wanting to collect greenery for decorating. But if I know Joe's Barbie, the branches will go into the fire as soon as she gets home."

It was sad that Bethany wasn't permitted such simple pleasures. When Silas was seven or eight, right after the family had moved to a more liberal district than the previous one, Mamm had decorated the home with freshly cut evergreen branches and clear bowls filled with red and green glass Christmas ornaments. They'd looked so pretty. So festive. Silas had wanted Mamm to keep them up all year. They'd lasted only a few days, until Daed had shattered all the ornaments and bowls during one of his rages. That had been the first and last time Mamm decorated for the holidays.

If Silas married Bethany, he would give her free rein when it came to the holidays. And he would do everything in his power not to destroy the work of her hands.

"I'll...." He swallowed a lump in his throat. "I'll go with her to collect some greenery after we get home, if it isn't too late. I mean, if we have time before your—that, uh, accountability thing you mentioned."

Preacher Samuel smiled. "You're a gut man, Silas Beiler. The Bible study will occur after dinner to-nacht, so you should have time. Josh Yoder is leading it because David—my sohn-in-law—won't be there. His frau—my dochter Rachel—is due to have a boppli very soon. The midwife says definitely before the end of the week. So David is staying close to home. It's their first."

"Congratulations, Grossdaedi," Silas said with a grin. "Your first, too, ain't so?"

Preacher Samuel chuckled. "Not exactly. Gott led Sam to adopt his old girlfriend's boppli. His name is Peter James, but everyone calls him Peanut. We'll be watching him while Sam and Abby go on their wedding trip. To-nacht, Abby's aenti Ruthie is taking care of him."

Silas nodded, unsure of what, if anything, he should say to that.

"I'm considering inviting Bethany to join us for the Bible study to-nacht. She would be the first woman to join us, since it started as a men's accountability group, but Josh has expressed a desire to include women at least on occasion. And it seems Gott is impressing on me the importance of Bethany being there. She doesn't have a strong male influence in her life right now. Let me rephrase: She doesn't have the strong influence of a man wholly committed to der Herr."

It'd be gut for Bethany to go. Especially with all the spiritual wounds she'd suffered. *Gott, please, heal her. I still love her, and….* Silas exhaled. He had his own painful past to work through. And something whispered deep inside him that even though he'd left home and hearth, he hadn't even begun to truly escape. It seemed Preacher Samuel had recognized the same thing, given the comment he made last nacht about Silas's needing to face whatever it was he was running from.

Silas certainly didn't want Bethany in the midst of his life when it all came to a head and unraveled. It wouldn't be pretty. Nein, he wanted Bethany to find healing and stability first, so that when his life unraveled, she'd survive.

Chores completed, Silas and Preacher Samuel returned to the haus. They entered the warm kitchen and were greeted by the delicious scent of fresh-baked raisin bread. A glaze-drizzled loaf cooled on the table, a dish of homemade butter beside it.

Silas's stomach growled at the sight of four bowls on the counter that were filled with oatmeal and topped with banana slices and granola bits. Then he looked at the table. A red candle was placed at either end, and on each of the four plates was arranged a green cloth napkin folded into the shape of a pine tree.

Elsie carried two of the bowls of oatmeal to the table, then turned around with a big smile. "This is fun. At home, I'm always sidetracked from creative activities with my quilting and the kinner. And it seems our Bethany has been stifled by rules and strictures. She would've done even more if we'd had time to gather the pine branches she wanted."

Bethany smiled, albeit not as broadly. "Not to sound like a complainer, but chores aren't usually this fun. I've actually enjoyed the morgen chores."

His family would scoff and call it impractical.

But it was pretty. Very pretty.

Silas looked at Bethany and smiled.

⁓

As soon as breakfast was finished, Bethany ran some water in the sink and added a squirt of dish soap. Chores weren't so terrible when she was appreciated. She'd received great compliments on the raisin bread, not so much by words as by actions, with Silas and Preacher Samuel going back for seconds and thirds, slathering each slice in her homemade butter. And they'd finished the oatmeal in short order.

If her efforts were greeted like this every day, she wouldn't mind doing them. Washing Silas's clothes had ceased to be a chore when he'd given her a grateful smile and a word of thanks. Nobody else bothered to thank her for doing that job. Or any other work.

She'd have to remember to thank her sisters and brother. Maybe they, too, suffered from lack of affirmation.

"Don't forget, you need to go into town and file a restraining order against Hen," Elsie reminded her as she carried several dirty dishes to the sink.

Bethany felt herself sag. Just like that, her gut mood evaporated.

"And pick up some special treat for yourself."

Like what? A candy bar? She'd merit more than just one for making that dreaded stop. Would she have to see him face-to-face in order to file the order? Hopefully not.

Elsie stacked another dish on top of the others. "I'm trying to think of someone to ask to kum stay with you and Silas to-nacht. Seems everyone I've considered has someone else to take care of. Maybe Josh and Greta could kum, if you wouldn't mind having a boppli in the haus over-nacht. We'll stop by their haus on the way home and ask. Greta might even be able to help get a start on your Christmas baking."

That sounded fun.

If only they didn't need a chaperone.

"I know Mamm went to Kansas City because Daed is having an emergency procedure, but I don't get why she left Silas and me here all by ourselves, and then told Hen I was alone. Why didn't she round up any chaperones? Was she hoping Hen would run Silas off and that Hen and I would be forced to marry? I know she's said several times it would make Daed happy, and that the only reason she let Silas stay here is that we need his help."

"I can't imagine your parents knowing what Hen had done and not trying to put a stop to it." Elsie shook her head. "It almost sounds like they encourage him. That's plain wrong. I probably shouldn't say this, but there's talk of—" She bit her lip. "Never mind."

"What is it?" Bethany prodded. "I won't tell. I promise."

Well, she would try not to, anyway.

The door opened, and Preacher Samuel peeked inside. "Ready to go, Elsie?"

A look of relief flittered across Elsie's face. "Jah. Let my grab my things."

Preacher Samuel looked at Bethany. "I'll be by after supper to take you and Silas to a Bible study."

"Me?" she squeaked.

"Jah, you." The preacher nodded. "Silas is hitching up your horse and buggy. You might want to get ready to go."

Elsie gave Bethany a quick hug. As she did, she slipped something inside her apron pocket. Then she put on her cloak and hurried out the door after her ehemann.

Without telling Bethany what it was that she'd almost said.

Suddenly, it seemed like something Bethany really needed to know.

Something of earth-shattering importance.

⁓

Silas hitched Chocolate Chip to the buggy and drove around behind the haus. Beneath the warm gloves he wore, his hands sweated. Nervousness over this date, of sorts, with Bethany. Even if they were just going to town to do an unpleasant errand. Maybe he could take her to lunch afterward. There used to be an ice cream shop on the square. Was it still there? But then, with the current air temperature, ice cream might freeze them from the inside out.

Speaking of freezing…he hurried inside and snatched a heated brick from the woodstove to stash in the buggy. That would help to warm them on the long trip into town.

Several minutes later, Bethany came out of the haus. She took a moment to tuck a slip of paper into her black clutch purse, then pulled on her hand-knit mittens. Silas jumped out of the buggy and came around to help her climb in.

"Danki." Bethany got herself settled on the seat. "Elsie said something about trying to get Josh and Greta Miller to stay with us. I hope she does, because Greta is a phenomenal baker, and it'd be fun to get some Christmas baking done before Mamm gets home and tells me I can't make special things because we aren't celebrating. Do you think we'll have enough time to stop at the store for ingredients?"

Silas rubbed his chin with the rough tips of his gloves. The bits of fabric caught and pulled on his growth of whiskers. He should've taken the time to shave earlier instead of deciding it wasn't too bad and trusting nobody would notice his five o'clock shadow. Should he urge Bethany to do what her mamm would expect, even though the older woman wasn't around to enforce it?

But then, what harm was there in Christmas baking? The family would need the goodies to offer to visitors throughout the holiday season.

He swallowed. "Jah, we can go to the store. And Preacher Samuel mentioned you wanted to gather some pine boughs to decorate."

Her smile was faint. "Jah. Some acorns, too."

Chocolate Chip tossed her head and snorted.

Silas looked at the horse, suddenly realizing he'd never prompted her to start their journey. He and Bethany could talk just as easily as they rode along. He flicked the reins and clicked his tongue, and they started down the drive.

"I'd love to hang some mistletoe, too."

His heart rate increased. Catching Bethany under the leaves, stealing a kiss.... A smile tickled his lips. "Mistletoe, huh? Why's that?"

"Because it's something I've never been allowed to do, and it sounds fun. My gut friend Susanna hangs it every Christmas. A different place every time. She said her grossmammi taught her. One year, she even hung it in the barn."

After all she'd been through, she deserved at least that small happiness. "I'll shoot some down for you."

Her squeal startled him. Even the horse quickened his steps. Bethany flung her arms around Silas's neck and hugged him, a big smile on her face. "You're beyond wunderbaar, Silas Beiler. Ich liebe dich. Really."

His face heated, and he looked away as she released him and settled back in her seat.

I love you. She hadn't meant it. She couldn't have. Because he wasn't worthy of her.

Chapter 23

Bethany hugged herself as she stepped out of the sheriff's office and started toward the buggy. Silas stayed close behind her, his hand held supportively at the small of her back. It'd seemed strange, and wrong, to press charges against a fellow member of the Amish community. The officers—none of whom she'd recognized from last nacht—had processed the restraining order, though Bethany wasn't sure about the logistics of enforcing it. After all, she and Hen lived in the same district; they would see each other at barn raisings, work frolics, church Sundays, and more. It couldn't be avoided.

The best option was for her to leave Jamesport.

A shiver coursed through her, and she tucked her coat more tightly closed. Her teeth chattered. It must be from stress, because nobody else seemed to be shivering. Silas certainly wasn't.

In the prison yard, a guard, and several inmates dressed in gray and white stripes, stood against the fence, smoking cigarettes and laughing. The prisoners wore gray-and-white striped shirts and pants. The smoke burned Bethany's nose, and she coughed.

"Kum on." Silas pressed his hand more firmly against her back, urging her to quicken her pace. "You're shivering. Are you cold? I wish the buggy were heated. At least there's a thick blanket in there. I'll help you bundle up."

The concern in his voice and his words reached deep inside her, and she forced a smile. Forced, because, as much as she appreciated his care and wanted to show her gratitude, exhaustion had overtaken her. The lack of sleep the previous nacht, not to mention the events of the previous minutes...hours...however long it'd been, had sapped all her energy.

She climbed into the buggy and kicked aside the heated brick that had long since lost its warmth. Meanwhile, Silas took out the blanket and unfolded it. The material was fleece with an Indian print, a gift from their Englisch driver to Mamm when Daed had started having

154 Laura V. Hilton

his bad headaches. Migraines, the doctor called them. Mamm had swapped out the old, tattered blanket they'd kept in the buggy, which was now kept in the barn loft for "strays." Men like Silas who wandered in and bedded down for the nacht.

Except Silas was much more than a stray.

She watched him shake out the fleece blanket, making sure there were nein spidery surprises in it. Then he spread it wide and draped it over her. "I'll let you tuck it in," he said, withdrawing as she adjusted it slightly. The musty, dusty odor of mothballs made her sneeze. She ought to wash the blanket next time she did laundry. Mamm and her sisters would appreciate it, even if they never said so.

Would she lose contact with her whole family when she left? She wouldn't dare write and risk having Hen find out where she'd gone.

Silas settled in beside her, his shoulder brushing hers as he reached for the reins. "Where do you want to go next? The Amish Market?"

She nodded.

Silas drove the buggy around the square, peering at the different shops they passed. Then, with a shake of his head, he steered them toward the main road.

"What were you doing?"

"Checking to see if the ice cream shop was still open." He shrugged. "Sign says it's closed for the season."

"A bit cold for ice cream, ain't so?"

He grinned. "It's never too cold for ice cream."

"Too bad there's nein place to get bus tickets here. I'll have a driver take me into Chillecothe or Cameron." A siren wailed. Bethany twisted around to look over her shoulder. A police car trailed them, its lights flashing. "There's a—"

"I see it." Silas's smile had vanished. He slowed the horse, preparing to pull over.

The police car sped around them and disappeared in the distance.

"I didn't think I did anything wrong." Silas's expression was sober. There was nein hint of his grin from earlier. "You mentioned bus tickets. Where are you planning on going?"

"Anywhere but here. A restraining order won't do any gut in our community. Since you won't take me with you to Pennsylvania, I guess I'll just go alone." She tried to sound flirty.

A sharp intake of breath was his only reaction. A long moment later, he sighed. "I'm serious, Bethany."

Right. And when would she learn not to flirt with him? They'd be getting along so well, and then she'd forget herself and ruin everything. "I don't know. I'm thinking about Montana."

"Changed your mind about the widower?"

Bethany sighed. "I lost that issue of *The Budget*. Again. Besides, I've decided I'll never marry, since Preacher Samuel said I couldn't marry you."

"Technically, he said 'Not yet.'"

Bethany ignored him. "I'm not gut enough. I'm defiled. And nobody would have me."

Behind them, another siren wailed. Silas glanced in the side mirror and saw a fire truck speeding toward them. There wasn't a safe place to pull over, so he stopped the buggy in place, holding as tightly as he could to the reins so the horse wouldn't bolt.

The engine screamed around them, followed closely by three pickup trucks, their emergency lights flashing. Silas sat there a moment after they passed, peering over his shoulder to see if any more emergency vehicles followed.

All quiet.

He flicked the reins again.

Bethany nestled further beneath the blanket, her expression sad. "You don't think it's another barn fire, do you? I mean, Daed and Hen are in jail, but—"

"They aren't the only reason there's a fire department in town." Silas studied her. "Not to change the subject, but what you said about being defiled…I, uh, I meant what I said, though I didn't mean to say it. I would marry you. But Preacher Samuel is right. You need to heal."

Her face brightened for a moment, them dimmed. She gave a half shrug. "And you need to face what you're running from."

A more threatening prospect than Hen's knife. Silas balled his fist to keep his free hand from shaking. "Someone will have you, Bethany. If not me, then someone else."

"If I can't have you...." She caught her breath, the flirty tone gone. Shook her head. "I just need to go someplace where I'm not known and can't be found. I won't even tell my family where I'm planning to go."

"There goes the option of any plain community. You know how news travels."

Pennsylvania wasn't the smartest choice for him, but at least it was a start. Until he found someplace better. Transitioned into the Englisch world. And vanished completely from the Amish world.

She looked away.

The Amish Market came into view. Silas didn't know where the police car and fire truck had gone, but they weren't at the store. The parking lot was full, however, and—he chilled—more than one of the cars were black.

He wanted to let Bethany shop alone while he hid beneath the blanket in the buggy. But Bethany still shook, and he wanted to stay near to protect her. Besides, what were the odds that *he* would be at the market today?

Silas pulled up to the hitching post, parked between two other buggies, and firmed his shoulders. He could do this.

Still, he was careful to keep his back to the parking lot as he got out of the buggy, tied Chocolate Chip, and went around to assist Bethany.

He adjusted his hat and lowered his head as he turned toward the store. Maybe none of the vehicles belonged to the man he feared.

Maybe one of them did.

He had nein way of knowing.

Then he saw it. The nonsensical bumper sticker. "Save the Frogs," it said.

A chill trembled through him.

He was here. Somewhere on the premises. And if he saw Silas, there'd be a price to pay. Maybe Bethany was on to something, wanting to get out of town sooner rather than later.

Silas tried to think of a reason to go back to the buggy and hide. Couldn't kum up with any.

A throng of people—Englisch and Amish alike—were gathered just inside the store entrance. He ducked his head further down and turned away from them, heading in the opposite direction.

There, the candy aisle. Gum. He could get a pack of—

"Silas! Where are you going?"

Did Bethany have to call his name so loudly? He swallowed his fear. *Everything is fine. Just smile.*

But he couldn't. It wouldn't kum.

"Silas?"

He blindly picked up a package of gum. The flavor didn't register. He swiped his hand over his jaw. Turned.

And looked straight into a haunting pair of dark eyes.

He whirled and barely kept from running down the aisle. Making a sharp turn around the endcap, he almost knocked the bags of pre-popped corn off the shelf.

There—a door. "Employees Only."

He made a beeline for it. Pushed through and let the door swing shut behind him. A brief measure of peace enveloped him in the silence. Nobody yelled or chased after him. The door didn't swing open again.

Maybe he was safe.

He hurried down a hallway. A large break room on one side, two messy offices on the other. A restroom. And through a set of double doors, a loading dock with a truck backed up to it.

A couple of Amish girls tried to help a delivery man who muttered something about the store needing more male employees. Silas approached them, hefted a box, and carried it into the storeroom. He went back for a second box. Then a third. And then—

"Who are you?" demanded a male voice behind him. "You don't work here."

Silas froze, bracing himself.

"You don't work here, but I've been watching you, and it seems to me you'd be a gut fit. Looking for a job? Part time. Delivery days only. We could use a gut, strong man like you."

Silas dared to relax. He turned slowly around, still holding a box. The Amish man before him was slight of build. His thick beard was trimmed, not long, unkempt, and stringy, like some men's. According to the tag on his shirt, his name was Joel. The manager.

Was he the same manager who'd dealt with Silas's brother Henry when he'd lost his temper and thrown a bag of flour that exploded all over the store?

"I might be looking. I'm Silas." He hesitated. "Silas Beiler."

Joel gave a slight tilt of his head and narrowed his eyes. "I knew your brother." Then he went silent, as if he might be reconsidering his offer.

A smile finally appeared. "I know you, too. Kum. We'll talk."

⌇

Bethany bounced the two-year-old bu of a local Englisch woman in her arms as the two women chatted. When the conversation ended, she handed the bu back to his mother, with a verbal agreement to babysit her kids the following week. Of course, that assumed Bethany would still be in town. The woman handed Bethany a piece of paper with the phone number of another woman who wanted someone to iron clothes and clean haus for her elderly father. Job opportunities were here, Bethany just wasn't sure she wanted to take them.

She sidestepped a somewhat-familiar-looking Englisch man who almost ran into her. For the second time. He'd almost plowed her over when she'd entered the store, too. Now, he muttered under his breath as he glanced around, as if looking for someone or something specific, before walking out.

Where was Silas? He had vanished suddenly, with a flash in his eyes of what might've been fear. Bethany had been expecting him to reappear. To see him standing behind her, a pack of gum in hand, when she finished her conversation. He was nowhere in sight.

She turned around and backtracked, looking down the next aisle. And the next.

She searched the whole store.

He wasn't anywhere.

For a moment, she stood still, feeling exposed and uncertain. Abandoned, yet again. At least, at a grocery store, she was bound to find someone who would offer her a ride home. Eventually.

She opened her purse to retrieve her shopping list. And fingered the note Elsie had slipped into her pocket right before leaving with Preacher Samuel. Bethany pulled it out and reread it.

Even if you are having a hard time loving Him, He's not having a hard time loving you.

Elsie had written her note on a card preprinted with a Bible verse—Psalm 27:13: *"I would have lost heart, unless I had believed that I would see the goodness of the* Lord *in the land of the living."*

Something resembling hope bubbled up inside Bethany. *Ach, Lord, let it be so.*

She put the note back and pulled out her shopping list. She had ingredients to buy. Baking items for all the brownies, cookies, and candies that her friends served at their holiday gatherings. Fudge...it'd been forever since she'd made fudge. Mamm had outlawed almost all the sweet stuff.

A sense of power at being able to do the things she enjoyed washed over her. And Elsie *had* told her to treat herself to something. Baking goodies would be just the thing. But the sense of empowerment was eliminated by a flash of guilt over her blatant rebellion.

She firmed her jaw. She would shop, anyway. Elsie had okayed it.

By the time Bethany had filled her cart with all the items on her list, Silas still hadn't surfaced. As she approached the checkout counter, she glanced outside. Chocolate Chip still waited at the hitching post.

"There you are." His voice came from behind her.

She turned around.

He held a can of orange cola in one hand, a can of root beer in the other. "Which do you prefer?"

"Root beer, please. Where'd you go?"

He set both cans on the counter, along with a pack of cinnamon gum, but avoided her gaze. "A delivery truck showed up, and I went to help unload. The manager offered me a job here, unloading trucks on delivery days. After some thought, I accepted it. Had to fill out some paperwork."

Nobody just walked into a store and got offered a job. And what about his frightened look before he'd run off? Had Silas just lied to her? She stared at him.

The cashier—Gizelle—stepped behind the counter. "Hi, Bethany. Did you find everything you needed?" She lowered her voice to add, "How are you doing?" Concern filled her eyes.

Bethany frowned. How had Gizelle found out already? But, wait. She'd been there immediately afterward. With Caleb. "I'm…I've been better." She searched for a different topic. "Did you hear all those sirens earlier?"

Gizelle shrugged.

"Car fire out on the highway, according to the delivery man." Silas lifted a bag of flour from Bethany's cart and set it on the counter behind the canned goods.

So, there really was a delivery man?

Silas heaved the bag of sugar up beside the flour.

Gizelle glanced up at Silas and batted her eyelids. "Gut to have you on staff."

Maybe he wasn't lying.

But what was Gizelle doing, flirting with him? Was he attracted to her, too? Bethany glanced at him.

His cheeks reddened. He still wouldn't look at her.

It would be so nice if something would make sense for a change.

Chapter 24

Silas settled into the buggy next to Bethany and waited half a minute for her barrage of questions to start.

She popped the tab of her root beer and took a sip.

Ignoring him.

Okay, then. Maybe he was safe from her questions. Surprisingly, it kind of hurt. Didn't she care?

He clicked his tongue at Chocolate Chip and backed the buggy away from the hitching post, then headed toward the road.

Finally, Bethany spoke. "You were hired at the Amish Market? Really?" She sounded incredulous. But her question wasn't the one he'd been dreading. "I've tried to get a job here for years and years, but they never seriously considered me. Then you just walk in, and they ask if you want to work for them?"

The hiring process had been slightly more involved than her summary. But how could he admit to the cowardice that had landed him in the right place at the right time?

He opened his can of soda and took a gulp, then glanced at Bethany. "What can I say? They need someone with my brawn." Definitely not his brains. He hadn't thought this through, because this job would put him in a public area where he was sure to see *him* again. Eventually. Unless they kept him in the back of the store, near the loading docks.

Bethany eyed his arms, opened her mouth, and shut it again without a single flirtatious remark about his strong muscles. Progress. Then she frowned. "Aren't you busy enough at home?"

"Home?" He forced back the painful memories that word evoked. He'd never really had a "home," but he hoped to create a happy family place someday. "Jah, there's more than enough to keep me busy at your haus." The words came out gruffer, harsher, and sharper than he'd intended them to. "There is much work to be done. How long has the bishop been gone, anyway?"

It was a rhetorical question, but she answered, anyway. "Too long." Bethany slumped. "The family dynamics have changed so much over the past couple of years. We lost our barn the summer Ezra died. He was smoking in the loft on the Fourth of July, and the hay caught fire. He died later that summer, at the end of August, in a car accident. And then, in November, Daed started suffering migraines, and spent much of his time in bed or holding an ice pack to his head. The doctors couldn't figure out the problem, at the time. Possibly too much stress, they said. That's when Hen started…hurting me, and the other fires began. And then, Daed was diagnosed with a brain tumor. He'd started trying to raise money for surgery—for himself and for another man in the community who got hurt in a farming accident—when he got was arrested. And my whole family fell apart. Birthdays and holidays became nonexistent. Mamm turned harsh. And…." Bethany sighed heavily.

Silas could relate. He reached for her hand. She grabbed hold and clung, reminding him of her grip when the rung of the loft ladder had broken, and she'd latched on to him to keep herself from falling.

When he got back to the farm, fixing that ladder would be the first item on his agenda, unless Bethany insisted on collecting pine boughs first. He'd also noticed a pile of shingles, covered in dust and forgotten, along a far wall of the barn. Further investigation had revealed that the haus roof needed replacing soon—definitely before the snow came. On the other hand, the barn looked almost new. Probably was rebuilt after that fire Bethany had mentioned.

"Then why did you take the job?"

Was that worry in her voice? Silas glanced at her. She bit her lower lip.

He squeezed her mitten-covered hand again. "I'll be able to buy new shoes sooner. You know I need them."

"And you'll be able to leave sooner." Bethany adjusted her hand in his. "Why do I sense that you're not telling me the whole truth?"

Silas frowned. "About what? They did hire me, part-time, and only on delivery days." He kicked his foot out to the side, closer to her, then released her hand and pointed to his holey shoes. At his socks peeking through. "And I do need new shoes, ain't so?"

She barely gave his foot a glance. "I don't know. It seems as if there's something you aren't saying."

Silas tightened his grip on the reins. The leather bit painfully into his skin. "Something"? Nein. There were a lot of things he wasn't saying. Wouldn't say.

What else could he do?

He shook his head. "Same thing I said before, schatz. If you know, you'll be in danger."

⌣

Bethany liked it when Silas called her "sweetheart." But the whole exchange niggled her. And she didn't understand his last comment. True, he'd said something similar when she'd asked him why he dragged her into the woods. She couldn't begin to guess what he was so afraid of, but maybe that fear would explain his sudden disappearance in the store.

She lapsed into silence and stared at the gray clouds. The air smelled like snow. Cold. Crisp. Invigorating. Winter birds flocked on the side of the road and pecked at the ground, as if intending to fill their stomachs before returning to their warm, cozy nests to wait out a blizzard.

Unlike the birds, Bethany didn't want to go home. But where else could she go? She had bags and bags of groceries, for the baking she'd been so excited about earlier. Now, she didn't want to be alone in the haus. Especially not after last nacht.

"I know what you're thinking." Silas's voice was quiet. "But I'm not quite sure what to do about it."

"What?" Bethany blinked. "How can you possibly know what I'm thinking?"

"You're wondering how your knowing would put you in danger. But I can't explain. I don't know what he'd do, but it would be something serious. And he's aware I'm here now. He saw me with you at the store, and probably heard you call me by name. We arrived together.

So you're already at risk." He hesitated. "You're right. We need to catch a bus out of Jamesport. Sooner rather than later."

Huh? For a moment, Bethany's mind whirled, trying to grasp what Silas was talking about. *Ach!* "I wasn't thinking that at all. And who is *he?*" Someone more dangerous than Hen? She shivered. "And if we did get a driver to take us to the bus station, where would we go?"

A vein pulsed in Silas's jaw. "I'd go to Pennsylvania. To my onkel's."

"And you won't take me unless we're married. Not to mention, Preacher Samuel said nein. Got it." Bethany lifted a shoulder. "I think I'd like to go to Montana. Or maybe Florida." Florida would be warm. With beaches. "Maybe both. I could travel."

Silas chuckled. "Jah, there you go. We could become Amish globe-trotters."

"We? You mean, you would travel with me, unmarried?"

"Who said anything about us not—" He tugged on the reins to make the turn into the Weisses' driveway. A buggy without a horse was parked by the back porch. "Expecting someone?"

Bethany stared at the buggy for a long moment. Then she spied a birdfeeder in the back. Grinning, she bounded out of her seat. "Josh and Greta."

"I'll take care of the horse and then bring in the groceries." Silas looped the reins around the porch rail.

Bethany dashed up the porch stairs, raced through the all-season room—the laundry had been taken down and folded—and burst into the kitchen as Greta lifted a steaming casserole out of the oven.

"I'm *so* glad you're here. Let me wash up, and I'll set the table." Bethany hung her coat and bonnet on a hook by the door, peeled off her mittens, and tossed them on a shelf before hurrying to the sink.

"Onkel Samuel said you needed us." Greta set the dish on the top of the stove and covered it with a towel, then slid a baking sheet of crescent rolls into the oven. She shut the oven door, then gave Bethany a hug. "You've been through so much."

How much did she know? Bethany couldn't imagine Preacher Samuel spreading gossip. She returned the embrace, then stepped back and looked around the room. "Where are Josh and Drew?"

"Josh is out in the barn. He was going to see if there was anything he could do. And Drew is sleeping." Greta pointed to the living room. "I brought a playpen for him."

"Can I peek?" Bethany didn't wait for an answer but tiptoed quickly into the other room. The one-month-old boppli had his thumb in his mouth, and his forehead was scrunched up as if he were worried. "Such a sweet thing."

Greta laughed as she stood in the doorway. "You won't think so when he screams during the nacht."

"Ach, he can't be that bad." Bethany inhaled the scent of baby powder. "Can I hold him?"

"Later, for sure. I just got him to sleep. Right now, we need to get supper on the table. Preacher Samuel tells me you have your mind set on baking to-nacht. Are you planning a Christmas frolic?"

Bethany's mood fell. "Nein. Mamm would never allow it." She returned to the kitchen.

Greta followed her. "Bethany."

She opened a cupboard to get four plates. "What?" She hadn't meant to snap.

"I just want to say that I've been th—"

The door opened, and Silas came in with the groceries. He set the bags at one end of the table. As he retraced his steps, he glanced at the covered dish at the back of the stove. "Smells gut."

"Danki." Greta smiled at him. "It's chicken casserole. I'll put a blueberry cobbler in the oven to warm as soon as the rolls have finished baking. And I have peas simmering." She pointed to a kettle. "Welkum back to our community."

Silas nodded, glanced at Bethany with a shy smile, then went out again. The door shut behind him with a quiet click.

"How's it going with Silas Beiler here?" Greta asked. "I never dreamed he'd leave his family. Ever. He's a couple of years younger than me. But I remember him being very quiet in school, and he seldom attended the youth events. I don't mean to gossip. I'm concerned, though. Is he anything like Henry?"

Bethany dipped her head to hide her smile. She'd forgotten that Greta had been present during the infamous flour-bag explosion at the Amish Market. In fact, she'd gotten covered in the stuff. "He's nothing like Henry, or any of his brothers."

"Gut." Greta opened the cutlery drawer and took out four sets of eating utensils. "You're not as talkative as usual. It must be so hard, worrying about your daed, what with the high-risk surgery he's having, as well as all the talk about asking him to step down as bishop."

Bethany caught her breath. All that was news to her. Well, Mamm *had* mentioned an emergency procedure in her note. Certainly not that it was dangerous. And she'd heard nein talk of his stepping down. But it figured, because if Daed did recover from his brain tumor, he would face time in prison. Not exactly a convenient place for a man of Gott to preside over an Amish community.

Then again, she wouldn't call Daed a man of Gott.

She kicked at an imaginary speck of dirt on the floor, then turned and opened the refrigerator. Cold air swept over her as she pulled out the four-bean salad, pickled beets, and homemade butter, then set them on the counter. She reached back inside for a jar of blueberry jalapeño jam that Greta had given them at the end of last summer.

Greta stepped in front of Bethany and gripped her shoulders. "I'm worried about you. I've never seen you so quiet. Ever."

"Maybe I'm finally growing up." Either that, or she'd run out of things to say. She pulled away from Greta. Hunted for some courage. Finding a shred of it, she said, "After supper, we can talk about what Preacher Samuel told you." Or what he hadn't told her. She dreading finding out, either way.

Wait. Relief washed through her. "Ach, I forgot. There's some kind of meeting to-nacht, and Preacher Samuel wants me there."

Greta shook her head. "He changed his mind. They're meeting here, and he wants me to talk to you."

What? The shred of courage vanished. Bethany's hands trembled. This meant Greta knew more than she had indicated. Either that, or Preacher Samuel thought she'd be able to help Bethany, due to her own experiences. Right now, Bethany's knowledge of them was limited to the rumors she'd heard. Something about a kidnapping. A sex-trafficking ring of drug dealers.

Greta took the crescent rolls out of the oven and arranged them in a basket, then glanced at the battery-operated wall clock. "Time for dinner." She opened the door and rang the dinner bell before putting the cobbler in to reheat.

Bethany reached for a couple of pot holders lying on the counter, lifted the dish of chicken casserole, and took it across the room, setting it on the cast-iron tile trivet in the center of the table, while Greta drained the peas and transferred them to a serving bowl. Bethany went back for the basket of crescent rolls when the door opened.

Josh and Silas came in. Josh paused long enough to kiss Greta on the cheek. "We've already washed up. Handy setup out there." He smiled at Bethany. "Hey."

"Hey, Josh." Bethany set the rolls on the table, then went to get the tray Greta had arranged with a glass pitcher of iced tea and four plastic tumblers.

Silas settled into his chair at the table. He winked at Bethany as she approached with the tray. "Hi, again, hübsch maidal."

Pretty girl. Bethany stumbled, and the pitcher of tea toppled forward, dumping brown liquid onto Silas's shirt and lap and the floor around him before falling and shattering on the hardwood.

Silas leaped to his feet, his eyes wide, and grabbed a cloth napkin. Red flooded his cheeks as he blotted at his clothes. The only part of him that'd escaped the deluge was his hair.

"I'm so sorry." Mortified, Bethany knelt to pick up the pieces of the pitcher and collect the tumblers. Thankfully, they were plastic.

Pretty. He'd called her pretty.

But she was a mess.

She stood and set the tray on the counter.

His eyes danced when she dared to look in his direction again. "You brought drinks."

She couldn't believe he was making light of the situation when she'd embarrassed him as she had. Her own family would've made snide comments about her klutziness. Even most of her friends would've, too.

"I made the attempt, anyway." She managed a weak smile.

"Danki for the attempt." He held her gaze in a way that conveyed more than just gratitude. Though she didn't understand his full intent, her heart raced.

Silas balled the napkin in his hand, and headed toward the all-season room, where the baskets of soiled laundry were kept. As he walked, he yanked his shirt up and off.

Bethany lost her balance again. This time, nothing fell, but she almost did.

Righting herself, she gave up all pretense of dignity and studied him openly.

Those muscles…. Oh, my. This absolutely would not do.

She struggled to catch her breath as the door shut behind him.

There was a soft giggle. A clearing of a throat.

Ach. They weren't alone.

Her face flaming, she ducked her head so she wouldn't have to see Josh and Greta's too-knowing smiles.

But wow, was he hot.

⁓

Silas dropped his soaking shirt and the damp napkin in a laundry basket, snagged a clean set of folded clothes off the table, and strode into the small bathroom to change. His face still burned with embarrassment. It'd been an accident, though, and maybe it was that knowledge that had kept him from exploding in rage. *Danki, Lord.*

He quickly changed into the clean pants and shirt, then washed up—again—just to have time to compose himself. What had possessed him to call her "pretty" and to wink at her? A bold move, and inappropriate, considering they weren't alone.

He'd flirted openly. Broadcast his heart to Josh and Greta, if they'd been looking. He was almost certain they had.

Lord, I want Bethany. I want to marry her. Someday. Heal her. Heal me. Make the way clear so that I'll feel safe taking a frau—and the preachers won't hesitate to allow it. If it's Your will.

He splashed another round of cold water on his face, to cool down faster, then patted it dry with a towel.

His heart still pounding, he opened the bathroom door and returned to the kitchen. This time, he avoided Bethany's gaze. Everyone's, for that matter.

Because, if they'd been alone, he probably would've pulled her into his arms—even arms soaked with chilled mint tea—and kissed her like he'd wanted to.

Still wanted to.

It would be a long nacht.

Chapter 25

Bethany quickly washed the supper dishes, anxious to start baking. After drying the dishes, Greta retrieved her recipe box and set it on the table. A gut thing she'd brought it, because Bethany couldn't find any of her longed-for recipes when she thumbed through Mamm's collection. It was as if Mamm had planned to remove all sources of sweet temptation from the haus.

Premeditated. That was the term the police had used in their report the previous nacht. And deliberately removing recipes fell under the same category of offense. Didn't Mamm know Bethany *needed* chocolate? Needed cookies, candy...sugar?

She would have to copy some of Greta's recipes and pack the cards away in her hope chest while she had the chance.

In the other room, Drew whimpered. Greta rose from her seat at the table. "I'll go change and feed him. You pick out what you'd like to make. Then Drew can have some time on the floor while we work and talk."

The whimper turned into a wail.

"Told you he can get loud." With a smile at Bethany, Greta hurried from the room.

Bethany slid the recipe tin closer and took out the stack of well-used cards inside. She knew they shouldn't be too ambitious, since it was after dinner, but maybe they could make a couple of different things. Like her favorite sour cream cut-out cookies with buttercream icing. And maybe some fudge. Ach, jah. Fudge was a must. With walnuts. Hopefully, there were some in the pantry. She'd forgotten to check before going to the store.

She stood and went to the pantry. *Joy!* There sat a jar of walnuts, already shelled and chopped, waiting to be baked into some sort of chocolatey goodness.

She would make the fudge and let Greta start the cookie dough. That way, Bethany could sample the chocolate to her heart's content.

With a smile, she assembled the necessary ingredients and bakeware, then went to work.

When Greta returned, carrying Drew, the fudge mixture was cooking away on the stove. Greta spread a blanket on the floor, laid the boppli in the middle of it, and set up an Englisch toy with colorful stuffed animals dangling from it that played music when you tugged on them. Bethany was familiar with the toy, since a woman she regularly babysat for had something similar.

"It was a gift," Greta explained. "Let me wash up, and I'll get started on the other recipe you selected." She straightened. "Smells gut and chocolatey in here. Sometimes, I think chocolate and soda-fountain pop are all that's needed to solve a woman's problems." She gave Bethany a knowing glance.

Bethany grinned. "The stuff of emotional self-medication, for sure."

"Silly, isn't it? We get so caught up in chasing chocolate, we forget that the ultimate Problem-solver is only a prayer away."

Bethany stifled a snort and turned her attention back to the kettle full of future fudge.

Gott. Again. She should've known He would kum up, somehow.

But then, He had helped. Before it was too late.

Even so, the vague reminder of the previous nacht formed a hard knot in her stomach. And she wanted a Coke. Not a root beer. A real, honest-to-goodness Coke. Big time.

"You *do* have some of those medicating drinks in pop cans with you, ain't so?"

Greta laughed. "I'm not supposed to drink any right now. Nein caffeine." She hesitated, then pointed toward the stove. "But I think I can have one tiny piece of that when it's cooled and set."

Bethany wiped her hands on her apron and reached for the candy thermometer. "Maybe I'll make some brownies, too." And eat the whole pan herself after everyone else had gone to bed. Was it possible to overdose on chocolate?

Probably not.

"Onkel Samuel told me what almost happened last nacht…and what *did* happen, many times before." Greta spoke quietly. "He told me that you feel Gott has forgotten you or doesn't care. That you aren't on speaking terms with Him."

So, she *had* known. Tears blurred Bethany's vision. She bit her lower lip so hard, it hurt.

Greta's words reminded her of Elsie's note. *Even if you are having a hard time loving Him, He's not having a hard time loving you.*

"I've been there. There was a time I was convinced that Gott had forgotten me and my family." Greta measured some flour. "But I discovered He *does* care, and often He waits for us to call on Him in complete surrender."

If only Greta would say something that would prove to Bethany that God truly did love her. To help her believe that Gott truly did love her the way Elsie had said He did.

Greta dipped the measuring cup into the sugar canister, leveled it, and emptied into the mixing bowl. Then she set the cup down and came over to where Bethany stood. "There's a passage in the Bible… Romans eight, verses thirty-eight and thirty-nine. Josh had me memorize it. '*For I am persuaded that neither death, nor life, nor angels nor principalities nor powers, nor things present nor things to come, nor height nor depth, nor any other created thing, shall be able to separate us from the love of God which is Christ Jesus our Lord.*' You know what that means?"

In principle, jah. But it didn't apply to her.

"There's a concept in Scripture that's known as 'the refiner's fire.' I don't know all the references, but it has to do with the pain of undergoing dramatic change—change for the better. Take baking, for example. Like the fudge you're making now. You took all the ingredients and mixed them up. Now you're heating them above the boiling point. If the ingredients were living beings, they wouldn't appreciate the process much. It hurts when we go through the fire, through painful changes. What we see as bad things happening to us are much like that. But what if Gott is using those bad things to shape and form us into the people He wants us to be?"

Bethany glared at the bubbling chocolate. "I don't like what He's done. And I don't see what gut it is."

"Nein, and the sugar and cocoa and other ingredients don't see what gut you're doing to them, either. But think of the final product you have in mind. You're seeing fudge. And that's the way it is with Gott. The heat is never intended to destroy you, only to conform you into the character of Christ. His gaze is always fixed on you, and even when the heat of painful circumstances has intensified in your life, Gott has never left you. Will never leave you. He loves you."

Longing filled Bethany. If only this were true.

"That's what those verses from Romans mean. Nein matter what we go through in life, gut or evil, Gott loves us. And nothing can ever separate us from His love."

"Nothing? Not even our sins?"

"Nothing. Nobody. Nein matter what, He loves us."

Bethany closed her eyes. *Gott loves us. He loves us. He loves...me.* But He'd allowed people to hurt her. How was that supposed to help her grow into the person He wanted her to be? She shook her head.

"Talk to Him, Bethany. Talk to Him, and listen for His voice."

Ach, Lord, help me to believe this. Help me to know it's true. Nein matter what may kum.

Greta touched her arm. "The fudge is nearing the soft-ball stage."

⌐⌐

Silas started up the ladder wearing a construction apron he'd found in the toolbox, a supply of nails tucked in one pocket, a hammer hanging from another. He'd already marked the steps that were cracked or weak.

Repairing a ladder was hardly a two-person job, but Josh stood at the base, a supply of short boards stacked beside him. Silas didn't know exactly what the other man planned to do. Catch him if a board broke, and he slipped?

Still, it was nice having a little extra help with the chores. Josh agreed that the roof repairs were urgent, especially since it was already

December, and the bad weather would start soon. With the two of them working on it today and tomorrow, the job wouldn't take long.

"Daed says they're forecasting average temperatures and clear skies for the next few days, followed by a cold front starting late Monday, with snow." Josh seemed to have read his mind.

Either that, or Silas had a bad habit of speaking all his thoughts out loud without realizing it.

Silas glanced over his shoulder. "That so?"

Josh shrugged. "I think he heard it on the radio in the driver's van. He and Mamm went to Pennsylvania for a funeral. They were picked up at the Jamesport bus station yesterday afternoon. It was gut to have them home again, to be sure. Work is slow right now, but my brother decided it would be a great time to reorganize everything in the barn and inventory our supplies. Plus catch up on bookkeeping for taxes next year. Headache inducing, Greta called it." He chuckled.

Silas frowned. "Think we'll have enough time to repair the roof?"

Josh grinned. "Jah, we should."

With a few knocks of the hammer, Silas replaced the first of the cracked steps.

Josh held up another board. "So, what brings you back to Jamesport?"

A muscle jumped in Silas's jaw as he ascended another couple of rungs. "Needed to get away."

"Home life get worse?"

"With every move we made." Seemed the word had gotten out about Daed and Henry's abusive ways. Someone in the new community always knew, thanks to the Amish grapevine.

"I see your brother Wade from time to time. He came out to the blueberry farm to pick berries this past summer. Brought his frau and their two little tikes. Cute girls. But guess you know that. Or have you seen him? I heard he was shunned—or was for a while. I do business with him, anyway. I left the Amish for a time, as well."

"I remember." And Silas had nein desire to get in contact with his oldest brother.

Because, if Wade knew, then....

But Wade *did* know. He'd seen Silas at the Amish Market.

Silas shuddered.

❧

The haus was quiet at last. Boppli Drew *finally* fell asleep in the cradle in Mamm and Daed's bedroom, where Josh and Greta were staying.

Bethany's chaperones. Silas's, too, since he was sleeping inside the haus rather than out in the barn.

He must have paced Timothy's room for a while after turning in, because Bethany had heard the floorboards creaking beneath his feet. She lay in the darkness and waited for silence to fall. She didn't want to risk his catching her in the midst of the gluttonous feast she had planned.

A pan of brownies. All. To. Herself.

Her taste buds broke into song. Her stomach joined in the chorus.

Ach, the yummy, delicious, chocolatey goodness. Fa la la.

When she was nearly certain Silas was asleep, Bethany slid her feet into her slippers, pulled her robe on, and fastened the tie around her waist, then sneaked into the hall, avoiding the squeaky floorboards. And the noisy steps as she descended.

In the kitchen, she set the flashlight lantern on the table and reached for the square glass baking dish filled with her chocolatey mid-nacht treat.

The refrigerator door shut with a soft whoosh.

All the breath left Bethany's body. She grabbed the edge of the table. Closed her eyes. Started to scream.

A cold hand covered her open mouth, muffling the sound.

"Shhh. It's just me. Silas."

He must be adept at avoiding noisy floorboards, too.

"Don't scream," he whispered. "I'm going to remove my hand now."

Her mouth uncovered, Bethany sucked in a breath.

"What are you doing up?" he asked, still speaking softly.

She glanced toward the pan of brownies that had captured her attention for what seemed like hours. Swallowed. "Couldn't sleep."

176 Laura V. Hilton

"Me, neither." He took out the pitcher of milk. "Want some?"

With brownies. "Jah." So much for eating that whole pan by herself. Now she'd have to share. She gestured to the baking dish. "Want one?"

He grinned. "Thought you'd never ask. Jah, danki."

She sliced the brownies as he filled two glasses with milk. Then she put a single brownie on two plates and sat down across from him at the table. "Why couldn't you sleep?"

He shrugged as he broke off a tiny piece of his brownie. "Worrying. About…things."

Same as her. But at least Hen's mamm hadn't shown up on her doorstep demanding repayment of the bond money. Tomorrow might be a different thing. And Daed…should she worry about him surviving the procedure he needed, if it was as dangerous as Greta said? Whether he would be asked to step down from his post as bishop wasn't a concern right now. It'd bring disgrace on the family, for sure, but Bethany was accustomed to bowing her head in shame.

Her concerns didn't matter right now.

Silas did.

He picked off another crumb of brownie.

How could he eat like that? Brownies were meant to be inhaled. Enjoyed as seconds, thirds, and even fourths. Bethany's first brownie had disappeared sometime during her musings. She plopped another square onto her plate. Hopefully, Silas wouldn't notice. "Was ist letz?"

Another shrug. He shook his head as he picked at the brownie again.

"Kum on, Silas. Don't torture that poor brownie. Eat it, already."

He raised his head. Looked at her, a slight smile on his well-formed lips. "I don't think the brownie feels any pain."

"Ach, but it does. And it will make you feel better, too."

"I doubt it." He took a bite, though. "Ser gut. Danki."

She grinned.

Silas looked away. "Thing is, I can't stay around here long enough for your mamm to get back and pay me. I need to leave."

"Monday, maybe?" Bethany perked up. "I can call a driver to take us to the bus station. That'll give me time to pack." And say gut-bye to a select few people.

"Um...I'm hitchhiking, Bethany. And I'm not taking you with me."

"You've said that. Multiple times. But I'm not staying here."

"I can't blame you. I would if we marri—" He shook his head.

Right. And he wouldn't marry her. Preacher Samuel had said nein. Unless....

"But you said you would marry me. Forget what Preacher Samuel said. What if we eloped, like one of my friends did?"

His eyes widened, and he jerked upright. "Disobey the preacher?"

Despite his obvious shock, there was an undeniable spark of interest in his eyes when his gaze met hers.

The same interest that probably glinted in her own eyes.

Her stomach clenched, and a shiver ran up her back.

Please, please, please.

Chapter 26

Silas stared at Bethany a moment more. Inside him, longing warred with a more than generous measure of common sense. What if he did marry her? What if they did run away together? Became the Amish globe-trotters he'd joked about earlier?

The answer—the smart answer—was still a firm "nein."

But the unmistakable pleading in her eyes made him want to say "Jah."

It would require a trip to town on Monday to apply for a marriage license. And they would need to find a judge who would agree to marry them.

Anticipation filled him at the thought of coming home after the wedding, for a nacht behind closed doors with Bethany in his arms.

Which was sure to make her freak out.

But he didn't want to be the one to extinguish the light of hope in her eyes.

The light that died a little with every second that passed.

She polished off her second brownie and reached for a third. Shrugged. "Well, it was just a thought."

"How about we think and pray about it over the weekend, then decide on Monday?" That would give him time to figure out a tactful way of saying that, as much as he wanted her, they couldn't be together. Because....

Well, because of so many reasons. Not just his problems.

Besides, he respected Preacher Samuel too much to blatantly disregard his advice.

A chance to marry Bethany…that was the stuff dreams were made of. His dreams, anyway.

Except that she still needed to heal.

A fourth brownie disappeared from her plate. And he'd taken only a couple nibbles of his first.

She reached for a fifth. Impressive. But also kind of scary.

As she reached for a sixth brownie, Silas shot to his feet and snatched the pan away. "Stop! Don't do this. You'll hate yourself in the morgen."

Bethany blinked. Looked down at her empty plate, then up at the pan. Tears shimmered in her eyes. "Forget I said anything. I should've known you didn't want me. Not really."

She stood. Wobbled. Her shoulders slumped as she started for the door, her long braid bouncing against her back.

A cuss word his brothers had used a million times crossed Silas's mind. He bit it back, unsaid. Slammed the pan on the table.

How had things gone so terribly wrong?

Two more steps, and she'd be out the door.

He hurried after her. "Bethany, wait." He closed his hand over her shoulder and spun her around.

Tears beaded on her lashes. Her lower lip quivered.

Silas groaned as he took her face in his hands and lowered his mouth to hers.

She responded with what seemed like reckless abandon, pressing against him, her arms encircling his neck.

His pulse pounded. His body warmed. *Ach, Bethany.*

He struggled to stay in control of himself. To take nothing more than what she offered—though he wasn't exactly sure how to measure that. As the kisses deepened, her fingers tangled in his hair, slid down his back, and then hooked in the belt loops of his jeans. She tasted of chocolate and desperation.

He wanted the same right. He slid one hand down her braid and grasped her neck. His other hand skimmed over the softness of her robe, coming to rest at the small of her back as he pulled her nearer.

She responded with her whole body.

Better stop. Now.

She moaned as he moved away. Pulled him nearer, her lips reclaiming his.

Passion flared. Again.

A boppli wailed.

A throat cleared.

Silas sprang back. "Sorry," he mumbled to nobody in particular. To everyone, in general. He turned and fled the haus. Trekked barefoot across the yard, shivering in his shirtsleeves. The icy temperature cooled his passions as effectively as, and maybe even better than, a cold shower.

He wouldn't sleep inside the haus. Not to-nacht.

Wouldn't be in the room right next to Bethany, thinking thoughts he shouldn't.

Nein. He'd stay in the cold barn loft, his teeth chattering as he shivered beneath a thin blanket, wishing for things that couldn't be.

Silas and Bethany. *In your dreams.*

He fell to his knees beside his cot. *Ach, Lord….*

⌒

There came another earsplitting wail from boppli Drew as Josh entered the kitchen. He passed Bethany and crossed the room, muttering something about a diaper change. He snatched the diaper bag from its spot by the door.

Bethany had nein words. Not when she fought for every breath. Still struggling for air, she grasped hold of the doorjamb and backed up until she reached the wall.

Chaperones…it was gut they had them, because, wow, could Silas ever kiss. Was she wrong for not wanting him to stop? The contrast with Hen's kisses couldn't have been starker. She hadn't freaked out about the intimacy thing with Silas.

She shut her eyes. Maybe there was hope for her, after all.

"Sorry for interrupting, but…." Josh chuckled. "You needed interrupting."

She bowed her head as shame coursed through her, leaving her weak. She fell to her knees. Tears flowed down her cheeks and dripped off her chin.

Still there were nein words.

She heard a soft huff from Josh, then the shuffle of slipper-clad feet leaving the room.

"Greta, I'll change the boppli," she heard him say. "You're needed in the kitchen."

Moments later, a hand patted Bethany's back. Then Greta slid down against the wall beside her, pulled her close, and held her.

Bethany didn't know how long she'd cried when she finally wiped her eyes with the sleeves of her robe. Her nose ran, and her throat hurt. Greta pushed a tissue into her hands. Josh sat down across from them, his hands clasped between his knees, and leaned forward as if in prayer. Greta must've released her at some point, since Drew now slept against his mamm's shoulder, a contented expression on his sweet little face. With a clean diaper and a full stomach, his life was complete.

If only it were so simple for Bethany.

"I'm sorry," she croaked. She pushed herself to her feet, dried her face again, and eyed the pan of brownies on the table behind Josh. They waved their chocolatey hands at her, promising to ease her pain.

They hadn't worked the first time.

Maybe now they would.

Josh raised his head as she neared him. He watched as she bypassed him and reached for a square of chocolate delight. And inhaled it.

Greta managed to stand without waking the boppli. "I'll be right back," she said softly. "I'm going to put him back to bed."

Bethany nodded. And reached for another brownie. A fresh round of tears filled her eyes. She blinked at the burn. Her throat still ached, and the brownie didn't help. She slumped into a chair and lowered her head to the tabletop.

"Want some chamomile tea?" Josh got to his feet. "I think Greta would probably take a cup. Better for you than sweets, ain't so?"

"But chocolate solves the world's problems." Bethany gazed at the pan that still held a few brownie squares. Waiting for her.

Josh gave a wry grin. "Looks like it's really doing that for you." He filled the kettle with water, then placed it on the stove. "In my experience, der Herr is the only One capable of putting wrongs to right."

Bethany snorted and sat upright. "Der Herr won't have anything to do with me." Even if Greta did say Gott loved her. Bethany knew better. "I'm not gut enough."

"Nein, you aren't. Nobody is. And that's the beauty of His love." Josh stepped away from the stove. "I'll be right back. Need to get my Bible."

What, Daed's German Bible wasn't gut enough?

When Josh returned a few minutes later, he had Greta with him, and he carried an Englisch Bible bound in orange. Bethany swallowed.

The teakettle whistled. Greta took it off the stove, put a filled infuser inside it to steep, and got out four mugs.

Bethany looked around for Silas.

"He's out in the barn," Josh said, answering her unspoken question. "But right now, I think we should leave him alone. I'll talk to him tomorrow."

"Except that tomorrow might be too late." Oops. Bethany hadn't meant to say that out loud.

Greta and Josh turned to look at her. Josh raised his eyebrows. "And why's that?"

Bethany shook her head. Shrugged. "I'm afraid he'll leave. Start hitchhiking across the state again. Without me."

"The road is nein place for a woman," Josh said. "You should be at home, where it's safe."

"In theory." Ugh, there went her unbridled tongue, again.

Josh scratched his neck. "I'll check on him." He hesitated a long moment, frowning, then finally stood, slipped his coat on over his robe, plopped his hat on his head, and went out the door.

Greta filled a mug with steaming tea, then set it in front of Bethany.

Josh came back inside a minute later. "He's fine. Spending some time in prayer, he says. Can't beat that. He's a gut man."

Jah, he was. Nein wonder Gott loved him.

Josh sat in the chair he'd vacated earlier. "A few minutes ago, you told me you weren't gut enough for Gott. If you're referring to what Hen did to you, jah, it was sinful, but it wasn't your fault. And, as I told you before, none of us is gut enough. Admitting to being a sinner is the first step." He opened his Bible. Hesitated. Then thumbed through it, until he'd apparently reached the page he was looking for. "Romans five, verse eight, says, *'But God demonstrates His own love toward us, in that while we were still sinners, Christ died for us.'* God showed us His love by giving us the potential to have life through the death of His Son, Jesus Christ. It goes on to say, in Romans ten, verse thirteen, *'For "whoever calls on the name of the LORD shall be saved."'"*

Bethany eyed his Englisch Bible. This wasn't what Daed taught from the pulpit. Though some of the other preachers had talked about it openly since Daed's arrest. Had Daed been not teaching the whole Bible? Or was this Englisch version different from the German?

If only the words Josh had read were true.

"My favorite passage"—Josh flipped ahead a few more pages—"is Ephesians two, verses eight and nine: *'For by grace you have been saved through faith, and that not of yourselves; it is the gift of God, not of works, lest anyone should boast.'"*

Bethany blinked at him. That definitely wasn't what Daed taught from the pulpit.

Josh grinned. "I know what you're thinking, Bethany, and you can be sure this is true. We aren't gut enough on our own. But God loves us so much that if we just believe, He'll save us, through His grace." His smile became more tender. "We are accepted in the Beloved. Ephesians one, verse six. Read it."

Bethany slid her fingertip over the page until she found the verse he'd indicated. "*'To the praise of the glory of His grace, by which He made us accepted in the Beloved.'"*

Her eyes stung. She shut them. Bowed her head. "I want to believe." Everything within her cried out for it. *Lord, help me. Forgive me for being who and what I am…a sinner. I'm sorry for every wrong I've ever done.*

A strange sense of peace that she'd never experienced before washed over her. Filled her.

Danki, Lord.

⌢

Silas's knees ached when he finally straightened and stood. He stretched his sore, stiff back. Maybe the kitchen was clear now, and he could get that glass of milk he'd abandoned in his flight. *Coward.*

Not that he was afraid of anyone here, really. It was more that he was ashamed of himself. Bethany was off-limits, and he'd taken advantage of her.

Though, crossing the yard again for a glass of milk that was warm by now, and had probably been discarded, was foolish.

He wouldn't waste his time.

And he wouldn't be sleeping inside, anyway.

The barn doors creaked, and Silas peered over the edge of the loft. Fear filled him.

It was a man's silhouette. Amish, by the hat.

"Josh?" His voice quivered.

"Jah. You sure you're okay out here? Pretty cold."

Silas grunted. "It's for the best. I know my place. And where I want to be—with her—isn't where I need to be. I've got to keep my distance. I'm a stray, as her brother called me. A wanderer. And I…I have goals. Dreams. I need to pursue them. Not her."

"Why not?" Josh stood at the base of the ladder and looked up.

Silas barked a laugh. "Are you kidding? I might not have lived here long enough for you to have known my family before you left, but I'm sure you've heard stories. Bethany has been through enough. She doesn't need someone like me bringing her down. She deserves someone like you. Like Preacher Samuel. A gut man. A man of Gott."

"And that's not you?"

"It's who I want to be." Silas swung his legs over the edge of the loft and let his feet dangle as he hung his head. "But you know where I'm coming from. I can't risk it. I just can't. I want to marry her. I *would* marry her. But I don't want to hurt her."

"I know what I've seen of you, Silas. What Preacher Samuel has seen. What Sam sees. And I think you *are* a man of Gott. You just need to accept yourself. Believe you are a new creature in Christ. The old things are passed away, and all things have become new. Even you."

Silas shook his head. "My oldest brother lives in Jamesport. He knows I'm back. You know how we parted six years ago? Probably not. I think you'd left by then. I turned him in for dealing drugs. And he swore he would kill me, and anyone close to me, if he ever saw me again." Silas shook his head. "The right thing for me to do is to leave. To go to my onkel's haus in Pennsylvania. It's been my plan all along. But I'm worried about Bethany. I don't want to leave her feeling rejected by yet another person. I know I've only been here a week, but we knew each other before. Had feelings for each other. And seeing each other again...."

Josh chuckled. "You don't need to explain your relationship. I know what it's like to have loved a woman for a long time. Greta and I, we grew up together. I've always loved her. I just remembered something I read in a book by Mark Batterson: 'If it's the right thing, the results are God's responsibility. Focus on doing the right thing for the right reason.'"

Silas nodded. "I'll continue praying for Gott's guidance, for me and for Bethany."

But with his brother knowing he was there, he couldn't help feeling that if he stayed, he was a dead man walking.

Chapter 27

Bethany's newfound joy still bubbled over when she got up the next morgen. She smiled at the low murmur of Greta's cooing to Drew in her parents' bedroom as she padded past on her way downstairs. The men's boots and coats were absent from the area near the door. Silas and Josh would expect breakfast soon.

Bethany put on her cape and a pair of mittens, grabbed a wicker basket, and hurried outside to look for any stray eggs. Most of the hens had stopped laying due to the cold. Gut thing she'd bought eggs at the store. She seemed to remember Preacher Samuel mentioning a way to keep the hens laying during the cold months. She would ask him about it.

If she stayed.

The dark, heavy clouds filling the sky overhead promised more bad weather. Daed called them "snow clouds." If it actually snowed, that'd be a gut thing. Bethany enjoyed the sight of the fluffy white stuff covering the dead grass and bare trees. Enough accumulation, and maybe she and Silas could go for a sleigh ride.

Deep in the recesses of the barn, a cow mooed. Sounds of thumping and bumping came from the area where Josh or Silas—or both—worked. Bethany hurried to the chicken coop, refilled the feed and water pans, and checked for eggs. Two lay in the straw. Not a lot, but better than none. Enough for pancakes. She could fry some bacon, too.

She carried the basket back to the haus and set it on the counter, then lit a burner on the stove to heat water for koffee and tea.

Greta came into the room, with Drew curled inside the sling she wore across her chest. "How can I help?"

"Gut morgen. You can mix up the pancake batter. I'll fry the bacon and cook the pancakes so the grease doesn't splatter your little sweetheart."

Greta smiled. "Danki. Did you sleep okay?"

Bethany shrugged as she got out a skillet for the bacon. "Well enough. For once, my trouble sleeping was due to excitement instead of angst. I can't wait to tell Silas I was wrong about Gott."

Greta began mixing the ingredients for pancakes. "Josh said they plan to work on the roof today. They want to get it done before the bad weather arrives. And before Silas leaves for Pennsylvania."

Bethany's joy faded as she transferred the crisp bacon slices to a plate lined with paper towel, then ladled a circle of pancake batter into the shimmering grease. Silas hadn't changed his mind, then. Of course, neither had she, for her own safety's sake. But it seemed she was nothing more than a temporary diversion. He had nein real plans to marry her.

Why did Silas have to be so stubborn about refusing to take her along? She could keep up. She would even pay their bus fares. They'd get there so much faster, traveling that way. And be ever so much warmer.

Josh came inside and set two pails of milk on the floor, then removed his shoes and outerwear before going to the sink to wash up. The door opened again, and Silas strode in. He stopped long enough to take off his shoes, hat, and coat, then smiled at Bethany. "Smells gut in here." His gaze dipped to her lips, then shot up again, pink rising on his cheeks.

After the meal, the men went back outside. Moments later, there was a thump on the side of the haus. Bethany glanced out the window. A ladder stretched past it. Silas ascended, hauling a bundle of shingles. Josh went right behind him with another bundle.

Bethany turned to Greta. "Will Drew still nap with them pounding overhead?"

Greta grinned as she kneaded bread dough. "A boppli can sleep through anything if his parents don't insist on silence. People are coming in and out of our haus all the time. My family, Josh's family.... We had some noisy repairs done recently, too. I won't worry." She looked up. "Besides, the more he's awake during the day, the more he'll sleep at nacht, ain't so?"

"Jah, but a tired boppli is a cranky boppli." And, selfish or not, Bethany didn't want to listen to a sleepy boppli screaming.

Greta shrugged. "Maybe so. He's fussy when he doesn't get his way."

The men came down the ladder, then made another trip up it with more shingles.

Greta set the bowl near the stove to let the dough rise. "Josh said Onkel Samuel would try to kum by and help, too. Maybe he'll bring Aenti Elsie. I always enjoy her visits. Ach, that reminds me—we need to bake those sour-cream cookies you wanted. The dough I mixed last nacht should be chilled enough for rolling out by now. Where do you keep the cookie cutters?"

Bethany retrieved the shoebox full of metal shapes from the pantry. "Mamm used to like using the angel ones, but when Daed became bishop, he forbade it, so now she only bakes circle-shaped cookies. And flower ones, in spring and summer."

Greta frowned. "A cookie is a cookie. Doesn't much matter the shape, ain't so?" She took the lid off the shoebox and sorted through the contents. "You have hearts, trees, flowers, angels, circles, ginger-bread men, and…is this a boot?"

"I'm surprised Mamm hasn't gotten rid of everything but the circles and flowers." Bethany sprinkled some flour on the old tablecloth they used for rolling dough. "We haven't been allowed to bake cookies at all since Ezra died, unless it's for someone coming to visit. Then it's all about appearances."

"I've learned that appearances are deceiving," Greta murmured. "Not just in your case. With life in general. People pretend to be what they aren't. They want to disguise themselves. To seem as if they're not wounded. Or…." She shrugged.

Bethany reached into the shoebox and pulled out the circular cookie cutter, then scowled at it. She didn't want boring circles. Maybe she'd reinstitute the use of the angel one. Or the heart, to symbolize her newfound discovery of Gott's love for her. And her growing love for Silas.

She set out both of them. Angels and hearts.

Mamm would have a conniption.

With a small shrug, Bethany retrieved the wooden rolling pin. She could relate to Greta's comment about the deceptiveness of appearances. Hadn't she acted like a normal, non-Amish twenty-two-year-old girl? Flirting in hopes of catching the eye of a decent man who would take her away from Hen. She'd pretended for so long, flirting had become her natural way of interacting with the opposite sex.

But it hadn't worked the way she'd hoped. She hadn't gotten any positive attention, and she'd ruined her reputation. She was now known as desperate, and the decent men weren't impressed.

She dumped a heaping handful of flour on the tablecloth and spread it out.

While Josh had shared several Bible verses to show her that God forgave her for everything, she still wished she could go back and have a redo. Avoid the mistakes she'd made.

If only.

"Did I give Hen the wrong idea? I flirted with him when he first came around. Teased him. I thought he liked me. And when he and Daed said we would marry, I thought it was wunderbaar. Exciting. Someone loved me. But…." She shuddered and released a heavy sigh. "It was awful. Beyond awful. I was so humiliated and hurt, and…and nobody cared."

Greta plopped the ball of dough in the center of the floury surface, then reached over to rest her hand on Bethany's arm. "It's not your fault. He's the one who did wrong. And don't ever confuse love with lust. They aren't the same. Someone who loves you will respect you, and never take advantage of you or hurt you intentionally. He'll wait for you."

Was it love that she felt for Silas? Or lust? Maybe she just liked the idea of someone loving her. She enjoyed his kisses, his touch. But what if it ever became more? Would he stop when she said "nein"? Or force himself on her, like Hen had done?

She bit her lip. She really was a mess.

She needed to pray.

Preacher Samuel had been wise in saying they needed to wait to marry. She shouldn't need to be in a relationship with any man until she was sure whether she was in love.

⌒

Silas glanced over at Josh as he positioned a shingle along the top edge of the roof, about ten feet away. They'd already repaired the leaky parts, Josh talking Silas through the process. Now they were adding a layer of new shingles over the old ones. With both of them working, the job went quickly.

They paused at noon for sandwiches, freshly baked cookies, and warm drinks. Bethany avoided his gaze, taking care not to even look at him. He hoped it wasn't because of something he'd done…or hadn't done. Then again, he hadn't exactly kum out and said he wouldn't elope with her. But the implication was there. And she was smart enough to figure it out.

With Wade's being aware of his arrival, his time in Jamesport was limited. Nein point in hoping Wade hadn't recognized him. You don't live with someone for years and not know his face. It'd be a matter of days, at the most, before his brother discovered him. Maybe as little as hours.

To be honest, he was surprised Wade hadn't found him already. News traveled quickly via the Amish grapevine. And even though the only "event" Silas had attended was Sam's wedding, everyone knew he was there, staying in the bishop's barn.

So why hadn't Wade shown up, guns blazing? Knives flashing? Swords slashing? Or whatever his method of murder would be.

Was he waiting like a cat waits to kill the mouse it preys upon? Crouched, ready to pounce. Toying, playing, with the poor, hapless creature?

Sharp pain shot through Silas's left thumb, and he blinked to focus his eyes.

He'd hammered his finger instead of the nail.

He set down the tool and shook his throbbing hand. When Josh glanced up, Silas stood. "I need to take a break. Be back soon."

Josh nodded. "We've been working pretty steady. Should be done by dinner, I think."

Silas's stomach rumbled. "I'll go see if they'll give us a few cookies. If so, I'll bring them back with me."

"Nein, I'll go with you," Josh said. "A hot drink and a couple of cookies will do us both gut." Josh laid his own hammer down, stretched, and made his way to the ladder.

The kitchen smelled wunderbaar. The oven was still on, a saucepan of something simmered on the stovetop, and freshly baked cookies—oatmeal raisin and peanut butter, from the looks of them—cooled on several wire racks. The cutout cookies Greta and Bethany had baked earlier that morgen had disappeared. They'd likely been placed in the decorative metal tins that were stacked at the end of the table.

Josh snagged a peanut butter cookie as he went by. Silas hesitated a moment, then grabbed an oatmeal raisin. He almost expected Mamm's wooden spoon to slap him across the knuckles for pilfering cookies.

But nobody yelled at either of them when they walked into the living room and found Bethany sitting in a rocking chair, holding Drew against her chest, while Greta sorted through a box of what appeared to be recipes, returning some of the cards to the box, and stacking others in a neat pile to the side.

Silas stared at Bethany for a minute, imagining her rocking his boppli. *Their* boppli. *Someday, Lord.* He blinked and looked away, glad nobody could read his thoughts. Especially Bethany.

Josh crouched next to his frau. "Are you looking for another recipe to make?"

Greta shook her head. "I'm sorting out the ones Bethany wants to copy for her hope chest, for when she marries."

"*If* I marry." Bethany glanced up at Greta with a frown. "And even if I don't marry, I'll still need to cook for myself." She didn't sound bitter but matter-of-fact. Maybe a bit sad and wistful, though.

"You'll marry." Silas couldn't keep the words inside. They burst out of their own free will. "I'll marry you. Someday." *If I'm still alive.*

"Maybe." Then he cringed. He shouldn't have tacked on that last word. "If I can." Hopefully, that addendum would suffice.

Bethany looked away, her cheeks reddening. Josh narrowed his eyes as he studied him.

Silas dipped his head, his neck and cheeks heating. "Someone will, anyway. You're a sweet, beautiful girl. Any man would be blessed to be loved by you."

He could only pray he'd be that man.

⁓

The next morgen, Bethany still wasn't any closer to finding answers. Just more questions. Her life was a puzzle she might never master.

Breakfast, on the other hand, she could manage. She tiptoed downstairs to the kitchen. Started the koffee on the stove, then got out a package of Cream of Wheat. That would be a great breakfast. Especially topped with sliced bananas, and served alongside toast with butter and jam.

She combined the water and cereal in a saucepan, which she then set on the stove to cook. Next, she grabbed her basket, threw on a coat, and headed out to take care of the chickens and collect any eggs she might find.

There were voices coming from the cow barn, but she couldn't discern the words being said. She thought she heard her name, so she stealthily moved closer. But the conversation must've ended, because the next sound she heard was Josh's whistling. Bethany didn't recognize the tune. It wasn't from the Ausbund.

In her journal, she'd recorded some of the lyrics from an Englisch song she'd heard on the radio in the driver's van. She hadn't journaled for days. Maybe now would be a gut time. With Mamm gone, she could even bring the diary inside the haus.

After taking a quick glance around, she snatched her journal from its hiding place under a loose board near the hayloft ladder. She stashed it in the egg basket, then turned to go.

Except that Preacher Samuel stood there, a scary expression on his face. Scary, in that she didn't recognize it. But it terrified her.

Josh's whistling faded into the background, lost in the weird buzz that filled Bethany's ears. Somehow, she knew. "Daed. He's...gone, isn't he?"

Tears filled Preacher Samuel's eyes. He sighed. Nodded. "Your mamm and sister are calling for a driver. They will soon be on the way home. Should arrive before noon."

Bethany swallowed hard and looked away. A myriad of emotions filled her, none of which was familiar. A lump formed in the back of her throat, making it hard to breathe. Her surroundings blurred. Somehow, she remained upright. Or did she? The room whirled and tilted. She swayed and lost her grip on the egg basket. And then the barn disappeared in a sea of darkness.

Daed. Dead.

She blinked, surprised to find Preacher Samuel kneeling beside her. She sat up and leaned back against the hay bale behind her.

But after that brief glimpse at her surroundings, they disappeared again into black nothingness.

When she came to again, a strong set of arms were wrapped around her, holding her close. Silas. She burrowed into his chest, allowing him to comfort her. To carry her burdens. To make her decisions.

At least for now.

She shut her eyes once more, and tried to force her mind to perform some semblance of logical reasoning. Her thoughts rambled worse than a chicken with its head cut off. Flapping around in nein definite direction.

She couldn't leave now. It would be selfish. But if she stayed, it meant things would get worse, not better.

At least Mamm wouldn't yell at her for baking. She probably wouldn't even know she'd done any, because as soon as word got out— in a matter of hours, probably—meals and desserts would start arriving. Women would kum over to clean the haus and help prepare it for the funeral. Men would gather to build the casket.

The cookies would be lost in the shuffle. Consumed within hours.

And the greenery she'd wanted to gather for decorations…gut thing she hadn't wasted her time.

Except, Mamm would kum home and wonder what Bethany had even done. Not laundry. That much would be painfully obvious.

She ought to hide her journal again. And the recipes she'd planned to copy.

"I'm picking you up now, Bethany," Silas murmured, scooping her in his arms before the words even registered. "Let's get you inside."

Daed.

Tears burned her eyes. Clogged her throat. But didn't fall.

"I'll grab her basket and notebook," Josh said.

Notebook? *Journal.* Bethany mentally corrected him.

And only then realized what he'd said. Her thoughts—her own painful memories, her dreams, her desires—they needed to remain private. Maybe even burned. She never wanted anyone to see her deepest secrets. Her doubt of God. Her brokenness. Her emptiness. Her despair.

I will never leave you nor forsake you.

Was that Gott? Bits and pieces of the verse Greta had quoted last nacht invaded her thoughts. Something about death not being able to separate anyone from the love of Gott.

Did Daed even know Gott?

Bethany felt an immediate stab of guilt. Of course, he did. He was Amish from birth. Never strayed. He'd served der Herr tirelessly as bishop.

Except for the crimes he'd committed.

She wouldn't think of those. One should never speak ill of the dead, or even think poorly of them. Hadn't she been around enough widows and widowers to know that even the most horrible people became perfect once they were gone?

Then it hit her. They would lose the farm. Mamm couldn't afford to keep it. And unless she remarried right away, they'd have nein choice but to move in with Onkel Ducky and his family.

Onkel Ducky was nice. His frau, on the other hand…Aent Zinnia was nothing like the beautiful flower she was named after. Prickly, thorny, and just as much about keeping up appearances as her sister. Mamm. Perfect on the outside. Not so much on the inside.

Things had gone from bad to worse.

Was this Bethany's fault? A penalty for embracing what Josh and Preacher Samuel had shared with her—and what Daed had called a "false religion"? The grace of Gott. His mercy. His love.

Memories surfaced of the peace that had washed over her the previous nacht.

Silas lowered Bethany to a chair, then knelt beside her, his hands on hers.

Greta rested a hand on her shoulder and whispered, "'For I am persuaded that neither death nor life, nor angels nor principalities nor powers, nor things present nor things to come, nor height nor depth, nor any other created thing, shall be able to separate us from the love of God which is in Christ Jesus our Lord.'"

Chapter 28

How quickly things changed. Silas ducked into the bathroom to take a quick shower before the men of the community started showing up. He didn't want to smell or look like he'd been sleeping in the barn, even though that was the truth. Grateful for a set of clean clothes, he dried off, dressed, and headed for the kitchen.

Greta had taken charge of breakfast, though Silas didn't think Bethany would stay down for long. He never would've expected her to faint. But the news of her daed's death, coming so quickly on the heels of the situation with Hen...it was enough to weaken even the strongest of woman.

In the kitchen, three men stood talking with Greta and Bethany. Silas stumbled to a stop when the men turned as one to face him. He recognized his cousin James, dressed in typical Amish attire. He didn't know the other two men, who wore black T-shirts and blue jeans. Their scowls were identical, indicating disgust with a hired job that was too easy.

"Kum with us," one of the strangers said to Silas.

Silas swallowed and looked at Bethany, who had moved to the stove and now stirred the bubbling cereal. She held herself stiffly, her movements rote, her gaze on the men. Then she glanced at Silas and shook her head. *Nein.*

"Wade?" Silas forced the single word past the lump in his throat.

James nodded.

"I have to go?"

Another nod.

Silas looked at Bethany again. *Gut-bye, my love.* This was it, then. He straightened his shoulders and looked around for Josh. He wasn't anywhere in sight.

Silas nodded at Greta, then gave Bethany another long look, one in which he tried to convey his love for her, hopefully without giving the men any ammunition to hurt her.

And then he followed them out.
To his death.

Chapter 29

Bethany trailed the men outside. "Don't go, Silas."

He didn't react, other than to stiffen his back.

One of the other men turned with a slight smirk.

"Stay, Silas. Please." She hated begging. He would really leave without his coat? Without his bags? Wouldn't he need them in Pennsylvania?

Something about this wasn't right, but she couldn't make her brain work well enough to figure it out.

How could Silas carry her so gently to the haus and then walk away with such nonchalance?

Finally he looked over his shoulder. "Go inside. Now."

Did he have to sound so harsh?

"Can't we talk? Please—"

"Nein," he growled. "Go."

"Fine! See if I care." With a huff, she retreated inside the haus and stomped into the kitchen. Out the window, she watched the four men approach a black two-door extended-cab pickup parked in the driveway. One of the men folded the front seat forward, and Silas and another man climbed into what appeared to be a narrow back-seat. When Silas was settled, he stared out the small window, his jaw clenched.

Maybe she should've tried harder to talk him out of leaving, instead of letting him order her inside like a little girl. She should've at least kissed him gut-bye, despite the smirking man escorting him out.

The driver shifted the truck into gear and drove away.

Bethany's heart hurt.

Silas hadn't even gotten the money he was due. How would he pay the man driving him? And what about his job at the Amish Market? Silas was the responsible type. Not the type to just walk out without warning.

"Who were those men?" Bethany glanced at Greta. "Did you know them?"

Greta shrugged. "I've seen them before. One was Silas's cousin, I think."

It wasn't adding up.

The truck engine roared as it picked up speed on the road. The same dirt road she and Silas were walking along when he'd yanked her into the woods. He'd been scared, because….

"He's afraid of motor vehicles," Bethany said.

"Really?" Greta raised her eyebrows. "Why?"

"He wouldn't tell me. Said my knowing would somehow put me in danger." She gripped the edge of the sink. "It's not as if a car or a truck would suddenly decide to chase me down. So, it's a person he's afraid of. But who...? I have nein idea." Bethany leaned forward to peer down the road but saw nothing beyond a cloud of dust, until a buggy appeared, turning into their drive. "Someone's here."

"There'll be a lot of people here soon." Josh came into the room and looked around. "Silas still in the shower?"

Bethany tried to answer, but all she managed was a moan. Fresh tears sprang to her eyes. Greta made a small, indistinguishable sound.

Josh frowned. "I thought I heard men's voices in here. Did they head to the barn already?"

Bethany swallowed and tried once more to speak, but she couldn't find the words. She began ladling the lumpy Cream of Wheat into bowls.

"Well, I should probably go help with the casket, but I'd like to have breakfast first."

"Jah, you need to eat." Greta handed him a bowl of cereal. "The men who were in here weren't Amish. Well, one of them was, but not the other two. They left, and took Silas with them."

Josh hitched an eyebrow at her. "Who were they?"

Greta lifted one shoulder. "One of them looked familiar. I thought he might be a cousin of Silas's. Anyway, the three of them came in without knocking and wanted to know where Silas was. I told them he'd be right in. I'd nein sooner said it than he entered the room, and then they ushered him outside."

Josh furrowed his brow. "Really." He walked to the window and peeked out, then glanced at Bethany. "Any idea where they went?"

Bethany shook her head. All she knew was, Silas had left. Without a gut-bye. Without his things. Unless he'd packed them ahead of time and left them out by the road.

Or unless something was wrong. Her stomach churned. If he was in trouble, what could she do to help him?

Not a thing.

Except pray. *Gott, protect him.*

Josh's lips settled into a grim line as he moved away from the window.

"Maybe he simply decided to leave," Greta suggested. "That's the way most Amish kids do it, you know. They pack their bags and go."

That would be exactly the way Bethany would do it. Pack her bags, hide them out by the road, and call for a driver. She'd make sure the driver knew not to kum to the haus. Silas must have neglected to make that clear.

But now, Bethany's hope of leaving seemed as impossible a dream as marrying Silas.

Once again, Daed had ruined things.

But what was it Silas had said to the men in the kitchen? "Wade"—a question. And then he'd asked if he had to go. What did that mean?

Bethany huffed as she ran the wooden spoon through the lumpy cereal again. Figured. Silas left, Mamm was on her way home, and Bethany's cooking skills had disintegrated considerably. Josh stood at the sink and spooned the congealed mess into his mouth. Definitely not a meal worth sitting down to savor. After a final bite, he bowed his head for a silent prayer, then set the bowl and spoon in the sink before heading out the door.

Bethany set two bowls of Cream of Wheat on the table for Greta and herself, even though her own appetite was mostly absent. She would serve the remains of the lumpy cereal to the hogs.

Bethany slumped into a chair at the table. Greta started water heating on the stove for tea, then sat next to her. "We'll need our energy today, for sure. It's going to be busy."

The door opened, and Elsie Miller and another woman came in, both of them carrying mops, buckets, and other cleaning supplies. "Morgen, Bethany, Greta." Elsie smiled. "Don't hurry on our account. We'll start in the other room."

Bethany forced herself to stand, not sure of the proper protocol. She'd never been a hostess for a funeral. "Danki for coming, Elsie and...." The other lady looked familiar, but Bethany couldn't place her right now. She looked to Greta for help.

"Mamm." Greta smiled brightly. "I'm glad you're here. I didn't know where to start."

So much for a name. Bethany merely nodded. "Jah, danki."

As the two women went into the other room, the door opened again, and several more women entered. Bethany forced herself to eat a bite of her flavorless cereal. She'd forgotten to add salt, and it amazed her that both Greta and Josh had ate theirs without complaint.

With breakfast finished and the kitchen cleaned up, and the haus filled with women wielding mops, brooms, and feather dusters, Bethany decided to do some laundry. If the clotheslines were laden with clean garments when Mamm returned, maybe she wouldn't criticize Bethany for being lazy the few days she'd been gone.

In the room where they kept the washing machine, Bethany stopped, stunned, at the sight of the schoolteacher, Dorcas Beachy, bent over the basket of dirty clothes as she sorted the contents.

The chores would be done, the haus would be thoroughly cleaned, and the meals would be provided for up to a week or so after the funeral. And then what?

Maybe the time to leave *was* now. Nobody would miss Bethany in the busyness of a funeral and the subsequent changes. Since Silas had already left, she could think of nein gut reason to stay. And she could take the money earmarked for Silas's salary, so it would not be missed.

She got to work feeding clothes through the wringer washer. Once the laundry was done, she would pack her bags and hide them out near

202 Laura V. Hilton

the road. By Monday afternoon, Bethany would be on her way to a new life.

Somewhere.

～

Silas's insides churned as the vehicle slowed to a stop in front of a haus in a small Iowa town. He didn't catch the name. His brother's black car, with the "Save the Frogs" bumper sticker, sat in the driveway, its trunk open.

A gut place to stash his body until they dumped it somewhere?

He swallowed the bile that rose in his throat.

Trust Me.

Right. Easier said than done.

I've got this.

Silas didn't see how that was possible. Unless his murder had been Gott's plan all along.

The three men with him had laughed and joked the entire way here, as if killing Amish buwe were an everyday activity. And one of them was his cousin. His whole family was bad news. Silas's stomach threatened to erupt any second.

This was wrong. So wrong.

Lord....

Would it be wrong to pray that he would survive this? Did he really want to?

Jah, he did. He wanted to return to the Weisses' farm and marry Bethany someday. Sooner than someday. Maybe right away.

Bethany could heal after marriage, ain't so? And if they were married, Silas would be able to protect her.

If only he'd been truthful with her about his reason for traveling to Pennsylvania. She'd pleaded with him not to leave, and now her last memory of him would be of being rejected by him.

She might never know he'd wanted to stay.

The front passenger seat had been folded forward to allow Silas to climb out of the truck. What would they do if he refused? He didn't want to see his brother. Didn't want to—

"Come along, now." The man spoke with impatience.

"Anxious to get the job over with, huh?"

That earned him an odd look. But nein comment.

Maybe he should've planned ahead and kum home bearing gifts and ready to recite an apology. Something along the lines of, *I'm sorry I stole several years of your life by sending you to prison.* Even though he would do it again if given the chance.

"Move it," the man growled.

Right. Silas pressed his hand to his stomach, willing the contents to stay put, and made the awkward climb over the seat belt. He landed on his feet on the ground next to the other man. Sort of. The driveway was a sheet of solid ice, and he skated around, his arms flailing, as he tried to find his balance. And keep it.

When Silas seemed somewhat stationary, he glanced at the other man with what he hoped looked like a smile but was probably more of a grimace. "I don't think we've been introduced."

"Dylan."

Would a murderer offer his name so easily?

Maybe, if he was positive there was nein way Silas would ever escape.

"You look kind of sick." Dylan studied him. "Maybe some water will help. Let's go inside, and I'll get you a bottle."

James and his other buddy had already gone in.

Silas scratched the side of his head. Oddly, his fingers didn't bump his hat. He must've left it at Bethany's haus. Along with his coat. He shivered in a gust of cold wind. Something icy hit his cheek, and he swiped at it.

"Freezing rain." Dylan looked up. "Wasn't supposed to start until tomorrow."

Silas's shoes lost traction again, and he grabbed hold of the side of the truck to stay upright.

"Obviously, the forecasters were wrong."

This was the farthest from any murder scenario Silas would've thought up. What, were they trying to put him at ease? Help him relax so he wouldn't attempt to escape?

Well, he could've escaped when they came for him. Could've turned and run out of the Weisses' kitchen. But he hadn't, because he'd been afraid they might shoot and kill Bethany. Or Greta or Josh or boppli Drew.

Could Silas escape? On this ice? Probably not.

But there was only one man guarding him.

"You got a gun?"

"What?" Dylan gave him another strange look, then shut the trunk of Wade's car. "Yeah, man. I'm licensed for conceal carry." His hand moved to his side. "Now, move along."

Great, just great. Either way, he was going to die.

⁓

Bethany's bags were packed and ready to go. She'd even managed to carry them out and hide them in the vegetable stand near the mailbox without anybody seeing her. As far as she knew, anyway. But someone who had seen her surely would've said something to discourage her from leaving.

The freezing rain wouldn't make for a flawless escape, however. What driver would want to take her to the bus station in this weather? It seemed as if Daed were still ruining her life, now from the great beyond. She could almost hear him cackling at his silly dochter before he roared, *I will prevail! You WILL obey! Or else.*

It was the "or else" that scared her. Daed was gut at designing horrible punishments, like the time he'd locked her in the chicken coop and forced her to spend the nacht with the smelly, noisy chickens, and the mean old rooster. She'd been certain the bird would kill her before Daed let her out.

That rooster had been made into a meal of chicken and dumplings before the dust had settled the day of Daed's arrest. Justice had been served. To the rooster, anyway.

Though Mamm had had plenty to say about it.

Maybe Bethany wouldn't stick around for Daed's funeral. Nobody would miss her until it was too late. Besides, Hen's family would be there, and his mamm probably had words for Bethany. And if her own mamm found out what had almost happened, and how things had ended....

Bethany shut her eyes. Mamm couldn't find out. Not from her, at least. Preacher Samuel would inform her, and explain why Josh and Greta had kum to stay awhile. Would Mamm even care?

She looked around the living room. The whole haus still hummed with women scrubbing floors, changing sheets, bringing in meals, and visiting. Out in the barn, the men worked, building the casket and waiting for the body to be delivered.

Bethany heard a vehicle door slam. She peeked out the window. Mamm and Rosemary were home.

Bethany pulled in a deep breath for fortification. Then she hurried into the kitchen, grabbed her coat, and the jar full of money Mamm had left in the hutch, and returned to the living room. She went out the seldom-used front door.

Nobody noticed. Or if someone did, she didn't say anything.

See? She wouldn't be missed.

She waved down the driver as his car neared the mailbox. Behind the wheel was his sohn, Stan. *Danki, Lord, for sending him by and providing a means of escape.*

Bethany leaned in through the window when Stan opened it. "I need a ride to the bus station in Cameron, please."

"Sure, babe." He winked. "Hop in."

Chapter 30

Silas followed Dylan into a brightly lit Englisch living room cluttered with dolls, stick horses, and stuffed animals. On the TV screen, an animated cartoon show played at an ear-piercing volume. A Christmas tree decorated with twinkling lights and colorful ornaments sat in one corner, near the fireplace, where several logs crackled upon the glowing embers. A young girl, about two years old, sat cross-legged on the overstuffed sofa, coloring with markers in the sketch pad on her lap. A girl who looked slightly older tried to braid a doll's hair while her own hair was being combed by a woman.

This was getting stranger and stranger. They would murder him here? With women and children present?

The woman looked up with a smile. "Go on into the kitchen. They're waiting for you."

Silas wasn't sure if she was addressing him or Dylan, or both of them. He trailed Dylan into a modern kitchen with stainless-steel appliances. James and the other unfamiliar man sat at the table, sipping from koffee mugs and working on short stacks of pancakes. In the center of the table were a platter of bacon and a pitcher of syrup. Silas froze at the sight of his brother Wade standing at the stove, a spatula in hand. Wade turned, set the spatula down, and crossed the room in several long strides.

Silas held his breath as his brother's arms enfolded him, wrapping him in a bear hug. Warm tears dampened his neck.

Was this a dream? Silas blinked several times, his eyes burning with tears. He awkwardly returned the embrace, overwhelmed by disbelief.

After a minute or so, Wade pulled away with a few slaps on Silas's back. "It's so gut to see you." He spoke in Pennsylvania Deutsch.

"I thought you were going to kill me." Silas rubbed his neck. It hurt, probably from tension.

"What? Nein. You changed my life." Wade nodded toward the table. "Have you eaten lunch yet?"

Lunch? He hadn't even had breakfast. Silas glanced at the microwave's time display. Ten thirty. It would be more of a brunch than lunch. "Nein, but...."

Dylan opened the refrigerator, took out a bottle of water, and handed it to Silas. "Here you go. Unless you'd rather have juice...?"

"Water's fine." Silas took the bottle.

"Eat, and then we'll talk," Wade said.

Silas eyed the window as ice pinged against the glass. He'd be stranded here over-nacht, at this rate. Bethany would worry. The way she'd followed him outside, begging him to stay—it had broken his heart. And likely hers, too. He'd hurt her. Unintentionally, but still. And now he couldn't get back there to fix things. To explain. Not right away, at least.

If only he'd listened to Gott's voice telling him to trust. Then he wouldn't have wasted so much energy fearing his brother. Wouldn't have run away from him at the Amish Market. Wouldn't have abandoned Bethany in her kitchen and gotten stuck with the painful memory of the tears in her eyes.

Dylan grabbed a few pancakes in his hand and headed for the door. "I'm taking mine to go. Need to get home before the roads get bad and my wife worries. See you later, Wade. Nice to meet you, Silas."

"I'd better go, too." The other man stood and carried his plate to the sink. "Nice meeting you, Silas. I'm Bo. Work with Wade at the cabinetry shop."

"We all do," Dylan said.

"I live right next door." James glanced out the window. "I'm probably over here more than there, though. My frau's working today. Got called to a birth this morgen. Gut thing we dropped the kinner off at her parents' place for the weekend."

Why all the introductions? Silas didn't care. He wanted to tell the men to cut the chitchat and get to the point. He focused on Wade. "Why'd you have me kidnapped? Will I be going home to Jamesport to-nacht?"

Not that Jamesport was home.

Wade chuckled. "Don't think so. We need to talk. And the ice storm ensures a captive audience."

"But my...my girl's daed just died, and I don't want to miss the funeral. I need to be there for her."

Wade sobered. "I'm sorry. I didn't know. Bo's the only one with an all-wheel-drive truck, so I'll have to wait till the roads clear to give you a ride back."

~

"What do you mean, the route's canceled? It can't be. I have to get out of here." Bethany wanted to cry.

The man behind the ticket counter shoved his glasses higher on his narrow nose. "The bus to Lincoln, Nebraska, is delayed because of the ice storm and the bad road conditions farther north. However, if your only aim is 'getting out of here,' there's a bus to Memphis, Tennessee, that's set to leave on schedule. They're boarding now. Departure's in ten minutes." He smiled, as if the news were helpful.

It wasn't. Not at all. She wanted to go to Montana, not Tennessee.

But then, she'd also considered going to Pinecraft, Florida. And Memphis was halfway there. Maybe this was her opportunity to reach the Florida beaches, sunshine, and fun, fun, fun. Far more appealing than gray skies and snow.

She glanced out the window of the bus station as a gust of wind drove ice against the pane. She shivered.

On second thought, why Montana? That'd be a summer trip, not winter.

A burst of hope burst through the gloom.

"I'll take one ticket to Memphis." With a grin, she handed him the money and accepted the pass he gave her.

After passing her bags to the driver to stash in the cargo hold underneath the bus, she climbed aboard and scanned the mostly empty rows of seats, save for a lone man seated near the front and a family getting settled near the middle. She selected a vacant spot and sat down. The air smelled stale, with an undercurrent of fried chicken.

She didn't see any signs of the food, but the thought of it made her stomach growl. If only she'd thought to pack something to eat. This trip, like so many other things in her life, hadn't been thought out. She'd seen an opportunity and jumped without a plan.

Maybe this trip could be a chance to heal and start making adult decisions.

Not thinking things through was childish. Or Mamm would say it was.

Still, it seemed to Bethany there were plenty of adults who acted without thinking. Maybe it was a personality trait and not a character flaw. Something to puzzle through on her journey south.

South. Nobody would ever think of looking for her there. Not that anyone would look for her at all. She'd left. End of story. And walking out was the same as dying. She wouldn't be spoken of again. They might wonder where she'd gone, but it would be a shameful thing to lose a child to the world.

Not that she was joining the world. She wasn't even considering jumping the fence. Just making a change of location.

And seeking a major dose of healing. She patted the pocket of her apron that held the small orange New Testament she'd asked to borrow from Greta that morgen. She'd read it on the trip.

She sighed as her thoughts drifted to Silas. Where had he gone? To his onkel's, as he'd talked about doing? Or had he chosen a different direction altogether, as she had?

If only she could write to him. Keep in touch. But she didn't know his onkel's name or address. Simply writing to Silas Beiler, Lancaster County, Pennsylvania, would achieve nothing. There were probably a hundred different men by that name in Lancaster County.

How differently her life turned out than how she'd planned. She'd always imagined that by twenty-two she'd be married with a boppli on the way. Instead, she was almost an old maud. Ruined. Doomed to eternal spinsterhood. If there was such a thing as being doomed to it.

The driver slipped into the front seat, addressed all the passengers with some words she couldn't make out, and then turned the key in the ignition. The bus rumbled to life.

Montana, here I kum!

It wasn't Montana Bethany was headed for, but Memphis just didn't have the same ring. Even if it was warmer there.

The adventure begins.

⌐

Silas reluctantly sat down at his brother's kitchen table and spread some butter on the stack of rapidly cooling pancakes on his plate.

He'd never expected a welkum like the one Esau had given Jacob fourteen years after his younger brother had stolen his birthright and then fled the country. It hadn't been fourteen years since Silas turned Wade in for dealing drugs. More like four or five. How could so much have changed in such a short amount of time?

Admittedly, that "short" span of time had dragged on endlessly for Silas, with his parents perpetually angry at him for betraying his brother and ruining the family's reputation—as if they hadn't already accomplished the latter on their own.

Silas reached for the pitcher of maple syrup. He poured enough to make a puddle on his pancakes, spread it around with his fork, and sliced off a bite. After a second's hesitation, he set the utensil down again and bowed his head for a silent prayer. *Lord Gott, comfort Bethany in my absence. Help her to realize I never would've willingly abandoned her during this difficult time. Danki that my reunion with Wade went so much better than I feared. Help us to continue to work through our differences and to heal from our shared family history. And help me as I start to plan for a future with Bethany, with Your blessing.*

He raised his head and met his brother's gaze. "Why'd you wait this long to let me know you'd forgiven me?"

Wade sat down across from him. "I wrote a letter, but it was returned, marked 'address unknown.' How are the family?"

"They're in Kansas, for now. They went to Oklahoma first, but they moved on from there after I called the police on Daed for abuse. More recently, I reported Henry for abusing his frau." He sighed. "They're moving to Nebraska now."

Wade nodded. "You did the right thing. We have to stop the cycle of abuse. I'm praying for the whole family."

"But why didn't you just kum to Jamesport to see me, instead of having me kidnapped and taken to...wherever I am? Iowa?"

A small smile appeared on Wade's face. "Because I didn't think I could approach you without scaring you off. Seems I was right, considering the way you ran from me at the Amish Market. I realized I'd need to use some measure of 'force' to get a face-to-face with you." His smile widened. "Besides, my wife is due with a baby any day." He stood. "Honey? Bring the girls in here a minute."

The woman Silas had seen earlier came into the room. Standing, she was clearly very pregnant. The two little girls clung to her sides.

"Meet my wife, Sandee, and our daughters, Hope and Joy. The next one's another girl, we're told."

"Nice to meet you." Silas nodded at Sandee. "Congratulations." Then he crouched down to the girls' level. "Hi, Joy. Hi, Hope." He wasn't sure which one was which.

The littler one stuck her thumb in her mouth and hid behind her mother.

"I'm Hope." The older one blinked up at him. "Are you my uncle Silas?"

He straightened to his full height. "I am."

"I'm looking forward to getting to know you," Sandee said. "But for now, I'll leave you two alone so you can talk. Come on, girls." They left the room.

"I am sorry for sending you to jail," Silas said when the brothers were alone again.

Wade propped his elbows on the table. "Don't be. Really."

"I had gut intentions when I turned you in," Silas said with a slight chuckle. "But you know what they say...the road to hell is paved with gut intentions."

A smile. "You aren't on the road to hell. And neither am I, now. I found God in prison. I discovered He isn't just the God of the baptized Amish. He's not the judge who decides whether we're worthy based on our works and deeds. He's a God who loves us all enough to send His Son to die on the cross so that we might be saved."

Amazing to hear his brother talk this way. Silas swallowed. *Danki, Gott.*

"The prison chaplain shared something with me." Wade pulled his wallet out of his pocket and removed a slip of paper. He unfolded it and handed it to Silas.

Not by works of righteousness which we have done, but according to His mercy He saved us....   —Titus 3:5

Something inside Silas shifted. He handed the paper back to Wade. "When the whole family was living in Jamesport, I was gut friends with Sam Miller, and I would hang out at his haus a lot. I'll never forget something I read in one of Preacher Samuel's books. It was a daily devotion that featured a saying based on Psalm thirty-seven, verses twenty-three and twenty-four, which say, in the *New Living Translation*, '*The* L*ORD directs the steps of the godly. He delights in every detail of their lives. Though they stumble, they will never fall, for the* L*ORD holds them by the hand.*'"

Wade slid the index card back into his wallet. "What's the saying?"

"Evidently it's inscribed in the clock room of Big Ben in London: 'All through this hour, Lord, be my guide, and by thy power, no foot shall slide.' It made me realize that I wanted to be one of the men who Gott delighted in. I wanted Him to direct my steps. And even before I understood the gospel message, I prayed, there in Preacher Samuel's living room, that Gott would be my guide." Silas's smile grew as he reflected on that momentous day. "I didn't know it then, but Gott heard me. Something warm and wunderbaar filled me. And even though I still make bad decisions, He is there by my side. Upholding me."

Wade nodded. "I will forever be grateful I found God in jail. I also earned my GED, and I'm going to school now, attending seminary. Online, for now, taking classes as I can. I want to be a preacher. More specifically, a chaplain, so I can minister to men and women who made wrong choices."

"That's amazing."

Wade sliced into his stack of pancakes with a fork. "So, tell me about your girl. Is marriage in your future? Any chance you'll consider settling in these parts?"

Chapter 31

The trip stretched on endlessly, from the quiet countryside to the bustling cities that caused Bethany to clamp the armrests of her seat with white-knuckled fingers. Finally, the bus pulled into a busy parking lot in Memphis, Tennessee. More than twenty-four hours of cramped muscles, and she urgently needed a bath and a change of clothes. Not to mention she was starving. But she was afraid to dig into her bag for the jar of money she'd brought, and risk getting robbed.

It didn't help matters any that the bus from Kansas City to Memphis was delayed due to the ice storm. Or that Bethany accidentally dozed off for a few minutes and missed the bus. Now, she had to wait for the next bus to Memphis. And trying to get serious sleep in a bus station?

Impossible.

Bethany was the only one in the Memphis station in plain garb. She found a vacant corner to sit in, and tried to make herself as inconspicuous as possible. She had an hour to kill before she would be allowed to board the next bus. After some time, she went to the bathroom to clean herself up as best she could without changing her rumpled dress. Then she dug a few dollars out of the jar that was buried at the bottom of her tote bag, and went to survey the food options in the vending machines. She settled on a package of peanut butter crackers and a bottle of water.

She averted her eyes from a man's stare, only to cringe as a young child pointed at her and yelled, "Why is she dressed so weird, Mommy?"

She didn't want to be a freaky sideshow. She just wanted to fade into the wall and become invisible. At least until she got to Florida. Then she'd be ready to have fun, fun, fun.

Except that she would have to find someplace to live, and a job. After buying the bus ticket and the snacks, she had a little over a hundred dollars left. When she departed Jamesport, she felt as if she had a lot of money, but traveling was much more expensive than she'd expected. What would she do when she got to Florida? Was there a "Hey, I just arrived and need a place to stay" network in the Amish community there? Maybe she would seek out the local bishop or a preacher and ask if anyone needed a mamm's helper.

She was missing her daed's funeral. And what about Silas? Had he changed his mind and returned to her haus, only to find her gone? Or was the reason he'd left somehow tied to his fear of motor vehicles, even if a truck had been his means of escape?

She shouldn't have left. She would probably end up homeless, shivering in a cardboard box under a bridge or in a dirty back alley.

On the positive side, she wouldn't be shivering quite as much in Florida as she would someplace up north.

Someone would take her in.

Maybe.

She probably should just go home. Now. Could she exchange her ticket for a trip on a northbound bus?

But, nein. If she didn't go all the way, she would always regret it. She needed to heal. And as long as she lived in Jamesport, she would live in fear of Hen's return. And of Mamm forcing her to marry him, especially once she found out Hen had dishonored her.

Bethany should've taken the time to pray about the trip beforehand. It wasn't too late to pray now, was it? She pulled out the small orange Bible Josh had given her, and found the verses he'd underlined in Romans 8. The verses where Paul said, in effect, "For I am persuaded that nothing will separate me from the love of Gott."

Gott, I'm still new to this praying business, except to thank You for my food. I'm in Memphis now, just in case You didn't notice. And I don't know what I'm going to do when I get to Florida. If You hear me, could You somehow….

In all your ways, submit to Me, and I will make your paths straight.

She stilled. Even stopped breathing for a moment.

Then she smiled as peace washed over her. *I will, Lord. I do. Make my paths straight. Please.*

Two days later, Silas stared out the front passenger window, his fingers clasped, as Bo maneuvered his pickup down the muddy, slushy road leading to the Weisses' haus. While he had wanted to return yesterday, he had been glad for an extra day with Wade's family, and a chance to reach complete reconciliation with his oldest brother as they talked things through and got to know each other again.

The yard was packed with horses and buggies. Englisch vans were parked along the sides of the road. The funeral must be today. A twinge of guilt worked through Silas. While he was reconciling with Wade, he'd completely forgotten Bethany's loss. And he'd been so eager to see her again that he'd forgotten they wouldn't be alone.

At least he was back in time to support her.

Assuming he could get close enough to her. Unfortunately, anything beyond a cursory "I'm sorry for your loss" would cause other people to frown at him, and, worse, would incite gossip.

He urgently wanted to pull Bethany aside to tell her why'd he'd left so suddenly and share how Gott had taken care of his past. His mind replayed Preacher Samuel's words about their not being able to marry until Silas had stopped running and Bethany had healed. The running was done. Silas was free to stay in the area. Now, all he needed was for Gott to touch Bethany's heart.

He swallowed and glanced over at Bo as the truck slowed to a stop. "Thanks for the ride."

Bo nodded. "There's a thriving Amish community where we live. I'm sure you noticed. Well, you saw James. He's still Amish. There's also an opening at the cabinetry shop, in case you decide to leave here and move a bit closer to your family."

Silas hitched an eyebrow. He had nein desire to move closer to his family, but the idea of living in Iowa, near Wade, held some appeal. He'd have to check with Bethany, though. And if she had her heart set on Pennsylvania, he'd see what he could do about marrying her sooner rather than later.

"I'll keep that in mind." It was nice to have options.

Silas rubbed his hands over his jeans and glanced from the haus to the barn. He'd need to change into his Sunday clothes for the funeral, but there was nein chance of escaping notice, as people were already turning to see who was in the truck.

There were visitors standing on the back porch, sitting on the steps, and lining the benches and picnic tables that had sprung up like mushrooms all over the yard. Silas recognized only a few of them: Preacher Samuel, Sam, Caleb, and Josh.

He didn't see Bethany, but she was likely inside, with her mamm and siblings, standing near the casket.

He thanked Bo again, then got out of the truck and hurried into the barn. Scrambled up the ladder to the loft, where the cat that'd been rooming with him was nursing several newborn kittens...on *his* cot. He scowled at the feline. "Ugh. Really?"

He dug in his duffel bag for his gut clothes, did a hasty wardrobe change, and went back down the ladder, greeting people as he made his way to the haus. Bo had gotten out of his truck and gone to talk to someone. He'd left the driver door open, and the telltale dinging indicated the keys were in the ignition. Silas checked to make sure the truck was unlocked before he shut the door to silence the irritating noise.

The kitchen was filled with ladies visiting. Silas scooted past them as quickly as he could and went into the living room. The casket was at the far end of the room, and Bethany's mamm, her brother, and her sisters stood beside it.

But not Bethany. Silas glanced around the room as he approached the casket. Nein sign of her. "I'm sorry for your loss," he murmured to Bethany's mamm. Her eyes were red and bloodshot, as if she'd spent more time crying than sleeping the previous nacht.

"You have a lot of nerve coming back here," she whispered harshly, her lips curled in a fake-looking smile. "After stealing all the money I had saved. And me a widow, with my dead ehemann's medical bills looming."

"Stealing all your...what?" He glanced around the room again as his stomach knotted. The note Bethany's mamm had written the nacht of Hen's latest attack had mentioned a stash of money in an envelope somewhere in the kitchen. She must think he'd taken it all. But who'd given her the idea? Had Bethany lied to her mamm out of anger at Silas for leaving? Josh's Greta would vouch that he hadn't taken any money when the men escorted him out.

"Pretending as if you didn't know." The words were delivered with a sugary layer, as if she were thanking the town drunk for stopping by and paying his respects.

"Wait. Where's Bethany?" Silas needed to tell her why he'd left.

Timothy moved closer to his mamm, his lips thinning, his hands balled into fists at his sides. "You stay away from my sister. Take your things and don't kum back unless you have our money."

The stolen money was more important than Bethany's emotional state? Whatever had happened to Preacher Samuel's attitude—that if someone stole something from him, that person must need it worse than he did?

Perhaps that attitude was unique to Preacher Samuel.

It'd do nein gut to deny their accusations, so Silas only nodded slightly and muttered his condolences again before stepping away. Then he headed for the kitchen. Maybe Bethany was in there, helping prepare the food.

A quick scan of that room didn't reveal any sign of her. But Greta was there, slicing a yellow cake. Silas leaned in close and whispered, "Have you seen Bethany?"

"Silas! You're back. I didn't see you kum in." Greta turned to him, the knife still clutched in her hand. "I haven't seen her, but I'm sure she's around here somewhere. There have been so many people everywhere since the day you left, I haven't had a chance to talk to Bethany to see how she's holding up."

An older woman Silas recognized from Sam's wedding perked up. "I saw her walking out by the mailbox a couple days ago."

He stared at her, baffled by the news and also hunting through his memory bank for her name.

"Zelda," she volunteered with a pat of his hand. "Always such a shame, wouldn't you say? And at such a time as this." She clicked her tongue.

"What?"

Zelda's gaze narrowed as she continued to stare at him. He couldn't understand what she was trying to say, exactly. Walking along the road at a time like this was a shame…how? Maybe Bethany had needed to be alone with her grief.

Or….

His breathing became shallower as he looked at Zelda. "She…she left?" Had she tried to go after him and gotten lost? Or had she taken advantage of the chaos and followed her own pursuits? She must have taken the money, meaning her mamm had jumped to her own conclusions.

Silas's heart ached. Bethany was somewhere all alone, and he wasn't there to protect her. Had he added extra pain to her already damaged spirit?

"Shhh." The older woman clasped his arm with an iron grip and pulled him aside. "The focus is on the deceased and his suffering widow, as it should be. Not gossiping about the poor lost lamb that is surely being condemned by der Herr even as we speak."

"What?" Did she have to speak in riddles?

"Montana." Zelda nodded solemnly, as if she spoke with the voice of authority. "I've heard the dear lamb bleat about it many times."

"Montana," Silas repeated. "Seriously? Now?"

"I know what you're thinking. It's freezing, we just had an early blizzard, and she heads north." Zelda shook her head. "And that's where you kum in. Go after her. Find that poor lost sheep."

Bethany had also talked about Florida and Pennsylvania. Anywhere but here. Becoming a globe-trotter…. But Montana was as gut a place to start as any. Except that Silas had nein money, contrary to popular belief. He glared in the direction of the living room.

Zelda tugged on his arm again. "Kum with me. I'll get you outfitted for your trip."

⌣

Bethany opened her eyes to see an Amish girl, about three or four years old, sitting quietly beside her. She had light brown hair and sky blue eyes with long, thick lashes. In her arms, she cradled a fancy white teddy bear with tiny rainbow hearts sewn all over its fur.

"Hullo." Bethany smiled. "What's your name?"

The girl smoothed her hand over her lavender dress. "Gabby."

A wave of longing coursed through Bethany. Gabriela (or Gabriel, for a boy) was the name she'd planned on giving to the boppli she'd lost. Even though she hated what Hen had done, she wanted a boppli to love. Someday. With the right man. They would cut out cookies in fun shapes and decorate with greenery and always celebrate birthdays with frolics.

"He told me to sit with you."

Bethany looked around for the mysterious *he*, but she didn't see any other Plain people. "Who's he? Where'd he go?"

"There."

Bethany's gaze followed where Gabby pointed, but she saw only a dark-skinned woman wearing blue jeans and a maroon graphic T-shirt printed with words she couldn't read from this distance. She chatted on a cell phone as she tugged a large wheeled suitcase through the bus station.

"Where you going?" Gabby gazed up at Bethany.

Bethany shrugged. "Pinecraft, Florida...I think." Almost anywhere would do.

"I'm going home. He said I'd see my mamm."

"Where is home?"

Gabby pulled her teddy bear closer but didn't answer. Maybe she didn't know.

"Do you like the bus?" Gabby said.

Bethany glanced at the flashing sign across the room. The bus to St. Louis was boarding now. The listing was right above the one for Florida. If they went in order, her bus would be next.

"I don't." Bethany looked around for an Amish man again—even one dressed in Englisch clothes, like Silas sometimes wore. Seemed strange that a man would abandon his dochter with a complete stranger, even if she was Plain. "Riding around in the big cities scare me. And the buses all smell stale and funny."

"Why are you running away?" Gabby studied her.

A chill shimmied through Bethany. For a young girl, Gabby had hit uncannily close to the truth. "I never said I was running away."

Gabby's eyes were wise beyond her years. As if she could somehow tell Bethany lied.

Bethany cleared her throat. "It's complicated."

The girl shook her head. "Grown-ups always say that. It's not, so much. He is always there. Even when we don't see Him. He said that. He'll never leave us."

Goose bumps formed on Bethany's skin. Was this a response to her prayer that Gott would make her paths straight? "But...."

"He's set a path before us and wants us to walk in it, not run away because we're afraid."

The girl spoke too knowledgeably, with too much certainty, to be a child. Bethany's throat dried. "Who are you?"

"I'm Gabby. I already told you." The girl gazed downward. "Don't run away. Go home. Nothing will separate you from the love of Gott, because Gott always keeps His promises." Then she lifted her gaze. "Here, hold my teddy bear a moment. His name is Rainbow." She thrust the bear into Bethany's arms.

Bethany looked down at the furry softness and then up at Gabby.

Except Gabby was gone.

Chapter 32

Danki." Silas pocketed the thick wad of cash Zelda handed him. He hadn't counted it. Hopefully, it'd be enough to get him to Montana. If not, he'd ride for as far as he could and hitchhike from there. Though he wasn't sure his shoes would hold out much longer.

"Bring the poor lost lamb home." Zelda patted his arm once more, then closed her purse and left the room, probably heading back to the kitchen.

Silas slipped off the enclosed porch and headed toward the barn. He was surprised to see Bo's truck still in the driveway. He looked around and found Bo sitting at a picnic table, talking to Preacher Samuel. Both men were bundled up against the cold.

Silas waved at Bo to catch his attention, then motioned to him to wait. Once Bo acknowledged him with a nod, Silas hurried into the barn, changed clothes again, and shoved everything into his duffel bag.

The mama cat never took her eye off him, as if she expected him to try to steal her babies.

"Don't worry, Puss," he assured her. "I'm getting out of your way. You can have the cot—at least for now." Silas hefted his bag and went back down the ladder. He tossed the duffel into the back of Bo's truck and then went to find him.

Bo looked up from his conversation with Preacher Samuel. "You're not staying?"

Silas shook his head. "Barbie Weiss told me to leave and not kum back." He glanced at the preacher. "She wrongfully accused me of stealing money. And I was told Bethany left soon after I did."

Preacher Samuel stood, worry filling his eyes. "I wondered why I didn't see her anywhere. Are you going to find her?"

"I'm going to try. Zelda thinks she went to Montana." He turned to Bo. "Can I catch a ride with you?"

"To Montana?" Bo's eyes bugged. "Much as I'd love to go there, no."

"To the bus station. The first one we pass on your way home."

"Oh, I can do that. Yeah. Give me another minute."

Silas nodded and started to turn away, then stopped. "I won't be back, Preacher Samuel, unless I find Bethany and she agrees to return. But if I do, can I sleep in your barn?"

The older man smiled. "In the haus. The door's always open, day or nacht. Just kum right in. I'd appreciate it if you did return, or, at the very least, kept in touch."

Silas nodded, acknowledging the preacher and Bo. Then, leaving them to their conversation, he trudged to the truck, opened the door, and got in.

A few minutes later, Bo climbed in beside him and twisted the key in the ignition. "Sorry about that. Samuel's daughter wants a specific style of hutch, and he was asking for a vague idea how much it'd cost to build one." He drove slowly down the driveway, kinner scattering in every direction. "So, Montana, huh? What's there for Bethany?"

"I have no idea." That was the honest truth of it. All Silas knew was who *wasn't* in Montana. He definitely understood the need to escape. And he would honor Bethany's wishes—if he found her.

⟶

Bethany held the teddy bear, half praying—was Gabby an angel Gott had sent?—and half waiting for the girl to show up again. When the light on the display board changed, indicating the bus to Florida would be boarding in five minutes, Bethany gathered her bags and the bear. On her way to the bus boarding area, she stopped at the information counter and held up the stuffed animal to the woman standing there.

"A young Amish girl left this with me a little while ago. I'd hate for her to lose it. Do you have a lost and found?"

The woman shrugged. "We do, yes, but there were no other Amish here today. Believe me, we notice when there are." Her gaze swept over Bethany from her rumpled dress all the way down to her plain shoes.

"But...." Bethany looked at the stuffed animal.

"Lost and found is that way." The woman pointed.

"Dank—thank you." Bethany cuddled the bear closer. There *had* been a too-knowledgeable Amish girl at the bus station, named Gabby, and Bethany had the stuffed toy to prove it.

But if Gabby had been an angel, then Bethany had to go home.

Everything within her rebelled against the idea. Silas was gone. What was there to go back for, except to live in fear of Hen? Her relationship with her family had unraveled, and her running away mere days before Daed's funeral surely hadn't endeared her to them any more. Most of her friends were married and starting their own families, so she couldn't exactly move in with any of them. Though maybe she could stay with someone else, like the Millers. Elsie had always treated Bethany with maternal care.

Her flight suddenly reminded her of the biblical story of Jonah. Except that Bethany hadn't been sent to Nineveh. Nor had Gott given her a message to deliver. She wouldn't dare tell anyone she'd had an angelic visitor. Nobody would believe her. They would only whisper all the more about her being "off in den kopf." *Crazy.*

With a sigh, she clutched the teddy bear tighter and made her way toward the ticket counter.

All the Englischers working for the bus company would likely think she was cray, too. Who in her right mind bought a one-way ticket, only to return it halfway through the trip?

Her stomach roiled, even though she knew what she must do. Gott had answered in an undeniable way she couldn't possibly ignore, even if she wanted to. And when her turn came, she choked out, "I need to exchange this ticket for a return trip to Cameron, Missouri."

~

Silas strode up to the ticket counter and set his duffel bag on the floor. "One ticket to Montana, please."

The man nodded. "Sure thing. Must be someplace spectacular. Beautiful Amish girl made the same request."

Silas straightened. He was on the right track.

"I had to tell her the roads were closed, though. That was the day of the big blizzard. Whiteout conditions, especially further north. So she decided to go south, instead. Florida. Popular place for Amish snowbirds to winter, you know. They come back talking about the beach, concerts, Christmas parades, and shuffleboard. Almost makes me want to go. Okay, one one-way ticket to Montana. That'll be—"

"Wait. She went to Florida?" Silas scratched his head. "I need to change my destination."

"You're following her?" The man frowned. "This isn't an abused wife making a run for safety, is it? Because I could refuse to sell you a ticket."

Silas ran his hand over his clean-shaven chin. "She's not my wife." Yet. But someday, Lord willing.

"Girlfriend, then?"

"Jah, girlfriend. But not abused." Not by him, anyway.

The man studied him for a minute. "Okay, but it'll be a while. The next bus going that direction leaves late tonight. Might want to come back—"

"I'll wait. I have a book." Nein food, but he'd survive without eating. He'd done it before. Water, on the other hand...well, there were some vending machines selling it at an outrageous cost. And a drinking fountain—hopefully, one that was routinely sanitized.

Silas paid for his ticket and headed for the waiting area. Plopped down on a hard plastic orange seat. And dug into his duffel bag for his book.

Time dragged on. Finally, at ten that evening, he boarded the bus. There would be a long layover in Kansas City. He hoped he could keep this straight. Otherwise, who knew where he'd end up?

Well, Gott knew.

As the bus rumbled into motion, Silas bowed his head. *Lord Gott, help me to keep the bus transfers straight, and help me to find Bethany quickly. It's a big world, and she could be anywhere. Guide me, guide her, and lead us to each other.*

Chapter 33

Still clutching Rainbow the teddy bear in one hand, her two zippered tote bags of belongings in the other, Bethany staggered wearily into the Kansas City bus station. She glanced around the crowded room, mentally preparing herself for a long, exhausting, sleepless nacht.

In the waiting area, travelers were stretched out on and under chairs, some even leaning against the wall, attempting to sleep. She wasn't sure of the time, but darkness prevailed. She hadn't noticed a single star in the sky. A thin sliver was all of the moon that could be seen. The air had chilled significantly, and snow and ice partially covered the parking lot.

She'd nearly dozed off on the bus but had forced herself to stay awake, afraid she would miss her stop and end up in another busy metropolitan area far, far away from where she wanted—needed—to go.

Now that she had stopped running away and was obediently traveling home again, peace filled her. And the presence of the teddy bear—a reminder of the love of der Herr—kept her sane during the long bus ride. That, and Josh's Bible, where she read the underlined verses in Romans over and over again. *Nothing shall be able to separate us from the love of God.*

An Amish man was sprawled out in a corner, a black hat over his face, an Army green sea bag under his legs. Silas had carried a bag like that. Bethany's heart raced. But it couldn't be him, since he'd left before she had. But just seeing a Plain man with a bag so similar to Silas's gave her a measure of comfort.

Gott, keep Silas safe, wherever he is. Help him to conquer his fear of... whatever it is he'd afraid of.

She went to sit beside him and dropped down one seat away, so she wouldn't encroach on his personal space. A little bit of protection in a great, big, scary world.

Gott....

She didn't know how to pray. Hadn't known exactly how since she'd made her impromptu decision to follow Gabby's advice and go home. Had that kum from Gott Himself? Had to have.

What waited for her at home? She'd run out on the family in their time of need. She'd missed Daed's funeral. Daed had never been a kind, loving father. More like a stern judge. And Mamm would have plenty of harsh things to say, especially when she realized the money she'd set aside for Silas's salary was gone. Bethany would repay the debt, someday, somehow. She would deserve those words, of course, as thoughtless as she'd been, and would completely understand it if she were turned away from home.

Well, she would try to understand, anyway.

Bethany swallowed the fear bubbling up inside her. She would trust in der Herr. He had cared enough to send a small angel to guide her. He knew what lay ahead, even if she didn't. He would provide.

Maybe He'd even help her find Silas. She longed to be back in his comforting embrace. To share a kiss…a hug…a touch.

She wouldn't chase after him. He'd left—whether willingly or unwillingly, she wasn't exactly sure. But if Gott wanted them together, He'd bring Silas back into her life. And if not, then she'd be happy alone. Maybe not happy, exactly, but she'd settle for content.

But Hen….

Fear threatened to boil over again.

Fear not; for I am with you; be not dismayed; for I am your God. I will strengthen you, Yes, I will help you, I will uphold you with My righteous right hand.

The words flashed through her mind with uncanny clarity. She didn't remember ever having memorized that verse. Couldn't even be sure where to find it in the Bible. The Old Testament, maybe. She reached inside her pocket and pulled out the Bible Josh had given her. *Gott, help me trust You. Help me learn to completely rely on You. And Silas, Lord, wherever he is, take care of him.*

"I recognize that Bible." The male voice was groggy but somewhat familiar.

Silas! Nein wonder she'd felt safe near him. "It's *you*." She squealed, then launched herself into his arms for a hug. "I thought I'd lost you for gut."

"Never." He wrapped his arms around her in a return embrace.

Too soon, he released her, but then he leaned toward her and grinned, his gloved fingers brushing hers. "I was looking for you. Never thought I'd find you here, of all places."

She held up the teddy bear. "An angel told me to go home."

He chuckled. "An angel? Really?"

Her face heated, but she nodded. "Her name was Gabby, and she knew way too much about me. She's the one who gave me this stuffed animal. Right after she told me—reminded me, really—that nothing could ever separate me from the love of Gott because He always keeps His promises."

"He does." Silas's smile spread. "So, you're going home?"

"Jah. It'll be kind of embarrassing. I mean, I just left, and now I'm slinking back in. I'm going to be in so much trouble. Stealing the jar of money Mamm had set aside for your salary...."

"I thought you might have taken the money. Or that maybe someone had moved it."

"Sorry. Wait, how'd you know it was gone? Where did you go, anyway? Are you on your way back home? Ach, you said you were looking for me. Did you change your mind about Pennsylvania?"

Silas chuckled. "Which question do you want me to answer first?"

"I—"

He put his finger on her lips. "It's a long story. But right now, I need to exchange my ticket for a return trip so I can go with you. Be right back. Wait here. Please."

Bethany cuddled the bear against her chest as Silas strode away. *Danki, Gott, for helping me find Silas.* A short time later, he returned, a slip of paper clutched in his hand. He stood beside her once more, his arm brushing hers. "Success. I'm all yours now."

She giggled.

He reached for her hand, his fingers intertwining with hers. "I mean that literally. We'll have the whole way back to Jamesport to talk."

Literally? She was too exhausted to figure out exactly what he meant. She leaned her head on his shoulder. "I already told you my story. I got as far as Memphis, then turned back."

"Because of the angel."

Bethany nodded. "Gabby. And she was Amish."

He sobered, his muscles tensing against her. He looked at something in the distance. "Why did you leave in the first place?"

"I'm afraid to be there. I can't—won't—live where Hen is." She tightened her grip on his hand.

"And yet you're going home. Ach, Bethany," he whispered. "We have so much to talk about. But our bus is boarding. Kum on."

⌒

Neither the station nor the bus was a suitable place for proposing. Silas knew that much, even though he desperately wanted to drop to one knee, hold Bethany's hands in his, and make promises to love, honor, and cherish her forever.

Was it too soon? They'd known each other for more than a few years. Courted briefly before he'd hidden behind his family's shame. But the feelings never died. Or if they had, they were quickly resurrected when he came back to town.

Bethany was the only girl for him.

They sat next to each other on the bus, holding hands, all the way to Cameron. Silas spent the entire journey telling her where he'd gone, why he'd been afraid, and what had happened.

At the bus station in Cameron, Bethany smiled as she stood to get off. "Gott's been working miracles for both of us."

"Jah." Silas followed her down the aisle. "I'm seriously considering moving to Iowa instead of Pennsylvania. It'd be close enough to Jamesport that you could go home to visit, yet far enough for you to feel safe. I would like to be near family."

Bethany dipped her head. "You'd take me?"

He didn't know what to say to that, so he simply nodded, biting his tongue to keep the proposal unsaid.

This was neither the time nor the place.

Or was it? The station was empty, except for the two of them—and an attendant, who appeared to be occupied with something on his Tablet.

Silas swallowed. Hard. He would pay a visit to Preacher Samuel and, if need be, the local justice of the peace. "I'll take you wherever you want to go."

Bethany squealed and propelled herself into his arms.

It wasn't a proposal, exactly. But she seemed to have forgotten the condition he'd set regarding marriage. Or maybe she thought things had changed.

A tight hug, a sweet kiss on his cheek, and then she pulled away. She blushed as she glanced at the attendant, who gave Silas a thumbs-up.

Silas nodded with a smile, then frowned at Bethany. "I don't have any phone number for a driver. Nein way to reach one."

"I do." Bethany pulled a slip of paper out of her pocket. "Stan gave me his number when he dropped me off here. In case I needed it. But I don't have a phone." She glanced back at the attendant. "Maybe he'll let me borrow his cell phone." Without a second's hesitation, she waltzed over to the counter and spoke with the man standing there. A moment later, the man nodded and then handed her a cell phone.

A few minutes later, she walked back to Silas. "Stan is on his way. Should be here in half an hour or so."

Silas nodded, but his stomach churned. What would they face when they got back to Jamesport, as a couple and as individuals? He wouldn't be welkum at Barbie Weiss's haus. Not without her stolen money, which he didn't have.

Bethany did. Maybe that would make a difference.

He somehow doubted it.

Preacher Samuel had said Silas could stay at his haus. He would head to the Millers' after making sure Bethany was safe.

Her mamm wasn't exactly the loving type. And after running away mere days before the funeral, would Bethany even be allowed to return home?

Well, her mamm was the one who'd told Hen Bethany would be home alone, so Silas didn't feel comfortable leaving Bethany there, even if she were permitted to stay. Maybe the preacher would invite her into his home, too.

Chapter 34

Bethany dug her fingernails into her palms as they sped up the driveway in Stan's red convertible. She looked out the window and swallowed the bile rising in her throat as the car came to a stop. *Gott, I'm scared. Mamm has every right to be mad at me, but, please, help this to go well.*

Not that she held out much hope. Especially when Mamm stepped onto the porch with a scowl, her fists planted on her hips. Her facial expression didn't soften at all when Bethany got out of the car.

"You're back." Her tone was as flat as her lips.

Bethany gulped. "I'm sorry, Mamm. I—"

"You are a horrible, ungrateful child." Mamm's voice rose in volume. "After all I've done for you, raising you as my own after your parents died in that buggy wreck. And me, with a toddler of my own. And all because Joe felt obligated. Felt it was expected of him, as a new preacher."

"What?" Bethany stumbled to a stop.

"Well, I'm nein longer obligated. I have enough on my plate with nein husband and my own kinner. I don't need to care for some orphan." Mamm turned away.

"Are you saying I'm not Bethany Weiss?" Her vision swam, and she swayed, reaching out blindly for something, anything, to hold on to. Silas wrapped his arms around her waist and pulled her back against him. Supporting her.

Nothing like having her identity stripped away without warning.

She was glad Silas was there, in spite of the shame that filled her because he'd heard her being lambasted.

Mamm glanced over her shoulder and scoffed. "You think I'd give my child a worldly name like Bethany? Your real mamm was just like you. Too talkative, too easily distracted, too flirty." Disdain filled her voice. "We were doing our duty, trying to get you married off. But you rejected the ehemann we found for you. Claimed he raped you. Preacher Samuel told me your story. Lies. All lies. Hen loved you."

Bethany swayed again, her vision darkening, as if she were about to faint. *Gott…help.*

"Kum, then," Silas whispered. "I'll take you to Preacher Samuel."

Mamm glared at Silas. "And you. *You.* I told you not to show your face around here again, unless you returned with the money you stole. Every. Single. Penny."

"I took the money," Bethany spoke up. "I figured if he'd left, he wouldn't need his pay. I'm sorry. I do have most of the money—half of, anyway." Bethany held her hands out, palms up. "Please." *Please, don't reject me. Tell me it was just a bad joke.* Though, if Mamm were going to force Hen on her, maybe Bethany would rather be cast away.

Mamm's glare transferred back to her. "You didn't take his pay. You took *my* haus-hold money."

"I'll give you all that's left. It's in my bag."

"I'll deliver it," Silas said quietly. "Let's get you back in the car."

Bethany allowed Silas to steer her back to the convertible. Behind the wheel, Stan sat, wide-eyed, staring at Bethany's mamm. He glanced at Bethany's reflection in the rearview mirror. "Wow. I never…that's rough, babe."

The trunk slammed shut, and Silas jogged back over to Mamm and handed her the money jar. Then he returned to the car and climbed in the backseat next to Bethany.

Stan shook his head as he moved the gearshift into drive. "Where to?"

"Preacher Samuel's," Silas said.

It was gut Silas had taken control, because Bethany didn't know what to do next. She'd expected to be turned away, not disowned.

Even so, she hadn't had a plan in place.

Her real parents were dead? She didn't even know who they were.

That explained why she'd always craved love and acceptance. Searched for them. She'd been denied them both all her life.

She picked up the teddy bear and held it tight as a silent, symbolic reminder that she'd always had the love of Gott. Always would.

Silas leaned forward and said something to Stan that she couldn't quite discern. Then he settled back against the seat, wrapped his arms around her shoulders, and held her.

She had his love and acceptance, too.

But even Silas's embrace couldn't breach the numbness that had settled in her soul at the shocking news she'd just received.

⟲

When they arrived at the Millers' haus, Silas helped Bethany out of the car while Stan unloaded their bags from the trunk.

Preacher Samuel and Elsie both stepped out on the porch to greet them. "Welkum back, Bethany," the preacher said.

"Her mamm turned us away," Silas explained. "Can she stay here, too?"

"Of course. Let's get your bags inside, then we'll talk."

Preacher Samuel helped carry their luggage into the haus while Elsie sliced an apple pie and prepared steaming cups of koffee and tea. When everyone had gathered in the kitchen, Preacher Samuel settled into a chair at the head of the table. "Okay, what's going on? Why did Barbie turn Bethany away?"

A tear—just a single tear—escaped from the corner of one of Bethany's eyes. "She said I'm not her dochter, and she's nein longer obligated to care for me." Her voice caught and broke.

Preacher Samuel hitched an eyebrow.

"That's nonsense." Elsie huffed. "You are most certainly hers. You look just like her. And I was there when you were born."

Bethany sniffed. "She said my real parents are dead."

"I suppose that's true, in a sense." Preacher Samuel drummed his fingertips on the table. "Your parents were in a terrible buggy accident when Barbie was pregnant with you. Barbie was in a coma for almost two weeks. You were born during that time, but she wouldn't accept that you were truly hers. She kept insisting her boppli died in the accident. Her personality was altered due to the trauma, and not for the better, I'm afraid. There was a time when Barbie was carefree and as talkative as you. Sweet girl, but a bit flighty."

Bethany flinched, as did Silas. So, both her parents were off in den kopf? One from a brain tumor, the other from head trauma suffered in a buggy accident? Well, at least she still had a real family around. A brother and two sisters who would still want her in their lives. And she'd apparently kum by her talkative nature genetically. He smiled at the thought of a talkative little girl in his future, Gott willing.

Elsie looked at her ehemann. "You'll talk to Barbie, then?"

"Jah. After she's had some time to grieve. She isn't accepting truth as fact right now. She up and called me a liar when I tried to talk to her about Hen. But she's had a lot of devastation in her life, especially lately. Two deaths, her ehemann's arrest and diagnosis, and I know the medical bills are overwhelming. What the auctions brought in hardly put a dent in the last one she received. I daresay she'll be putting the farm up for sale soon and moving in with her brother and his family." Preacher Samuel frowned, then shifted his attention to Bethany. "You can stay with us for now. Until we get this settled."

"Danki." Bethany brushed away her tear with the back of her hand.

"Actually...." Silas pulled in a breath, then blew it out. "I'd like to revisit our discussion about marriage."

Bethany emitted a tiny gasp, and he glanced at her. Was it too soon to plan their wedding? Did she need more time?

Hope glowed in her eyes.

Preacher Samuel glanced at her. "She still needs to heal." Then he leveled his gaze at Silas. "And what of your issues?"

Silas exhaled a sigh as he recalled a terrifying truck ride he'd taken for a pancake breakfast. He couldn't believe he'd lived in fear for so many years. "Wade and I have made peace. He found Gott in prison. I still need to work through forgiving my daed and Henry, but...." He hesitated. "I believe I can forgive them now. Just saying the words will help it to be true, ain't so?"

Preacher Samuel nodded. "Jah, that's the beginning. Some gut came out of it, too. It brought you back to us. For now. But forgiving is an ongoing thing. You must mean it, and not let bitterness take root."

So, Preacher Samuel agreed. Silas had finally resolved his "issues," clearing the way for him and Bethany to marry. Hope for a future with Bethany began to build. But he needed to let Preacher Samuel know they would be leaving Jamesport.

Might as well get it over with, even though Preacher Samuel might not approve. "I'll be leaving again." Silas rubbed his hands together. "Either Pennsylvania, as originally planned, or Iowa, to be near Wade and work at his cabinetry shop. It'd keep Bethany somewhat near her family and friends, yet far enough away for her to feel safe from Hen."

The preacher remained silent as he tugged on his beard, appearing to be in thought. Hopefully, he would see the wisdom of Silas's plan. As soon as the preacher gave his approval, the first thing Silas would do would be to invite Bethany on a walk so he could propose, for real.

Lord Gott, please help her to heal quickly so we can begin our future together if it is Your will.

⁓

"Bethany?" Preacher Samuel's eyebrows rose as he turned to look at her.

"Um." She swallowed her nerves as she pulled the teddy bear closer. "I'd like to marry Silas, someday." She glanced at him and caught the flare of joy in his eyes. Maybe desire, too. Her cheeks heated. "And I'm willing to go to Iowa, if that's where he wants to go."

A new beginning, in a new place where she'd be safe, would be wunderbaar.

Silas wiped his palms on his pant legs, as if he were nervous or needed to do something with his hands. She wanted to hold them for courage. She hadn't expected to be questioned about the possibility of marrying him.

"What about…?" The preacher cleared his throat.

She frowned, confused. Then…*ach.* Her eyes widened at the preacher's implied question. Her face burned as the memory of the heated kisses she'd shared in the kitchen with Silas. "I know the difference between Hen and Silas, and I'm not afraid of Silas."

Silas smiled, relief lighting his eyes. He reached for her hand.

"And…." Bethany pulled in a breath as he entwined his fingers with hers. But her healing was more than just physical. It was spiritual. "I'm on speaking terms with Gott again. I discovered He wasn't the doing the hiding. I didn't want to see Him. Greta showed me a verse I've been hearing over and over in my head, and I believe it is true: *'For I am persuaded that neither death, nor life, nor angels nor principalities nor powers, nor things present nor things to come, nor height nor depth, nor any other created thing, shall be able to separate us from the love of God which is Christ Jesus our Lord.'"*

Preacher Samuel and Silas both smiled and nodded.

Bethany fingered the soft fur of the teddy bear. Hundreds of miles on a bus hadn't separated her from Gott's plan for her life. Gott had showered her and Silas alike with blessings. He'd brought them back together after several years apart, in different states, and helped them to find each other in a crowded bus station. Gott had even provided a place for her to stay after she'd been kicked out of her home.

"Mamm's rejection isn't going to change that. It hurts, but I understand a little bit better now. I'll still keep in contact with my family. With my brother and sisters, at least."

Preacher Samuel turned to Silas and nodded. Winked. "When you're done working things out with our girl, kum talk to me. I'll be in the barn." He got up and headed for the door.

"If you'll excuse me, I have sewing to do." Elsie pointed to a room off the kitchen, where Bethany could see a quilting frame set up. She giggled as she made a hasty departure.

They were leaving her and Silas alone?

Anticipation churned inside Bethany. She dipped her head so she wouldn't appear too anxious for his kisses.

An endless moment passed before Silas turned to her. "Would you want to take a walk?"

Something about his tone set her nerves to tingling. *Jah, jah, jah!* Bethany pushed to her feet and set the stuffed bear on the kitchen chair. Silas lifted her coat from the wall hook and helped her into it, then shrugged his own coat on.

Hand in hand, they strolled outside, toward the road. Sunlight glittered on the piles of leftover snow. Happiness filled her. *Danki, Gott, for the strength of Silas's character and faith.*

As they got out of sight of the haus, Silas stopped walking and pulled her into his arms. "I know this isn't coming as much of a sur-prise"—a gentle smile and a wink—"but ich liebe dich, Bethany. Will you marry me? Sooner, rather than later?"

Bethany grinned at him, joy bubbling up inside her. "Ich liebe dich." And despite their being on the road where anyone could kum along and see them, she flung herself into his arms and kissed him with the strength of all the wonder inside her.

Passion flared.

When they finally pulled apart, she giggled, her smile growing. "I thought you'd never ask."

About the Author

A member of the American Christian Fiction Writers, Laura V. Hilton is a professional book reviewer for the Christian market, with more than a thousand reviews published on the Web.

Laura's first series with Whitaker House, The Amish of Seymour, comprises *Patchwork Dreams*, *A Harvest of Hearts*, and *Promised to Another*. In 2012, *A Harvest of Hearts* received a Laurel Award, placing first in the Amish Genre Clash. Her second series, The Amish of Webster County, comprises *Healing Love*, *Surrendered Love*, and *Awakened Love*. A stand-alone title, *A White Christmas in Webster County*, was released in September 2014. Laura's last series, The Amish of Jamesport, included *The Snow Globe*, *The Postcard*, and *The Birdhouse*. Prior to *The Amish Wanderer*, she published *The Amish Firefighter*.

Previously, Laura published two novels with Treble Heart Books, *Hot Chocolate* and *Shadows of the Past*, as well as several devotionals.

Laura and her husband, Steve, have five children, whom Laura homeschools. The family makes their home in Arkansas. To learn more about Laura, read her reviews, and find out about her upcoming releases, readers may visit her blog at http://lighthouse-academy. blogspot.com/.

Welcome to Our House!

We Have a Special Gift for You ...

It is our privilege and pleasure to share in your love of Christian fiction by publishing books that enrich your life and encourage your faith.

To show our appreciation, we invite you to sign up to receive a specially selected **Reader Appreciation Gift**, with our compliments. Just go to the Web address at the bottom of this page.

God bless you as you seek a deeper walk with Him!

WE HAVE A GIFT FOR YOU. VISIT:

whpub.me/fictionthx

WHITAKER
HOUSE